RAVES FOR SÈPHERA GIRÓN!

"Girón deserves a place beside the top mistresses of the dark."
—*Hellnotes*

"If Poppy Z. Brite and Nancy Kilpatrick turn your cold blood to hot, then welcome Sèphera Girón to the short list of dark mistresses of terror truly worthy of that title."
—Stanley Wiater, author of *Dark Dreamers*

"Girón at no time lets up on the horror quotient."
—*Fangoria*

THE BIRDS AND THE BEES

"An aesthetic experience that at once both celebrates and vivisects humankind's relationship with nature and himself. . . . A straightforward, artfully rendered narrative."
—*Cemetery Dance*

HOUSE OF PAIN

"*House of Pain* is horror at its best."
—*The Midwest Book Review*

"A powerful and unflinching novel."
—Peter Atkins, author of *Wishmaster*

"Girón's prose is smooth as silk; the pacing is dead on. I devoured this book in a single sitting."
—*Horror World*

"*House of Pain* is a perfect—if far from safe—place to lose yourself on a stormy fall night."
—*Fangoria*

"Genuinely creepy."
—*Cemetery Dance*

"*House of Pain* rocks with good old-fashioned creepiness."
—Edo van Belkom, author of *Teeth*

THE TRANSFORMATION

The woman walked over to an altar comprised of a wooden plank and several candles. A pot of incense burned thickly, and there were other assorted instruments. An anthame, black crystals, a crow carcass festering with ants, a few assorted bones, and a baby alligator head from a trip to Florida. She lowered her head, her hand touching the anthame.

As she continued to pray, her flesh burned and crackled. Her face seemingly melted into its own river of emptiness. She raised her arms, returning to the nonsensical singsong she was chanting earlier. She tore away her clothes until she was standing naked. Her flesh bubbled and rolled into itself, cracking and then oozing. She screamed as the flesh sizzled and boiled. The pain grew so great she sank to her knees, screaming more than she ever had in childbirth. At last, the sharp burning sensation was ebbing, and she was able to open her eyes and breathe deeply once more. She smiled as she looked down. . . .

BORROWED FLESH

SÈPHERA GIRÓN

LEISURE BOOKS NEW YORK CITY

LEISURE BOOKS ®

March 2004

Published by

Dorchester Publishing Co., Inc.
200 Madison Avenue
New York, NY 10016

ISBN 0-8439-5257-1

Visit us on the web at www.dorchesterpub.com.

BORROWED FLESH

For Derek:
Thank you for opening my heart and mind to the endless
possibilities of life's grand adventure and for proving to me
that there is such a thing as a second chance.

For Adrian and Dorian:
Wherever life may take you, remember that I love you
and that you will never be alone.

ACKNOWLEDGMENTS

I want to thank all my friends, family and colleagues for being wonderfully supportive of me in so many ways. Neighbors, parents, relatives, staff and students at the dance studio, far away friends . . . I am surrounded by fantastic people who inspire me and I am grateful for their presence in my life.

I especially want to thank Don D'Auria for his faith in my ability to tell a story, and to thank the tireless staff at Leisure for all their hard work and support!

Preface

In the dark of the night, shadows reach with long elegant fingers toward that which humans hold dearest. What seems real and true in daylight becomes a misty uncertainty ready to be snatched away once the sun sinks below the horizon.

Hesitation replaces confidence. Vows of truth collapse into a crumbling facade of lies.

Dancing on weakness.

Poking holes in resiliency.

Even the strongest can only withstand so much grief.

Every day that dawns is a new creation. A new journey of discovery. A new villain to conquer. A new war to win.

In the end, it always comes down to the same common denominator.

Matters of the heart.

1

With love, we can draw strength and power to face all that is placed in our way.

With love, we can walk on glass, shiver in the cold, follow blindly into pits of pain. Love can surround us with comforting arms and nurture us. Make us believe in the child within us once more. Love can raise kingdoms and raze them simultaneously. We can love ourselves and all that we touch. We can draw upon the love of the spirit and angels that protect us. With love, we can feel whole. We can raise children and survive times of strife. We can accept things in our life that disappoint and dismay us.

Those without love wander along the earthly coil without focus or meaning. Their lives are dry without existence. They grow bitter and cold, seeing only darkness and sorrow. They elude happiness, finding resolution in the pain of others.

For those with stones for hearts, life is not a blessing but a curse. They covet all that they cannot have or understand.

Where humans can spend a lifetime trying to justify their spot in the universal scheme, matters of the heart can help focus and bend their understanding. Those that crave power, that desire to master others, can manipulate will, but can't manipulate love.

Shadows dance in the dusk, in the dawn, on a clear summer afternoon. Where there is light, there is darkness. Where there is hope, lies despair. Each day dawns full of promise. Each night drains away the fever of the day. What looms in the darkness with snatching claws, ready to drive away the most cherished aspect of life?

Each step taken is one step closer.

Desire. Lust. Power.

Love is fragile against the beating wings of omnipotence.

Even trees would wither up and die if they tasted the venomous visions of those seeking to conquer.

In the end, it is about power.

The power to love. The power to control. The power to forget.

The strongest use the power wisely.

The frivolous waste their knowledge, sending ripples through the universe that can turn a mud puddle into a tidal wave.

The power is dangerous. A curious balance of harmonic, melodic, and discordant. A teeter-totter of light and dark.

The next chapter of the journey is unfolding. Grief and despair open the doorway to a new path.

A new road weaving through a wonderland of all that has been and all that will become once more.

Chapter One

Vanessa parked her car down the street, out of sight from the school yard. She checked herself in the rearview mirror. Violet eyes stared back at her. No visible makeup. She didn't look like herself without any color or eyeliner, especially today. No matter, she had to do what she needed to do to get through this. Of course, she had practically used a trowel on her face to achieve the youthful, plain facade. But no one could tell.

She pulled the hood of her baby-blue sweatshirt over her long black hair. As she got out of the car, she was pleased to see that no one noticed her. Although the students around her wore school uniforms, nobody paid any mind to her rapper gear. She was just another teenager wandering down the street. Maybe she was a student at the other high school, a few blocks away.

She chuckled to herself. It would be pretty pathetic to still be in high school at her age. But no matter. She blended in and that was what counted the most.

She walked nonchalantly along until she reached one of the hedges that lined the path up to the gates of the school property. She stood, sketchbook and purse hanging half-assed in her arm, as she assumed the slouch of a kid waiting for a friend.

Vanessa smoked a cigarette. Long-legged schoolgirls in plaid skirts and white knee socks walked past her, books hugged to their budding breasts, heads lowered in giggling whispers. Boys dressed in gray sweaters, white shirts, and dress pants yelled and ran, teasing girls and each other. Autumn was definitely in the air as school flung into full throttle. The more eager students were hurrying as the second bell rang. High-pitched chattering echoed off the stone walls. All that remained on the outside were stragglers and rebels. Dragging their feet. Pulling one last puff from a smoke.

Vanessa looked up at the corners of the school, under the eaves and along the roof. All schools had security systems these days, and the cameras mounted above the doors were the ones that could be seen. Who knows where other cameras were hidden? She could almost hear the humming of electricity, and her fingers tingled. She figured there were at least twenty cameras on the outside of this school, and even more on the inside. For that reason, she never actually set foot on school property.

Vanessa was no student. She was a forty-year-old woman and she couldn't let herself be seen watching the students. She was dressed in baggy oversized hip-hop gear, along with a baseball cap, and was carrying a notepad. She hoped that there weren't cameras aimed beyond the fenced grounds, and maybe there were. As long as she wasn't actually on the school grounds, she wasn't trespassing, and therefore, wasn't breaking any laws.

Were there laws about watching the parade of students filing in and out of the school, though? Loitering? Stalking?

Perhaps.

But she was just watching.

And waiting.

The last of the kids flung her cigarette to the ground, and now the stairs at St. Mary's the Tormented were empty. The building was huge and old. Probably one of the oldest Catholic schools on the East Coast. Vanessa loved the architecture of these little New England towns. All the weird carvings and cobblestone fences. The gargoyles and the Latin words carved around the doors and windows were so interesting. It spoke to her of a time when people took pride in themselves and their workmanship. Now buildings were slapped up in weeks. Square buildings of cold indifference.

Vanessa pulled out her notebook and flipped it open. The hairs on her arms were standing on end, even here in the warm autumn sunlight. She started sketching the gargoyle peering over the doorframe of the side entrance. Her heart was pounding and her fingers tingled. She had to remain calm.

Composed.

Looking in the mirror that morning, she had been distressed at what she had seen.

7

She had woken up not feeling great. Maybe her period was due soon. The days blended into one after the other so fast she couldn't keep track. And it had seemed like forever since she had been with a man. She was tired, creaky, horny, bloated. She just didn't feel like herself in any way.

Pulling herself out of bed had been hard. Her bones ached and her head felt stuffed with cotton. It was a scary thought, to feel so old and crappy at forty. How was she going to feel in a hundred years? Or two hundred?

She had walked over to the mirror. Walking barely described the numb, stumbling lurch as her legs didn't want to wake up. She was beginning to feel like Frankenstein's monster. In a way, she supposed she was, since part of her body wasn't originally her own. Maybe that's why every so often, some days were harder than others. It made her wonder about things like breast implants and face-lifts. How did those things feel? Those were normal procedures, less dramatic than skin-grafting and limb-rebuilding. Still, she always thought that it must hurt like hell, every day, to have breast implants.

She sat on the toilet, relieved that simple things like peeing were still normal. When she was done, she dared to look into the mirror. The circles under her eyes were larger and darker than yesterday. The scar around her neck was starting to leak with a pussy green ooze, and she dabbed at it carefully with peroxide and cotton swabs. The scar around her neck would never heal properly and seamlessly. It had been nearly twenty years since that day, and still, the flesh would only adhere for so long before it slid off and the infection came back.

It was sloppy work, being forty. Amazing how from one day to the next, the face could fall, the breasts could fall, how a day without careful eating could affect the body instantly and dramatically. Yet, adding extra moisturizer and lifting a few weights could tip the balance back the other way, for a while.

However, Vanessa's body, Vanessa's flesh, needed more care. She was only forty, but that was nothing compared to how old she would be one day, so she needed to take extra steps to preserve her youth.

A few years ago, she had found out that there was more to eternal life than met the eye. If she wanted to remain youthful-looking, she had to start taking steps now. The scars of her past would haunt her. They would bleed through new layers of living flesh. She had pored through spell books at the library. Searched the Internet for information. The Fountain of Youth was more than a place. The Fountain of Youth was attitude and information.

Eventually she discovered the combination of properties that would keep aging at bay. She had hoped it would only be once a year at the most, but now it seemed that it would be more than once a year. Maybe it would be every solstice. How she prayed it would never be every month. Every day. It wouldn't be possible. She wouldn't survive. Even if she didn't go mad, she would be caught.

With eternal life, they could burn her at the stake. They could rip her head off. They could stretch her, hack her up. It didn't matter. She would still survive. She had survived gruesome misfortune before, and she didn't relish the idea of living through more.

She had to be careful. Cautious. Prudent. No one could know her secret.

This high school, an hour's drive from her humble abode by the ocean, would do for this time. How many high schools had there been? Five? Six?

She liked the Catholic schools. There was something ironic about Catholic schools that made her grin. Was it the short skirts that flipped up? The daring attitude of those that were supposed to be so rigid to the calling, yet smoked, drank, and had premarital sex as much as those of any other faith.

The Catholic girls stirred a sense of irony in her, for certain.

Her arms tingled right down to the whorls on her fingertips. Her long black hair, tucked away beneath her hood, swayed and coiled, like a snake rolling in the hot heat of the sun. She squinted and saw, far down the road, a lone figure shuffling along. Her lip curved into a smile. Her fingers fumbled through her little purse, finding another cigarette.

A girl walked slowly towards the school. In the sunlight, her golden red hair gleamed like a precious jewel. Her crisp white shirt was a startling contrast to the gray world around her. Her skirt lifted jauntily in the breeze, at odds with the slow, shuffling gait of the girl, who seemed to be headed toward the gallows.

Vanessa lit her cigarette and drew the smoke deep into her lungs. She looked at the girl's high white knee socks, her black loafers, her gleaming firm thighs.

The girl was now close enough that she could ignore Vanessa no longer.

"Hi." The girl looked at Vanessa, then dropped her gaze.

"Late for school again, Alex?" Vanessa asked.

Alex nodded. "First class sucks. Last class sucks. All the classes in between suck."

"I remember how much I hated high school." Vanessa offered the opened pack of cigarettes to Alex. The girl took one and placed it expertly between her lips.

Vanessa lit it. "Maybe you'd like to go for a walk with me again. You're late anyway."

Alex looked at the school, at the foreboding stone staircase. Her gaze traveled up to the snarling gargoyle peering out from the trough of eaves, straddling a video camera.

"I hate school."

"Then let's go."

Vanessa's heart pounded as she pulled the hood of her sweatshirt further over her head, tucking wayward strands of long hair beneath it. As she walked beside Alex, she adopted the swagger of a rapper. If the cameras picked up Alex walking away, or if anyone else spotted them, they would think Alex was with a boy, or so Vanessa hoped.

They walked for a while. Away from the school. Away from the town and toward the woods.

"Sometimes I think you're the only one who understands me," Alex said as they sat down by the creek. Vanessa pulled out a joint and handed it to Alex.

"I know what it's like to be an outcast," Vanessa said, lighting the joint for Alex.

Although it was cooler in the woods, it was still a balmy day. The creek burbled and glittered. Alex took a couple of drags from the joint and lay back onto the grass. She stared up through the trees.

"Will I ever stop feeling so fucked up?" Alex asked.

Vanessa studied the joint, flicking the ash onto the ground. She looked over at Alex, who wasn't watching her. She pretended to haul the joint and handed it back.

"Feeling fucked up is normal for a teenager," Vanessa said. "Hell, feeling fucked up is pretty normal for most anyone."

Vanessa scratched her neck, feeling more of the flesh peeling away under her nails. She pulled the sweatshirt higher.

They finished the joint in silence. Alex toking, Vanessa going through the motions.

When it was done, Alex sat up. Her large round eyes were glassy, and she was grinning.

"Why do you come around?" she asked.

"I'm an artist. I like to go for walks to clear my head. Meet interesting new people." She patted her notepad. Alex nodded as Vanessa flipped up the pages to show the gargoyle sketches.

"You draw the coolest stuff. I don't know why you aren't famous yet," Alex said.

"I draw for myself." Vanessa put her hand on

Alex's knee. "And like I said, I get to meet interesting people."

"What's so interesting about a fucked-up teenager?" Alex asked.

"What isn't interesting? Everyone has a story," Vanessa said.

"Mine sucks. I can't even get a guy."

"You don't need a guy," Vanessa said, running her hand up to the spot on Alex's thigh where her skirt ended. "Men only give you heartbreak. They lie. They cheat. And at your age, hell, at any age, all they want is to fuck you and move on," Vanessa said.

"I know lots of girls who are going steady. They fool around and the guys don't leave them."

"Believe me, Alex, the boys will move on soon enough. They'll screw those girls for a while. Maybe one night. Maybe for a year or two. Who knows why men do what they do? But I know from experience, all they want is pussy. To taste and try as many different kinds as possible. You're lucky you haven't been abused yet."

Alex sighed and fiddled with her fingers, making steeples and unfolding them. She chewed on the inside of her cheek before she finally spoke.

"But I want it. I want to try what everyone else tries."

Vanessa touched Alex's face with one hand while the other stroked higher up her thigh. "You're lucky to get out of high school still a virgin."

"I don't want to be a virgin. I want to try it. I'm not that ugly, am I? I don't even really want a boyfriend, I just want to try it."

"Then what happens? Some guy shoves his dick in you, he lasts about a minute 'cause he's only a kid, and before you can relax from the pain of his rough penetration, he's filled you with come. Come that can get you pregnant or full of disease. Where's the fun in that?"

Vanessa's fingers touched the top button of Alex's cotton shirt. She looked at the girl, who seemed to vacillate between stoned obliviousness and growing passion. Vanessa twisted and turned the button, trying to fiddle it through the button hole. The button popped off and landed somewhere in the dirt. Vanessa slid her hand along the top of the swell of Alex's bosom, spreading the shirt open a little wider.

Vanessa's other hand toyed with the elastic of Alex's underpants. Alex spread her legs.

"If it's so horrible, why do so many people do it?"

"It's not horrible at all, if you're with the right person and they know what to do. If you can find that rare man that wants to please, that can last long enough to let you ride your wave, over and over again, sex can be the most mind-blowing experience in the world. But unfortunately, that comes with age. You won't find that in high school. Some people may not find that at all, ever."

Vanessa's fingers teased Alex as she leaned over to kiss her. Alex's lips were soft. Young and shy. Vanessa slid her fingers in deeper as Alex searched her mouth with her tongue. Vanessa felt the flesh around her own neck slipping and dripping. She hoped it wasn't oozing through her sweater. Even the fingers that swirled and danced between Alex's legs felt odd. She plunged them in deeper, stroking the way she herself loved to be touched. It had been so long since she had been with a man and she missed it so much. She wanted to please Alex, let her enjoy experienced fingers circling passion. If she could bring a brief happiness to this girl's young life, then she would do it.

Alex sat up, squeezing her legs together.

"This isn't right," she said.

"Why? Because I'm a woman?"

Alex nodded.

"That's all right. We're just playing. You said you wanted to try things, so I thought I'd show you some. I can't help it if I'm a woman."

"Maybe I'm just afraid of where we are. Like I'm paranoid. What if a cop comes by or something?"

Vanessa grinned. "You're right. We need privacy." Vanessa kissed Alex along her neck. Alex moaned softly, the sound womanly for such a young girl.

"Would you like me to get a hotel room?"

"A room? Why can't we go to your house?"

"I don't live around here."

"Do you live alone?"

"Yes."

"So, can you take me to your house?"

"But it's far. You might miss even more school . . . I mean, days of school before I come back this way."

"I don't care." Alex wrapped her arms around Vanessa and kissed her. "Take me home with you, please. I can't stand this anymore."

"Okay."

Vanessa let Alex smoke another joint while she

15

drove the hour to her home. She hoped that no one had seen them. In her mind, she imagined them traveling in a big blue bubble, invisible to the world. If people saw them, they would pay no mind to the Catholic schoolgirl and the androgynous person in the hooded sweater and baggy pants. What a joke it was really. This girl, this virginal child, wanting nothing more than to taste the sins of the flesh, to break beyond the forbidden coupling of man and woman, and explore her luck with a woman. What would the Pope think of that? Of this large-breasted girl sucking a joint, her skirt hiked to her waist, her feet on the dashboard. The radio was blaring Godsmack's "I Stand Alone."

Vanessa turned off the highway and down the narrow gravely road that wound for what seemed like miles through scattered cottages, until she reached her driveway. Slowly she drove down the little hill and parked the car. Alex jumped out, looking at the small cottage.

"Cool," she said, running up the cobblestones.

"I call it home. For now," Vanessa said as she reached the door and unlocked it.

Once inside the house, Vanessa led Alex to the back sunroom. The ocean swelled before them.

"High tide," Alex said.

"Yes, it seems to be. Good swimming water."

"Can we go swimming?" Alex asked.

"It's chilly. Maybe later."

Vanessa patted a large wicker chair and nodded. "Sit here while I get us something to drink."

Alex sat in the chair, mesmerized by the beautiful view across the cove.

Vanessa went into the modest kitchen and got two coolers out of the fridge. She didn't want to leave Alex alone too long, so she hurried back.

Alex had lit a cigarette and unbuttoned her blouse. She sat back provocatively in her chair. Vanessa thought that Alex certainly acted wily for a virgin, but of course, she had seen girls act that way and more that were years younger. She had seen thirteen-year-olds on talk shows that she could swear were twenty. This beautiful creature before her now seemed to know all the right things to do to entice someone to her. A pity no man had thought her worthy. She surely would have been an enthusiastic lay for some lucky teenager, if only they had bothered with her.

Who knows why people went for the people that they did? How did someone as voluptuous and eager as Alex pass through high school a virgin? It was an odd world. Obviously Alex wasn't part of the cool crowd, if in fact it was cool at all to be spending the weekends tangled up in Daddy's car's backseat, playing Russian roulette with baby seeds.

Alex was somewhat of a loner, but that didn't mean a thing in the scheme of life.

Vanessa resisted the urge to scratch her neck. She wanted desperately to take off her sweatshirt, but she couldn't be sure how much of her flesh was leaking and scabbing. It wouldn't be long before the pus soaked right through.

"You are very pretty, Alex," Vanessa said, sliding a chair next to Alex. The girl giggled and played with the button on her blouse.

"Thank you." Alex blushed.

Vanessa ran her fingers along the girl's arm. Alex stared at her cooler bottle. Vanessa leaned over and kissed her softly on the cheek. Alex turned her face toward Vanessa.

"Why do you like me?" Alex asked. Vanessa stroked Alex's face, tracing her cheek, down to her firm strong chin. A beautiful face. The face of an angel. An innocent. For a moment she thought of the Our Lady Peace song, "Innocence."

"I see something in you. It reminds me of me," Vanessa said. She ran her fingers through Alex's hair, gently tugging it. A gentle buzzing resonated through Vanessa's hands. Surging through her blood. Pumping through the beating of her heart. Alex rested her head on Vanessa's shoulder.

"I wish I could stay with you forever," Alex sighed.

"Maybe you could," Vanessa said, pressing her lips against Alex's again. She kissed the girl hungrily, running her lips along her neck, her shoulders, down to her breasts. Alex sighed and threw her head back.

Vanessa's body burned. The scars rubbing against her clothes set off an electric heat. Her wounds would soon split open and the barrage of blood and infection would be unstoppable.

"Would you like to see my home?" Vanessa asked, standing up.

"Sure."

She took the girl's hand and led her back into the small kitchen.

"Modest, but home," Vanessa said. They walked back through the kitchen and into the tiny living room. Vanessa kept the home looking somewhat normal on the surface for clients and visitors. Alex ran her hand along a large TV.

"That's a big screen," Alex said.

"I don't watch TV much, but when I do, I want to enjoy it."

"Yeah."

Vanessa led her into the bedroom. It was large, with a queen-size bed, an ancient wooden dresser, and end tables. Off to the side was an oval tub with three brick steps up. Beyond the tub was a small bathroom, with a shower stall, toilet, and sink. There were shelves set in the wall, with many odd-shaped jars on them.

"Oh, wow!" Alex said. "I love that tub! I've never seen anything like it."

"It's a Jacuzzi, actually." Vanessa walked over to the tub and pointed to the jets set in the sides.

"I've never been in a Jacuzzi," Alex said. "What's it like?"

"Would you like to try it?" Vanessa asked.

"Please!"

The itching was growing unbearable. It wouldn't be long before Vanessa would have to rip her clothes off to keep from screaming.

Vanessa turned the large brass handles of the tub and pressed the stopper. Water rushed into the tub. Vanessa took a canister of purple oil from a shelf lined with various bottles of assorted shapes and sizes. As she unscrewed the top, lavender and other herbs permeated the air. She poured some into the water. She took a couple of toy bath animals from the shelf and placed them on the side of the tub.

One was a black cat, the other a pink pig.

"Would you like another drink?" Vanessa asked, noting that Alex's bottle was empty.

Alex nodded.

Vanessa went into the kitchen and got another drink.

When she returned to the bedroom, Alex was in her bra and panties. Vanessa looked at the girl's large breasts, hugged snugly in a white lace bra.

"Here." She handed Alex the bottle, staring sharply at the girl's swollen cleavage.

"My . . ." Vanessa said, turning away. She set to work lighting candles all around the room. Once they were lit, she dipped her hand into the water. It was deliciously warm. Not hot. Just warm. How she yearned to rip off her clothes and dive into the water. But she had to be patient.

"It won't be long before it's ready," Vanessa said. Alex stood before her, preening in the mirror. Such soft young flesh. So supple. So firm. So unblemished.

As if following a siren song, Vanessa walked over to Alex and stood behind her, watching them both in the mirror. Vanessa's violet eyes gleamed vibrantly, meeting Alex's in the mirror. Alex smiled. Vanessa pressed herself against the girl's nearly naked back, slipping her hands around Alex's front and running them along her breasts. Such full breasts. Heavy in her hands. She could imagine them swelling with milk. A baby suckling on them. Men dying to suckle them.

Vanessa kissed Alex's neck. Her shoulders. Her back. Alex alternated between giggling self-consciously and letting passion sweep across her.

Vanessa's fingers unhooked Alex's bra. She slipped the straps carefully from the girl's shoulders, and watched in the mirror as large breasts slid from the bra cups. Her nipples were hard little cherries. Vanessa rolled them in her fingers. She nuzzled Alex's neck as her burning fingers toyed with her breast.

Vanessa kissed Alex one last time and looked over to the Jacuzzi.

"It's ready," Vanessa said.

"Are you going to come in with me?" Alex asked as she slipped off her panties.

"Not just yet. I want to enjoy watching you first."

Alex stepped into the tub and sat down. She smiled and shut her eyes as she leaned back.

"This is amazing," she sighed.

The candles flickered as Vanessa sat on the bed. The itching was beyond annoying. Now it ventured toward pain. Liquid drops ran down her back, trickling like sweat, but she knew, she *knew* it wasn't sweat. It burned. Her wounds ached and burned, splitting open. In the dim light, she looked at her own chest and saw the wounds seeping through the jersey. Her legs ached, and splotches of pus were seeping through there as well. The girl in the bathtub was now washing herself, flirtatiously batting her eyes at Vanessa. Vanessa forced a grin, hoping it didn't look like a lecherous leer. She stifled a gasp as her wounds throbbed and burned.

How she hated this. Eternal life. What was she thinking? She hadn't even finished a normal first life yet and she'd suffered so much already. What powers had she that she couldn't even manage to alleviate this pain?

But she *could* alleviate this pain. No question.

In a few hours, by the light of the moon, she would be young and strong again.

She would be the voluptuous Queen of the Night, of Day, of all that she saw, all that she wanted.

A delicate balance, deciding what was worth having.

Trial and error. How much power did she really want? Really need?

Every time she exerted energy, she had to replenish it. So it was necessary to pick and choose what was truly important.

Before she became a witch, she had seen it as an amazing way to cast spells. To manipulate people, places, and things. She hadn't understood the balance of nature. Of energy. She hadn't realized that even in magic, for every action there is a reaction. Nothing should be frivolous.

The first fifteen or so years after she had reached her power, she had had many frivolous moments. But since turning forty, she was starting to pick and choose where to spend her energy. What was really worth fighting for and what was worth letting slide.

Even lying awake at night, wishing for the strong arms of a man around her, knowing she could *have* the strong arms of any man she desired in the world around her, didn't give her the comfort she sought. She had wished a couple of men into being over the years. To pay attention to her. To make love to her.

It was never worth it. She would rather be alone than know she had manipulated the affections of others. As ruthless as she had been in the past, she wanted to fall in love. Real love. To be truly loved back, for herself.

She knew Demian loved her, and she loved him. But they were too different, too far apart. She hadn't even seen or heard from him in years. He was still alive. Still playing his guitar somewhere. Still luring beautiful women to him with his vivid green eyes and haunting melodies. She could sense that much.

Perhaps he could sense her as well. He knew she had eternal life. And he was a mortal.

Wishing for men and their strength was going to do her no good right now. Alex sat in her bathtub, playfully fiddling with her own nipples, shyly glancing over at Vanessa.

Vanessa put her hands against her own breasts. God but they ached where the flesh had been patched together. She didn't dare touch them too hard in case they slid right off into her hands.

"Why don't you play with the toys I put out for you?" Vanessa asked. Alex giggled as she grabbed the cat and pig.

"They're so cute! Look at them!" she cried, rubbing the soft terry cloth against her face.

Vanessa's breath hitched as she watched the girl, almost in slow motion, rub the animals along her breasts, her body, until they touched the water.

There was a buzzing noise and instantly a huge blue spark showered over tub. The water lurched up and bubbled. Alex screamed, as electricity surged through her. She quivered and shook, her hands unable to let go of the toys. Puffs of smoke rose from her hair, followed by bursting clumps of sparks. Her eyes rolled back into her head, then melted into a steamy mush. Liquid ran down her cheeks as her mouth was freeze-framed into a scream. Her tongue bubbled, and a billow of smoke rose from her mouth.

Vanessa stood up and raised her hands into the air, shouting a sequence of rhyming words. The toys flew from Alex's grasp and landed on the floor. The water stopped boiling. The girl's lifeless body slid down until her face was nearly submerged.

Vanessa carefully peeled off her sweatshirt and pants. She had been right. Blood and pus was all over everything. Bits of her flesh tore off from being stuck to the clothes. She practically ran to the shelf of bottles against the far wall and grabbed several before climbing into the tub.

She cried out as the boiling stew hit her legs. Ignoring the stench of the bubbling body, she opened the stoppers of the premixed potions and dumped them into the tub. They steamed and boiled; odors ranging from sweet ambrosia to decaying flesh filled her nose. The potions stung as they seeped into her gaping wounds. After a while, the burn of the acidic water soothed her. The heat was beginning to dissipate.

Her anthame was on the floor, by the tub, under a towel, and she grabbed it. She swirled around in the tub, grabbing Alex, trying to sit her upright. Alex's body was slippery, but at last she had her propped up.

"Sorry, Alex . . ." Vanessa said as she slit the girl from her groin to her throat. Blood poured out into

24

the bathtub. Vanessa put her hands inside the huge wound in the girl, rubbed her fingers against organs, squeezing as much blood out as she could. She was sitting on Alex in such a way that she wished that the girl were still alive. Maybe she should have raped her first . . . but then she wouldn't be a virgin, would she? And it was the virgin blood she needed.

So Vanessa kissed the poor girl on her opened mouth several times, muttering words of sorrow as her hands squeezed and pulled on her innards. When she had pulled out enough of the guts, she carefully started to cut away large flaps of skin and patched up the leaking spots on her own. It was interesting, painstaking work.

She would take a piece of the flesh and press it over one of her own battle scars. Then she would take one of the potions and dribble a few drops over the flesh while uttering a magical phrase. The flesh bound itself to her, molding as if there had never been a scar there at all.

The flesh-bandaging itself took several hours, for Vanessa had an unbelievable amount of scars from all her battles. As she covered each badge of her journeys, she thought about how the wound had been received and then sought to banish it.

Once the superficial flesh was repaired, Vanessa turned the Jacuzzi on high. Blood and guts still simmering in the tub swirled and bubbled. Vanessa put her face into the mixture many times, her body totally immersed.

The pain of her wounds was ebbing. Power was slowly being restored to her like a battery charging. Her blood boiled with a new vibrant energy. By the time the clock struck midnight, she was ready to step out of the tub.

She gathered up as much of the leftovers as she could in a pail, and prepared some new jars. Once she was finished uttering words and organizing her latest catch, she was ready for the next round of cleansing.

She rinsed off in the shower, watching blood and bits of debris swirl down the drain. She washed her hair with her favorite herbal shampoo, inhaling the fresh aroma. It was a pleasure after the stench of death.

When she was done, she sashayed over to the mirror.

She laughed long and loud as pleasure surged through her. She flipped her hair back and turned around, examining herself from all angles. The flesh blended with her own so perfectly she couldn't tell where the patching had even been done. Even the pain was gone. Her breasts were high and large once more. Her stomach flat. Her ass round and firm. Her thighs were as taut as Alex's had been and there wasn't one wrinkle on her face. Not one gray hair in her head. Even the scar around her neck was gone.

New, improved Vanessa didn't look a day over twenty-five.

Chapter Two

"Tell me the truth."

Cheryl Smith was a dark-haired woman in her thirties. Her hand-knitted blue sweater was unraveling at the cuffs, and her socks had holes in them. She sat on the edge of her chair, alternately watching Vanessa's face and the tabletop. Her fingers played with the long strap of the large black purse that she held in her lap.

Vanessa laid the tarot cards out carefully in front of her. She stared at them, waiting for the pictures to form patterns. She was inclined to believe there was more here than met the eye.

"Well, first of all," Vanessa said, picking her words carefully, "your gut instinct is probably right, Cheryl."

Cheryl's eyes filled with tears. Her fingers picked more urgently at the vinyl strap.

"Who is it?"

Sèphera Girón

Vanessa stared at the cards, letting colors and emotions wash over her. A picture formed in her head. Blurry. Almost flittering at the corners of her mind. She scrambled to put words to the images she saw.

"Young. Blond . . ." Vanessa shook her head. "You don't know her."

"Seems almost impossible to not know everyone in such a small town. But it's true. There are a shit-load of people I don't know."

"She means nothing to him," Vanessa said quickly.

Vanessa felt an ache in her stomach. It was a lie. The man would leave his wife in a heartbeat for the blonde if he thought the blonde would be true to him. But he felt she was a cheater.

Once a cheater, always a cheater.

He felt secure with his wife. Secure in the thought that she would never cheat on him though he was a lying bastard himself. How could Vanessa say that to a woman who was watching her face for every nuance? Clinging to every hope that the marriage could be saved?

"I take it that there have been problems in the bedroom between you two," Vanessa said. Cheryl nodded, rustling in her purse for a tissue as the tears fell. Vanessa reached over to the coffee table beside her and placed a box of tissues in front of the sobbing woman.

"It's like . . . I don't know. I'm so tired from dealing with the kids all day. It's like someone wanting one more damn thing from me."

Vanessa nodded.

28

"I mean . . . I like sex. Don't get me wrong. I used to be insatiable before the kids came and I know I could be again, if I wasn't so tired. So drained. So nervous about so much. Maybe it's the way we go about it? God, how can something so simple be so complicated?"

"Sex is the great mysterious complication of life, isn't it? It *is* life. The beginning of life. The urgency that drives us through life. It has the power to destroy people and even countries."

"Marriages."

"Always marriages. I see it over and over. One partner looking for more excitement. Maybe there is truth in that. Maybe the grass is always greener in every aspect of their lives."

Vanessa sighed.

"You know, if I found someone who loved me for me, and we were able to please each other, I would never leave him," Vanessa said.

"But boredom sets in." Cheryl said. "On one side or the other, boredom sets in."

"It doesn't have to. Does it? Wouldn't love carry you through?"

"Apparently not." Cheryl's eyes filled with fresh tears and she fought to keep her voice from trembling. "Giving a man children, keeping his house, working part-time. All to build a future. And it's not enough. It's never enough. I've seen it in my friends, and now it's happening to me."

"Maybe he's just ungrateful."

Vanessa flipped a few more cards.

"He's scared."

"Scared of what?" Cheryl asked.

"Scared of you."

"Me?"

"He thinks you love the children more than you love him. He feels like he doesn't belong in the family anymore."

"But he *is* the family."

"I'm just telling you what the cards say."

"So he's fucking around. He's the one leaving the family. We're all right here."

"He knows you know. He's waiting for you to confront him."

"I don't think so."

"You should."

"Why? What's the point? There'll just be tears and denial."

"Maybe . . ."

Vanessa flipped another card.

"There's more to it, though."

Vanessa frowned and flipped a few more cards over.

"What is it?" Cheryl asked.

Vanessa stared at the cards. A strangeness washed over her, but she couldn't quite put her finger on what the message was that she was supposed to convey.

"I don't know. I'm sorry."

"What's that supposed to mean?"

"You know what, Cheryl?" Vanessa said as she scooped the cards together. "Can you come back in a week? I'll only charge you half price for today."

"Sure." Cheryl dug in her purse for her money. "Should I confront him then?"

"I'd wait on that. For a while. But in the meantime, reassure him that he's the most important person in the world for you. Maybe that will turn him around enough."

"What did you see that you aren't telling me?" Cheryl asked.

"I can't say right now. It will be more clear as time goes on."

Vanessa led Cheryl to the door and watched her get into the car. She felt weary and drained, and that was only the first reading of the day.

There would be Mrs. Bunting coming to see her in an hour, and she had to get composed. Recharge her fading energy. Try to understand what she saw in the cards.

Sometimes, though, she forgot what she saw in the cards almost the minute that she finished conducting a reading. She would say and see things, and then it would fade from her mind as if it had never been at all.

The living room where she conducted her readings was in a state of casual disarray. Her altar was covered with a sheet so that her precious tools wouldn't absorb her clients' energy. She hadn't dusted in a few days, and dust motes danced in the glint of the sun. She moved around the room, straightening things up, her mind churning a mile a minute. She had long suspected Cheryl's husband of cheating. Things like adultery barely fazed her in the cards anymore. Usually people asked because they had a gut feeling, and nine times out of ten, the cards indicated they were correct in their suspicions. It was more like people needed some sort of confirmation when, in fact, their own intuition was working just fine.

Adultery, though, was common. It was a practice as old as man. The great untold secret. Almost everyone fell into its path at some point. It was a sad, sorry state of affairs.

Why did people bother to get married? To swear their devotion to each other? And then go and cheat?

She had seen so many instances where one partner was disgruntled with the other for whatever reason. Yet so many things were working too. Financial. Children. So many partnerships. All thrown away for the sake of touching another person's flesh.

Vanessa had never been married, but she knew if she ever was, if she ever found someone who instilled a sense of devotion in her enough to stand up before friends and family, that she would never betray him. Never. No matter how angry he made her.

She had been through so much. If anyone could truly love her, if anyone could truly penetrate her elusive heart, why would she bother to betray them?

She hoped that one day she would trust someone enough to not betray her as well.

Was it even possible to trust like that again? To trust body, mind, and soul in the hands of another? To trust giving her heart, her love, to another human.

Would she ever get married?

She would have to reveal her eternal life if she did, wouldn't she? Or would she just be ageless while her spouse grew old and died? How many husbands would she end up burying over eternity? Would her first love be her only true love? Or was it possible to love over and over again as her life entered different phases?

She had loved Demian once. Maybe she still did. She felt a connection with him that went beyond lust and love. But marriage with him? It was laughable. He'd drive her insane within a month.

There had been others in her life she could have loved. Men. Women. People that had a spark of something in them that attracted her on some primal level. But in the end, or even before it began, there would be a disappointment. She wondered sometimes if maybe her expectations were too high. Could any mortal really live up to what she wanted?

Did she even know *what* she wanted?

Ah, but that was the secret.

The key to witchcraft, wasn't it?

Intent.

Knowing what she wanted. It was all fine and dandy to know what she didn't want.

But what did she really *want*?

Vanessa found a pen and paper and wrote down what she really and truly wanted in a human mate. It didn't seem that difficult or unreasonable.

1. Beautiful eyes
2. Kind
3. Sense of humor
4. Love of sex
5. Employed

6. Honest
7. Loyal

Man or woman. Was it that hard to find someone with those qualities?

It was always the honest and loyal part that got screwed up.

Humans just couldn't seem to be honest and loyal. At least, not in her experience.

And she was one to talk.

She hadn't been terribly honest and loyal in the past either.

Age and experience had given her great insight, should she choose to use it. She deeply hoped that her more selfish moments were behind her. For that had always been her fatal flaw.

Self-absorption.

She would be loyal and honest if she found the right partner.

If she ever found the right partner.

Vanessa rolled up the piece of paper and tied it with a red thread. She stuck it into the corner of her bookcase.

With her mind more focused, she was able to resume tidying things until Mrs. Bunting rang the doorbell. She had counseled Mrs. Bunting twice previously and found her to be a difficult read. It wasn't Mrs. Bunting's fault. She wanted desperately for Vanessa to be able to pluck facts from her mind, but they always slipped away. Like shadows. Vanessa could see them, but whenever she tried to articulate her visions, it was like trying to wrap her hands around a sunbeam. Her tongue couldn't convey what she saw, nor could she fully understand what it was she saw either.

It was odd, but not uncommon. Mrs. Bunting wasn't the first person she had problems reading, nor would she be the last. And who knows, maybe today would be different.

Mrs. Bunting was a tiny slip of a thing and reminded Vanessa of a grandmother, although she wasn't, yet. Mrs. Bunting was only in her late forties, but she looked much older. Or maybe she looked the way a person who ages naturally really looks without the benefit of nips and tucks and eternal-life baths.

Vanessa showed her to the table and lit a candle. They sat in silent prayer for a moment, focusing their thoughts. Vanessa handed Mrs. Bunting the cards, and she took them with the tips of her fingers. Cautiously, Mrs. Bunting shuffled, staring at Vanessa now and again with wide apprehensive eyes.

"I need to know more," Mrs. Bunting said.

"I know."

"I need to know if he'll come back to me."

"I know, Mrs. Bunting," Vanessa said patiently as she watched Mrs. Bunting pick several cards.

When Mrs. Bunting was finished, Vanessa laid them out and proceeded to turn them over. One at a time. When all the cards were turned, Vanessa leaned back, her eyes glowing as she absorbed feelings and pictures.

"It's the same," Vanessa said at last. Mrs. Bunting nodded.

"I should expect no less," Mrs. Bunting said.

They looked at the cards a bit longer.

"He feels guilty. He wants to stop, but he is powerless."

"Under her spell, no doubt. Who wouldn't be?"

"She has him bewitched, but not with magic."

"I know what she has. Thousands of dollars of work is what she has."

"It's not just that." Vanessa leaned forward as a ripple of energy passed through her. She shuddered. "Hmmm . . ."

"Something new?"

"I think there is something new coming to pass. I can't quite tell. But she isn't who you think she is."

"You mean I have the wrong woman?"

"No, she's the one all right. It's just that she isn't who you've always thought she was. She has a secret side. Darkness."

"We all have a secret side, honey," Mrs. Bunting said as she patted Vanessa's arm. "Evil thoughts for evil deeds. Humans are always perched on the edge of destruction, but it's our humanness that keeps us from falling all the way over." Mrs. Bunting stared out the window. "Actually that's not true at all . . . look at the suicide bombers, terrorists, Nazis . . . lots of humans fall over all the time. Who decides when to fall and what it's worth?"

Vanessa nodded, hoping that one day, she would feel as wise as she deemed Mrs. Bunting to be. Her own thoughts were cluttered with nonsense and day-to-day clatter. She needed deeper thoughts, and she needed to understand them enough to share them with her clients. Sometimes she felt that any woman over sixty could be a counselor. Nothing magic about experienced advice. Human nature was always the same; it was just a matter of living long enough to watch the patterns and learn which ones to avoid.

The candle spit, hot wax spattering both the women. They jumped up, wiping away the pain.

The flame shot higher, flickering a bright red, and more wax sprayed out. Vanessa grabbed the candle snuffer and placed it over the flame. Her arm grew hot, her fingers burning on the metal of the snuffer. She dropped it.

"What does this mean?" Mrs. Bunting asked.

"I'm not sure, but it can't be good. . . ." Vanessa said, rubbing her hands. The candle still burned bright and furious. Vanessa looked around the room. There was a flickering in one of the corners, like a shadow twitching. She shuddered. A sensation like she was being watched prickled her arms. She flexed her fingers. A blister was forming on one of them.

"What do you see?" Mrs. Bunting watched Vanessa as she stared at the corner. The candle flame danced and the shadows danced with it.

Vanessa shook her head. "Nothing."

In the shadows, Vanessa thought she could make out a face. A leering face with thick eyebrows and sharp teeth.

Vanessa pointed her fingers at it, and a blue stream of electricity shot forth. The elusive face melted back into a maze of shadows. The candle flame returned to its normal size.

Mrs. Bunting looked from the corner to the candle.

"Did something happen?"

Vanessa flexed her fingers. "Not really."

"I thought I saw . . ."

"What did you see?"

Mrs. Bunting shrugged. "Probably an optical illusion or something. I thought it looked like something was coming out of your fingers. And then the shadows changed."

"Well, you would be right. I was trying to rearrange the energy. I think it worked. Look."

Vanessa pointed to the candle.

Mrs. Bunting smiled. "That's better."

Mrs. Bunting stood up. "I guess that's all the excitement one needs for one day."

"Yes it certainly is."

Mrs. Bunting slipped several bills into Vanessa's hand.

"Tell me, Vanessa. Did you see anything else? Anything I should know about? Anything I should be doing?"

Vanessa touched Mrs. Bunting on the shoulder. "There is nothing you can do right now. Just keep living as you have been, doing what's right and good. As long as you do that, then peace will find you eventually."

"I hope you are right."

Vanessa watched Mrs. Bunting drive away.

She turned back to the room. The darkness in that same corner shifted. She blew out the candle.

Vanessa stood on a large rock that rose out of the shoreline like the back of a dinosaur. Below her, black sea waves undulated in the glow of the moon.

Dark secrets lurked beneath the waves. She had been there. She remembered.

No sooner than she'd think about one thing, another would pop into her mind. The moon flipped into the sun, and before long, her pale flesh was glistening with sweat.

The sun rose high into the sky, hurting her eyes with gleaming rays that bounced from the ocean like darts ricocheting from a target. The waves crashed higher, splashing her with stinging salty shards. She raised her arms, embracing the heat and coldness, reveling in the sharp burn of sun and sea. Power circled through her and the sun began to set. Orange-red rays burned across the top of the ocean. Steam rose as it rippled until the setting rays found Vanessa. The sun burned into her, dissolving the new flesh she had just bandaged around herself.

"Don't take her from me," Vanessa cried. Behind her, she heard laughter, sharp as a staccato on the E string of a violin. She turned around to face her mocker.

It was a pathetic rendering of what was once a woman. Two women? She wasn't even sure.

"How do you like it now?" The low raspy voice was now like gravel being poured into a pit. Vanessa tried to focus on the person—the thing in front of her. It wavered, as if it were film out of focus. One minute, it seemed to be a woman. A frumpy plump woman with dark hair and pudgy fingers. The next, it was animal. An odd animal person, like something out of *Alice in Wonderland* or some other fantastical place. Long wiry whiskers protruded from a stumpy snout. Triangular pink ears waved and twitched like a periscope. Vanessa recognized Sophie. A woman she had thought she was finished with long ago.

"How do I like what?" Vanessa asked.

"All that you hoped for. All that you dreamed."

"What did I dream?"

"Eternal life. You wanted it so badly and now look at you."

Vanessa narrowed her eyes. The woman rippled. She was a glimmering fountain of glitter. She was a pink wrinkled lump. She was a fat woman with small brown eyes and a pouty mouth.

"I am fine."

"Where are your friends now, Vanessa? You killed them all. You even drove away Demian."

It was dark again. The woman before her glowed pink. Her pig snout was now on the side of her head, as an ill-formed conjoined twin might be.

"That's not true." Vanessa turned back to the ocean, but it was gone. There were only rocks before her now. Mountains and miles of huge boulders.

"Where's Demian then?"

"He went to pursue his music career. Why would I go with him?"

" 'Cause you love him. . . ." The woman sneered. "Or as much as a selfish bitch like you can love anyone."

"Isn't the saying something like, 'If you love someone set them free'?" Vanessa said.

"Oh, sure. Enjoy your little platitudes. You've always done what serves you best."

"We all should live for what serves us best. That was *your* problem. You were too busy serving others."

"Compassion?" The woman lay on the rocks and rolled back and forth. Vanessa watched the gelatinous mounds of pink flesh flop. Was she human? Was she animal? Did it matter much in a dream?

"Passion? Yes . . ." The woman chuckled. "Yes, you always had passion. Horny witch with a perverted itch . . ." The laughter rebounded from rocks and sky and circled until it was a seagull scream. The sun flashed like a strobe light.

"Compassion. How many children have you murdered in the past twenty years, Vanessa? How many fruits of other people's loins have you violated for your own needs and pleasures?"

"It's the curse. . . ." Vanessa said. "I just wanted a peaceful life. A long full life where I could explore the mysteries of the universe."

"What would happen if you just let nature take its course? If you left the young alone?"

"I'm not going to be reduced to the role of zombie freak."

"So you murder . . ."

"It's not murder. It's survival of the fittest. Plain and simple." Vanessa turned her back on the woman rolling on the rocks and looked out to sea. Instead of water or rocks, there floated rows upon rows of shadows. They flickered, with red glowing holes where eyes would have been.

"You took our innocence. . . ." They moaned. They wailed. Vanessa laughed.

"You guys are worse then a cheesy horror movie. Come on now." She pointed at each one.

"I only took those that didn't have a chance. Sorry, guys and gals, but misfits are misfits. I needed your flesh to build mine. I needed your virgin blood to fuel mine. Pure and easy."

"She took mine first," Sophie told the shadows. "I was the first."

"So what, Sophie? Now you all live here. How wonderful."

The moon was back, glowing green. The shadows reached for Vanessa, but were unable to move from their spots.

"Think of how much more good you will do now, helping me help others." Vanessa said.

"You only help others 'cause you need money and that's the only way you can think of to get it."

"Not true. There's a lot I can do."

"Sure there is. You could have your own TV show. Or you could write a book. Or design museums and dig for dinosaurs. There's lots you can do. No kidding." Sophie crossed her arms.

"Okay, Jiminy Cricket, get the hell out of my head. I've had enough."

"I want my mommy." One of the shadows stepped forward reaching for Vanessa. It seemed to be stopped by some invisible barrier.

"Stay where you are. You're done." Vanessa raised her hand and pointed her finger. The shadow slipped back in among the others before it could experience Vanessa's anger.

"One day, I'll be the weaker, of that I'm sure. But so far, in forty years and several lifetimes of experiences, that has not been the case. I always win. I always will."

"Why did you lie to me?" Alex's voice was a sigh.

Her shadow wasn't as dark as the others. It shimmered.

"I needed you. I still need you. We're not done yet, you and I." Vanessa said.

"I thought you cared. I thought . . . maybe . . ." Alex stammered.

"Whatever you thought, you now know the truth. You are beautiful. Well, were. And men *are* scum. I saved you from a lifetime of heartbreak. This I know. I'm a fortune-teller, right?" Vanessa sneered.

"I don't know. Maybe I would have found a good man."

"There aren't any." Vanessa laughed. "No, there aren't."

"Maybe for you there aren't. If you hadn't been such an asshole to everyone," Sophie said.

"I was never an asshole to you."

Sophie's laugh was loud and caustic. The sun burned bright red and drops of blood fell from the sky.

"You made me what I am. Maybe I will one day find it in my heart to be grateful."

"You were always a pig. A big fat pig taking up space. Maybe one day I should just finish you off with some eggs."

"What goes around comes around, Vanessa. Remember that."

"Yeah, yeah. The circle of life, the threefold rule. All that shit. I know. But I have the power to make it not so, as well, don't I?"

"Just how powerful are you, really? Vanessa? How powerful do you think you could be against an army of witches?"

"There aren't enough witches to make an army. I'm not too worried about what my dream demons tell me."

"Maybe I am the worst dream demon you can imagine."

"Then maybe I already know I'm safe."

The crowd of shadows began to fade, squealing like air being released from a balloon. The rocks beneath Vanessa's feet shifted and shuddered. She adjusted herself for balance.

She looked toward the sun, now a glowing ball of red sinking quickly into the sea. The shadows were gone; only Vanessa and the rocks remained. She raised her hands in the air. Her waist-length hair rose gently in the wind.

"Oh mighty spirits of north, south, east, west,
I give you thanks for giving me Alex.
Bless her spirit into your giving arms,
and embrace her for all eternity."

The wind grew stronger, and Vanessa smiled as she felt it blow against her cheeks. She opened her mouth to consume it. The wind tunneled through her mouth and shot down her throat. Power vibrated through her, soaring from her chakras.

"Thank you mighty spirits of earth, wind, fire, and water,
for giving me power once more.
I will use it wisely
and in reverence to your generosity."

44

She bowed down and crossed her arms before raising them once more.

The wind died down and when she looked up again, the moon was full and the only sound was the lapping waves.

Vanessa knelt down and picked up a pile of seashells that lay scattered around her feet. One by one she tossed them into the waves, where they landed with a splash.

When she had finished the last one, there was lethargic clapping behind her. Sophie stepped out from a ripple in the air.

"Lovely ceremony, Vanessa. But tell me, do you think it will work this time? Maybe the gods grow angry at your frivolous ways."

"I'm not frivolous. I work for a living and I pretty much keep to myself. I don't even have a dishwasher."

"See? Dishwasher. All this power and all you can think about is dishwashers."

"I was thinking of something frivolous."

"And I was thinking in terms of more important matters."

"Such as?"

"Why do you pick on these poor girls and boys? With all your power, there must be another way to mend your battered flesh. What about the spell book?"

"That *is* from the spell book. You think in all this time I haven't looked for other answers? I've even tried some nonsense from the Internet, and nothing worked. Believe me, Sophie, I hate it as much as anyone."

Sophie raised her lip in a sneer.

"Somehow I doubt that."

Vanessa shrugged. "Yeah. Right. That . . . Man, that was years ago. Two decades ago. You sure hold a grudge."

"I think you would too. You're still alive."

"Yeah. I am." Vanessa stared off toward the ocean. A smirk crossed her face. She put her hand over her mouth to stifle a giggle, but it burst forth in a realm of laughter.

"I'm alive. Forever . . ."

Vanessa burst awake with a gasp. Her bedsheets were soaked with sweat.

"Boy, that was some dream," she said to Katisha, who sleepily watched her from the foot of her bed. Vanessa stumbled up to go get a glass of water. She flipped on the bedroom light and the glow streamed out into the hall. She felt a sense of unease as she wandered down the shadowed hallway. Snippets of her dream returned to haunt her. Goose bumps peppered her arms as she crept down the hall. As she passed through the living room toward the kitchen, she looked out the front window. It was heavily shadowed by branches, yet it seemed darker out there than usual. Perhaps there was someone looking in. Someone or something pretty large. After all she had seen, she was ready for anything.

She continued on until her shaking hands poured a glass of water and she downed it like a dying man. When she passed by the window again, she could see out toward the road and her car parked in the driveway.

There had been someone or something there.

Chapter Three

Vanessa stared into her morning cup of coffee. A great sense of unease coursed through her. How could it be that she had all those tarot readings with that same unanswerable question? What was the question?

It was as if there was something she could almost glimpse out of the corner of her eye, yet she couldn't put her finger on it. It was the same sensation she had from the cards. There was something there, something in common for several of her clients, yet she couldn't quite pull it into focus.

It was a puzzlement and one that distressed her. She didn't like it when the cards played tricks on her. There was no magic in tarot cards themselves, or even in how they were read. The only magic was in how the cards seemed to know when to reveal themselves to someone at precisely the right time.

Yet this sense of something not quite being right

was akin to magic. It was unanswerable right now, and smacked of occult or unknown activity.

She had hoped for peace in this little town, but now, after five years of avoiding unusual activity, aside from her own, there were indications that something was rippling the fabric of normalcy.

Lord knows, she had been through quite a few bizarre things over the past twenty years. Things most people couldn't even imagine, unless they had lived through them themselves.

Now, her intuition was gnawing at her.

Something new was in the air.

She needed to pay attention, for who knows what the warning would be, if there would be any at all.

Like when the Towers fell.

There was no warning. Nothing out of the ordinary that morning. She had been living in this very house, breathing in the warm fall air while she puttered around in her tiny garden, harvesting herbs for the solstice and grateful for how warm it had been that day.

Later on, she had turned on the news, and there they were. Smoking and wounded, until they fell.

She would never forget the ache of that moment. She had felt terror many times in her life, she had many enemies, but nothing prepared her for the ache of three thousand lives shattered in mere moments. She felt like she would never be able to do anything again. Everything seemed like an echo after watching that.

But she survived. Everyone survived. And the world was never really quite the same again.

Now there was the prominent threat of terrorism

daily. What had been before something lurking in the shadows now came forward full throttle. What she had always feared would happen now suddenly was happening.

The world was perched on the brink of war. Yet again.

And how could it not be?

People couldn't even get along within their own countries. How could they get along with other countries?

Husbands murdered wives, mothers abandoned their children, guns were everywhere, and the air always had the scent of chaos bubbling just below the surface. So how would this divided land ever get its shit together to unite and stand against Third World terrorism?

How could man think that more killing, bomb dropping, and environmental pollution were the answers to the questions?

She didn't know the answers, but she knew that dropping nukes on impoverished people wasn't a plan that she was proud of.

If she wasn't so afraid, if she hadn't been so wary of her powers, she would take a plane over and destroy all the terrorist supporters. But did that make her any better then them? A murderer was a murderer.

She was a murderer.

Who was she to judge the murder of three thousand or of one Catholic schoolgirl?

She needed air. She needed to go for a walk to clear her head.

Katisha ran under her feet, circling and rubbing, suddenly in need of great attention.

"You're so weird, Katisha," Vanessa said, stroking the rich black fur. Katisha rubbed against her legs, purring loudly.

"Stay here, I'll be back soon." Vanessa grabbed her keys and locked the front door, gently pushing the cat back into the house.

Vanessa walked out into the warm sunshine. It was much better out here, where she could think. The house was too small. Too many vibrations for her to concentrate. She liked to walk around in nature, to smell deeply of the earth, to watch the leaves turning, splashing vivid green with slashes of red and orange.

She walked down the winding path that led from her driveway and toward a wooded area that hugged the cove. Over the past few years, she had grown very fond of the woods and walked through them nearly every day, except when it was cold and snowy. One thing she hated more than anything was the cold and the snow. If the summers weren't so beautiful and the seasons changing so thrilling, she would move farther south in a heartbeat.

But she wasn't so willing to leave the East Coast right now. It had a part of her. It called to her on some primal level. She loved the rich earth and the changing trees, and even the unpredictable weather patterns of the past couple of years.

There was something in this rich changing earth that clung to her and she clung to it. She wasn't allowed to leave just yet. No matter how much the snow and darkness got her down.

She walked into the woods, feeling the temperature drop noticeably as she did. There was a path that people wandered along, and she followed it for a while. No one was around today. She figured they were all off at their day jobs.

A short way down the path there was a fork. If she followed the new path a while, it would fork off again toward a little pond. In all the times she had been here, she hardly ever saw anyone else around this area. She figured that people were either afraid of coming here alone, or just didn't have time during the day as she did.

The pond was hardly a pond anymore. It was fenced off by two winding sets of rusty barbed and chicken wire, with weeds and trees growing wild around it. The pond itself was a luminescent green from algae growing unchecked along the surface. She was always amazed to hear frogs burbling along the edges. She could only imagine how thick and murky the water would be and how horrible it would be to touch or drink or swim in it.

She went around the far edge of the pond, where the path swerved away, found her favorite tree with the roots that sprawled out like legs, and sat down in between them. She leaned back against the tree and stared at the green of the water.

Green.

Green was the color of growth.

Of money.

Of prosperity.

Of health.

Green was the color of Demian's eyes.

She wondered where he was. She wondered even

more why he was popping into her thoughts yet again when for so long, she had nearly forgotten his existence.

Too long without a friend.

Too long without a man.

She had to figure out how to make friends.

Sure she had acquaintances and clients. She certainly had people to talk to on a regular basis. But friends?

A confidant.

Someone to talk to who could talk back, unlike a pet.

Someone who would hold her when she was sad and laugh with her when things were good.

Someone to have a beer and burger with on Saturday night, watch *MAD TV* and have sex with till the sun came up.

That was her wish.

She was a witch, she could make it so.

But she didn't want to make it so in an unnatural way.

She didn't want to manipulate someone's free will.

She wanted someone to love her for her, and she wanted to love him for him.

So easy.

So human.

Was she still human?

Maybe she wasn't considered human at all.

She thought about those months after she had cast the spell. The horrible events that had transpired and how she was lucky to be alive, or was she merely un-dead?

Thoughts like that made her brain hurt. She wasn't sure at all what she was.

She was human.

She was a woman.

A woman that yearned for passion.

A woman that yearned for something new.

She sat and stared at the pond some more, reflecting on the green, watching a frog make his way from one side of the pond to the other in a series of plops and splashes and swims.

She must have been there quite some time, and daydreaming even longer, for when she snapped back to reality, there was someone else sitting and staring at the pond.

He sat almost on the other side, on the large flat rock that she sometimes liked to sit on.

She had never seen him before, but of course, being the hermit she was, that didn't mean a damn thing.

He sat in contemplation, and she felt that he didn't know that she was there either. He was staring into the pond.

She wondered how many secrets the pond held. How many people had come here over the years, staring and thinking and wishing and wondering.

Even though he was a fair distance away, she could tell he had a nice face. His hair was short, dark brown. His mouth was closed, his hands clutching his knees.

Vanessa stood up, and his concentration was broken.

He glanced over toward her, and a smile touched

his lips. He turned back to looking at the pond, only now he seemed self-conscious about it.

Vanessa made her way back to the path, taking the side that wound around the man. She walked slowly, feeling his eyes on her. When she was close enough, she looked directly at him. Her heart skipped a beat.

He had green eyes. Vivid and clear, like shiny dots of glass.

"Hello," she said.

"Hello."

She was about to walk on when he spoke again.

"Excuse me . . ."

"Yes?"

"Are you . . . are you the tarot reader?"

"Yes."

The man nodded. His face was pleasing to look at, more pleasing than she had realized from a distance. Strong-jawed and young. He must only be in his late twenties, early thirties.

They stood there, looking at each other in silence.

"Can I come to you for a reading sometime?" he asked.

"When would you like?"

"Well . . . when do you do it?"

Vanessa looked at the man again. She felt a surge of warmth run up her back, and her fingers tingled. It was as though a flower had sprung to life inside of her and was weaving its way through her veins.

"If you have time, we could go back to my place right now," she said.

"Now?" The man looked uneasy.

"Or we can do it another day."

"Now's fine," he said, and stood up.

My, but what a fine young man he was. Tall with broad shoulders. He walked with confidence.

They made their way back to Vanessa's place, mostly in silence. Swells of lust were rippling through Vanessa in a way that she hadn't felt in years. What was it about this man that was affecting her this way?

When they reached the house, Katisha was waiting at the door.

"What a pretty cat," he said as they entered. Katisha wove herself around his legs, purring loudly. He reached down to pick her up and she nuzzled his chin.

"I'm surprised she's taken to you like that. She's not usually that friendly."

"I like animals." he said.

Vanessa led him over to the table and indicated where he should sit.

"Would you like a tea or water or something?"

"Water would be fine. It's hot in the woods today."

"Do you go there often?"

"Now and again. I've seen you there before."

"You have?"

"Yes, I heard about you and didn't want to bother you."

Vanessa took her cards out of the silk kerchief.

"What do you want to ask about?"

The man sat and thought.

"Maybe I should ask, what is your name?" Vanessa said.

They both laughed.

"David."

"Hi, David. I'm Vanessa."

She touched his hand, and a jolt shot up through her. Instead of the usual heat and turbulence, the sensation was warm and peaceful. Her mind was filled with pink for a second, and then it cleared.

"So . . . your question."

"Well, I guess it's typical. A typical boring question for you." David sighed.

"Nothing is typical when it's from the heart."

"And it is. I had a girlfriend for the longest time, but she left me for another man a couple months ago. And I'm just wondering, will I ever fall in love again? Can I fall in love again? Will this ever happen to me again?"

His face was pained, and it was all Vanessa could do to keep from reaching over and taking it in her hands and kissing him. Sometimes she forgot that men were human too. That they hurt just as badly as women, that they felt the same highs and lows of love and passion. It had been too long since she had connected with a man emotionally.

With the cards shuffled and dealt, she stared at them for a moment, feeling the pain of his betrayal. The ache of his broken heart.

"Was she even worth all the agony you've put yourself through?" Vanessa asked.

"In hindsight? No. Of course not. Who is? But at the time, you always live for the dream. The what-ifs and hope-fors."

"We all do. Nothing to feel ashamed of for that."

"So, what else do you see? Anyone new?"

Vanessa smiled. "Yes. There is someone new."

"When? Where?"

"You have already met her."

"Who is it?"

"You will know."

David looked at Vanessa and sighed. "How . . . how will I know?"

"Listen to your heart. Your emotions. It will just feel right."

"I hope you're right. I don't put much faith in this stuff, but everyone says you are so good."

"It's not me, I just read the cards. We all are in control of our destiny. We have to make things happen."

"How can I make this happen?"

"Be patient and listen to your heart."

"Can you tell me? Give me a hint? What does she look like? Where do I know her from?"

"You live in town, right?"

"Yes."

"You work with people . . . a salesperson, bartender, or something? Something with your hands."

"I work at the hardware store. Sometimes I get to go out on calls, but usually I just sell stuff."

"Oh, the hardware store. I know the one."

"Yeah. It's okay for now. I'm not sure what I really want to do."

"You will figure it out."

"It's tough being thirty and not knowing what I want to do with my life. How do people just know? Sometimes it doesn't seem fair, how some people have a calling and others don't. Some of us just work to get by with no greater plan."

"I didn't know I would read tarot until just a few years ago."

"So you were young when you knew. That's what I mean."

"I'm not so young." Vanessa smiled.

"Women . . . they are always so coy about their age. What are you? Twenty-eight? I know you've been here a few years, living alone, so you have to be in your late twenties, but I swear you look eighteen."

"Flattery will get you everywhere."

"So back to the love thing . . ."

"There is love. There is hope."

David leaned back in his chair, smiling.

"You made my day, whether you are telling the truth or not."

"I always tell the truth. In tarot."

"What do I owe you?"

Vanessa leaned forward. "Dinner."

"Dinner? Surely you want to be paid in cold hard cash."

Vanessa grinned. "Always. But for some reason, from you, I want dinner."

"Then dinner you shall have. Tonight?"

"Yes."

"Seven?"

"Sure."

"I'll see you then."

David got up and nearly stumbled out of the door. Vanessa was light-headed as she watched him walk down the street.

Dinner? Was she nuts?

Yet there was something about David that she

liked. Something familiar and pleasant. A sense that they had met before, though she knew they hadn't. The time was right for him to find a new woman, and why shouldn't that woman be her?

In the bathroom, several jars on the shelves began to jitter. They clacked against each other, dancing around like jumping beans, until one fell over and shattered. A vague puff of smoke spiraled up from the debris and floated out the door. The stream, snakelike in its journey, wriggled through the air until it was lost among the trees.

As Vanessa was putting the final touches on her makeup, the phone rang.

It was Betty.

"I need your help," Betty said.

"What's wrong?"

"It's Larry. He's missing."

"What do you mean, missing?"

"He didn't come home from work yesterday. He didn't come home today. No one has seen him."

"Oh, my."

"What can I do?'

"Did you call the police?"

"That was the first place I called, but they can't help yet. He hasn't been missing long enough. They seem to think he's just going to show up on his own."

"What do you want me to do?"

"I need you to help me. I need you to look at your cards and see where he is."

"I have an appointment

"Please, Vanessa."

"I'm sure he'll be all right. I didn't see him coming to any great harm any time soon."

"But the cards can change. They change all the time. You told me that yourself."

"I know, Betty, but right now is just not good. I have another client to see who is just as important. I'm sorry."

"Can I call you in the morning?"

"Yes, of course."

Vanessa hung up the phone. Another hazard of the job. People thought you could drop your life for their little crisis. Betty already knew her husband was a snake, so why would she be surprised he hadn't come home?

It was the same old thing. No one can believe it's happening until it happens to them.

She finished getting dressed, putting on a little black dress, black nylons, and black high heels. She knew she looked great. She certainly didn't look like the rapper that lured unsuspecting schoolgirls to her Jacuzzi of death.

She went into the bathroom to finish up.

Vanessa noticed the glass on the floor as she stepped back from the mirror.

"Godammit." She knelt down to pick up the larger pieces and threw them into the trash.

She ran into the kitchen to grab a broom, and returned to hurriedly sweep up the mess. She pushed the rest of the jars back into place, trying to figure out which one had fallen off. She was too excited about getting ready for David to ponder over it too long. She looked at herself in the mirror and smiled. She would be young and beautiful for a while now. At least long enough to get to know David and to see if he was as wonderful as he appeared. She looked back at the jars again. The doorbell rang.

"Oh, I hope that it was one that was all used up anyway." She hurriedly gathered up the rest of her belongings.

"I must remember to check when I get back."

Betty hung up the phone, her whole body shaking. There was something wrong. Really, truly wrong. And Vanessa wouldn't help her.

She went over to the piano and sat down on the bench, plinking along the keys as she stared at the wedding picture of her and Larry perched on top. How time had flown so quickly. How a lifetime had passed her by. She had lived. Lived a good life, raised good kids, been dutiful wife and mother. Everything she had ever done was for the good of others. Yet it wasn't enough.

It was never enough.

She stayed home with her children, cooking good meals, taking pride in her housework. She always made sure Larry had clean, ironed clothes in the closet and fresh towels daily. She gardened and jellied and cooked and scrubbed.

Whatever home they lived in, she made a shiny palace.

It was never enough.

Larry was never mean. Larry never hit her. Larry could get sarcastic and made sure she knew her place.

She could never understand why Larry had to fool around on her, though.

When did he start?

Was that what he was up to now?

She remembered the day she found out for certain her husband was stepping out on her.

It was a summer day, and she was home with the baby. She was doing laundry when she found the matchbook from the strip club, with the phone number on it.

Funny how he had been working late, so he said. A lot lately, yet the paycheck was always the same.

She dialed the number, after blocking her name, and a young lady answered.

Betty knew in her heart what he was up to, she didn't have to ask.

It was weird, though, because she adored him so much, loved to make love with him, do anything he'd ask in the bedroom. Yearned to be his madonna/whore.

It was never enough.

She knew the police thought he was with one of the strippers. It was known around town and no one knew that she knew all about his affairs. She had never confronted him, never asked him why. Why she wasn't good enough.

Of course, now that she was in her fifties, she knew the lure of pretty young women would always captivate him. Even though she kept herself in shape and always wore makeup, she knew that she was old.

But still, he was missing.

It wasn't like him not to come home at all.

And the feeling in the pit of her stomach told her something was dreadfully wrong.

He had been acting odd lately.

She thought back to the last time she saw him. He was getting his briefcase ready to go to work at the office where he was an insurance adjuster. He wore his good suit and smelled fresh, like a clean-shaven man should. Being in his fifties had given him a distinguished air. Salt-and-pepper hair, a bit of a potbelly, and a face that had been rugged since the day they met.

"Will you be home for dinner?" she asked.

"Yes. I don't have any late meetings today."

"That's good. I'll make your favorite then. Roast beef with those little potatoes."

"I love your cooking."

"Maybe for dessert, we'll feed each other fruit sorbet." Betty winked. Larry laughed.

"You're so good to me." he said as he kissed her on the forehead. Betty wrapped her arms around him, pressing against his suit, smelling his hair.

"I love you so much. Even after all these years."

"I love you too, Betty," he said, kissing her again as he unlocked her arms.

Betty was going to tell him how she had bought a new negligee, but she held her tongue. Maybe she'd surprise him by being dressed up when he came home. She had done it a few times, and he always seemed to appreciate it. It had been a while since she had been spontaneous like that, so it seemed like a good time.

She waved good-bye to him from the window, and she never saw him again.

That night, she waited with her dried-out roast, her curled hair wilting, her red negligee growing stale from nervous sweat. By the time she went to bed at eleven, she was in tears. The phone never rang. His car never rumbled up the driveway.

By morning she was a wreck. She called his office several times over the course of the day, but no one had seen him.

Betty sat, playing the same keys over and over again. She wondered what she should do. Where would she begin to look?

Hookers? Strippers? College kids? Who knows what had turned his fancy.

Why would he say he'd come home for dinner and then not?

He always called to say he'd be late for dinner.

Even if he was with someone else.

Betty slammed down the keyboard lid and picked up their wedding picture. She blew on it, to rearrange the newest dust motes settling in.

Larry.

Even looking at his picture, even knowing that he was never truly hers alone, she still loved him.

Her body still ached for him.

He was her life, her reason for waking in the morning.

And now, he was gone.

Vanessa sat across from David, watching him finish his burger. It was refreshing, to share a meal with someone for a change. Especially someone so nice-looking. She didn't realize she was staring at him so intently until he swallowed.

"Is something wrong? Is there slime on my face?" he asked self-consciously, wiping his mouth with a napkin.

"Nothing's wrong at all." Vanessa smiled coyly at him and picked up her fork to resume eating her own meal of chicken salad.

"Tell me about yourself," David said.

"What's to tell? I live here and help people with their problems."

"There must be more to it. How did you know you were a witch?"

"I was always interested in occult subjects. When I was in the university, it was almost like I had a calling. I really got into it. Reading every book I could get my hands on. Meeting people . . ." Vanessa stared off for a moment, thinking about how turbulent life had been when she first found her powers. She gave a little laugh, knowing she could never explain it. "Things just evolved until I am where I am today."

David nodded. He leaned over and whispered in a jesting tone, "Are you an evil witch?"

Vanessa laughed. "I don't believe in good and evil. Witches try to exist within the laws of nature. Although when there's always that taste of power lurking, it's hard to have self-restraint."

"Are you going to cast a spell on me?"

Vanessa fixed him with bright blue eyes. "What sort of spell?"

"I just wondered. Maybe you already have."

"No. I haven't. Why? Do you want to be my zombie love slave?"

David blushed. "You wouldn't have to cast a spell on me for that."

Vanessa laughed. "You don't even know me. Maybe I would have to!"

"Tell me, then, beautiful witch, why are you single?"

"Now I feel like I'm on one of those dating reality shows."

"Maybe you are! Look into the camera!" David joked as he pointed to one of the low-hanging lights.

"Seriously, though. Have you ever been married?" David asked.

"No. No marriage for me. Not yet anyway. What about you? What's a nice boy like you doing having dinner with a witch?"

"You saw my cards. I've been through hell. But despite it all, I'm an optimist. I may be kicking myself in a month or two, but right now, I'm open to new opportunity."

Vanessa raised her wine glass. David raised his beer bottle.

"Here's to new opportunity."

They clicked their glasses.

Vanessa saw in David's eyes something she hadn't seen in a very long time.

And she liked how it felt.

Chapter Four

Darkness.

The air was thick with incense and candle smoke, the room lit with a hundred flickering flames.

Wizened fingers picked and pulled at the flesh of a dying blackbird. The bird's eyes glared darkly, its beak opening and shutting as muffled squawks of agony emitted from its throat. It was too exhausted to peck at the intrusive fingers.

In the fireplace, a heavy metal pot hung. Putrid liquid inside boiling and bubbling. Bit by bit, pieces of the bird were dropped into it.

On a nearby wooden table lay several straw dolls smeared with blood. Feathers were stuck into them. Tiny pebbles were pushed in for eyes. Bits of colored cloth were wrapped around them.

An old woman hobbled from table to fire and back again. She wore a black cotton dress with a black shawl wrapped over the top. Her tangled hair was

67

long and gray, reminiscent of the old fishing net that hung along one wall. She muttered, words that were a combination of chanting and singsong.

As she poked at the pot one last time, she smiled. "Ready."

With large towels, she carried the steaming kettle into the next area. She put it down on a wooden table. The room was lit by many tea lights set in gothic candelabras set into the wall. Around the whole room was painted a black circle. There were more lines on the floor, similar to the design on the candelabras.

Between each Celtic design, a naked man hung on a meat hook. There were no scars on the men, they just hung from the fleshy scruffs of their necks, heads down as if sleeping. One of them snored in a corner, his buzzing getting louder each passing moment.

The woman clapped her hands sharply.

"Enough of that blasted noise."

The man shuddered and fell silent except for a much lower rasp of regular breathing.

The woman surveyed her collection. They ranged in age from early twenties to late fifties. A fine-looking lot they were too. Each one she had chosen because they had something pleasing to offer.

She returned to the kettle and scooped out a cupful of the wretched liquid. She wrapped it in a dark cloth to keep her hands from burning, and retrieved a small spoon from the collection of odd utensils on the table.

She walked over to the first man. He was the youngest and the most handsome. She poured a spoonful of the soup over his head, and another one over his breast. She turned the spoon over and rubbed it in the soup that was dripping down his chest. She pressed the spoon lightly into several places on his arms, legs, feet, hands, and forehead. The man continued to sleep as the hot liquid ran down his body.

When she was done, she did the same to each man until they were all consecrated in the same manner. She put the spoon down. She stood by her altar and faced her men.

Her voice was low and creaky, as if it were a rusty old door hinge that could fall apart at any moment. She drew in a deep breath and raised her arms.

"I call upon the dark forces of revenge and loneliness.
Heed my cry, fill me with your power.
Repair my life to where it must be.
Let these men invigorate me,
obey me, comfort me, submit to me."

She returned to the first man. With shaking fingers, she took the tangled mane of her hair and entwined it until only a small stem remained, sticking from between her index finger and thumb. She swished the little brush along the first marking on the man, and proceeded to drag it along him until she reached the second marking. She swirled her hair once more and continued on to the third. The man still slept, his breathing deep and even. She connected all the marks until it formed a symbol much like a star.

She stood back and examined her work. She was breathing heavily, the strain of walking from man to man after hours of preparing for the ritual was taking its toll. It took her a moment to compose herself before she proceeded to the next man.

Again, she performed the ritual. Exhaustion taunted her to sit down, but she wouldn't. She couldn't. She was compelled to continue the ritual.

When at last the men had all been painted, she returned to her spot by the altar. She continued with her prayer.

"Be within my power to give thanks to the Darkness
by amusing you with games of decadence.
Let these men become the fools they are
to follow blindly their emotions
And ignore all logic.
Let their folly be my power!"

She sank down to her knees, her arms raised to the ceiling. Her voice was scratching at the air as she struggled to speak louder.

"Four corners of the world,
come together in me,
unite as one,
fill me with possibility."

Around her, the black circle painted into the floor began to glow red. Puffs of smoke rose up. Before long there were little flickers of flame. She hummed as energy surged through her. The flames danced violently, growing longer. They vibrated until they were just a glow, melting into each other. A red light shot up and toward the center of the ceiling, swirling like a tornado. She laughed as the wind tickled her lips. The light made her skin hot and she felt itching as the power surged forth.

For many hours, she enjoyed the vortex, singing and dancing with joy and hope. If anyone had seen her, they would never have believed that a woman so feeble could move so vigorously. She danced until she felt the wind growing softer. Her body pulsed with power. She looked over to the men, who were breathing harder and twitching their fingers and toes. Their heads bobbed as if they were on the verge of waking up.

"Thank you, oh, Dark One,
for bringing me this power.
Thank you, four corners of the earth.
Thank you, dark spirits of earth, wind, fire, water.
Vengeance will be ours."

She made another sign with her fingers into the air.

"Men, foolish men,
go out now about your business.
Wreak havoc on those that you loved
in ways you can best betray them.
Let them feel worthless and powerless
so that women are weakened
and I shall be the leader."

She pulled a little footstool out from under the table and went to the first man. His eye lids fluttered and he pulled his head up. His eyes were wide and glassy as he stared at the woman now fiddling with the hook on his back.

"Mistress." His lips were dry as he struggled to form words.

"Yes, your mistress. You will speak of me to no one."

"Yes, mistress."

Her fingers managed to finally unhinge the hook so that the man slid down to the floor. The hole in his back where the hook went through closed up instantly as if it had never been there. The witch led him to his clothes and helped him dress. It was an arduous process, like helping a retarded child. At last, the handsome young man was clothed and ready for the outside. He clumsily shuffled toward the door and went back out into the world.

One by one, she unhooked the rest of the men and dressed them. As she watched them leave, she had a sudden glimpse of herself as Snow White watching the seven dwarves hi-ho-ing off to work. But she was no Snow White right now. She was the hag. Maybe she was more like Fagan watching the pickpockets slink off to do their dirty deeds. She rubbed her hands and hummed a snatch of song from *Oliver*.

"Be good, my boys. I'll see you soon."

Once the last of the men had shuffled away, the woman hurried around the hut, collecting up all her tools and quickly washing and putting them away. Her fingers moved quickly with great agility. She hummed and sang until she was done. Then she wandered aimlessly around the room for a few moments, picking up knickknacks and putting them down again. Each one held a memory of her long life. All the terrible deeds she had done or that had been done to her. Not many of her possessions brought her pleasure. Her life had always been one of hardship, and now, even as a witch, she still had the same bottom line as everyone else.

"Now the bullshit. Money."

The woman walked over to an altar comprised of a wooden plank and several candles. A pot of incense burned thickly, and there were other assorted instruments. An anthame, black crystals, a crow carcass festering with ants, a few assorted bones, and a baby alligator head from a trip to Florida. She lowered her head, her hand touching the anthame.

"Oh, powers of darkness,
the dark mistress of night and death,
help guide me on this night
toward money and lots of it."

As she continued to pray, her flesh burned and crackled. Her face seemingly melted into its own river of emptiness. She raised her arms, returning to the nonsensical singsong she was chanting earlier. She tore away her clothes until she was standing naked. Her flesh bubbled and rolled into itself, cracking and then oozing. She screamed as the flesh sizzled and boiled. The pain grew so great she sank to her knees, screaming more than she ever had in childbirth. At last, the sharp burning sensation was ebbing, and she was able to open her eyes and breathe deeply once more. She smiled as she looked down at her hands. Smooth long fingers, like the neck of a swan, with a trendy French manicure on top of each. She ran those lovely fingers up her arms, the saggy flesh gone. She ran them along her face. Her lips were sticky with bright red makeup. Her hands ran to her breasts.

"Yes!" Her 38-triple whatevers were back. Firm and high, with large suckable nipples that pointed to the ceiling. Thank God for silicone wonders. She stood up and ran her hands along her hourglass waist, then slapped her large firm ass.

"Oh, yeah, time to go make some money. Before I turn back into a frog."

Her mood turned grim once more. She wondered if she would ever figure out another way to make a living. But even at her advanced age, knowledge meant nothing without a degree. She couldn't stay in her young body for months on end; it was too exhausting to perform the ritual and the effect lasted barely a day. Sometimes it lasted a couple of weeks. Sometimes mere hours. The last couple of months were taking their toll already. She would spend an eternity rejuvenating herself. And the past couple of decades were much more difficult than the previous ones had been.

She didn't think it was her age. She felt as if there was something much more serious going on. Someone else was draining her energy resource, that giant power generator of the universe. Someone else had found the secret and was draining her source. It had taken her years, but at last she had tracked down the suspect to a small nearby town.

Now it was just a matter of the most efficient way to deal with the problem.

Where had Alex gone?

Ashley couldn't understand it. It wasn't like Alex to run away. At least not as far as she knew. And she had known Alex for a very long time.

They had met in kindergarten when Ashley first moved into the neighborhood. Alex had taken her under her wing from the start, growing from crayon advice to how wear her hair, and when they were older, showing her how to put on eyeliner. They used to spend hours after school, hanging out at the park, smoking illicit cigarettes, and giggling over boys. Alex was her very best friend in the world, the only one who really understood her.

No one else understood Ashley or would give her the time of day. Well, some of the kids at the community center got what she was about, but she hadn't clicked with any of them on more then a superficial basis.

Alex was the one that realized Ashley was different from other girls. She was tomboy tough and when they weren't in their uniforms, liked to hang out in baggy sweats with a toque on her head, like the rappers she adored. Alex was just a jeans and T-shirt gal herself, so they got along pretty well most of the time. Alex would lie on Ashley's bed, watching as Ashley posed and shouted in the mirror, emulating her idol, TnT.

It was Ashley's goal in life to be a rapper, maybe even bigger then TnT, if she could find something to say. Something cool and good. Something as moving and real as a song like "Evasion," which had been a huge hit for him. Of course, she had the misfortune of being born a girl, and it just wasn't the same when a girl rapped.

She would just have to be different, find a new niche.

Figure out that something to say.

Ashley put her headphones on and cranked up her TnT CD. She stared over at the poster of TnT on the wall. She loved his music. His look. He was so nasty, yet funny. Sexy, yet a total pig.

He was a typical guy, she figured.

Saying out loud what a lot of people kept stuck rattling around in their heads.

She had gone to see his *Peeps* movie about twenty times before it came out on video. Then when the DVD came out, she'd snatched it up, playing and replaying it, searching for the Easter eggs, rerunning the scene over and over again where he was fucking that chick in the factory. So nasty, yet so sexy. She wished TnT would do *her* in a factory. Or anywhere for that matter.

Ashley was saving herself for him. So what if he was nearly old enough to be her dad? That just meant he'd have to show her everything!

He could be *her* superman, oh, yeah!

Her glance fell on a snapshot of her and Alex sticking their tongues out in a photo booth. What to do about Alex? She had been missing for a while now and there wasn't anything anyone knew. Ashley had been questioned by the police a couple of times because they knew the girls had been tight. But Ashley knew nothing at all.

They had sat her down and played the school surveillance tape for her. The last time Alex had been seen she had been talking to someone in rapper gear, and for the longest time the cops had thought the person was Ashley, but Ashley said it wasn't her. And eventually the cops believed her.

The person in the video had their face hidden, and no one could even tell if it was a guy or a girl. Ashley didn't have a clue who the person was. It could have been anyone. One of their friends, girl or boy, or a total stranger. The person wasn't tall, but that didn't mean anything. The clothes were so huge and formless that there wasn't even a sense of weight or age.

Ashley had spent a lot of time after school, hanging out on those very steps where Alex had disappeared, wondering if the person would ever come back. In her gut, she knew that the person on the camera had to be connected to Alex's disappearance. But how to find the person? And if she *did* find the person, then what? Would she be abducted too?

Was the person even related to the disappearance?

She missed Alex terribly. She stared at TnT and wondered, "What would TnT do?" He wouldn't take this sitting in his room. He would go out in full force and hunt the person down. TnT was a do-bee. And so was she.

Ashley threw on a baggy shirt and her toque, and tucked her CD player into her pants. She decided enough was enough. The police were doing sweet fuck-all, and probably had even closed the file on what they presumed was a runaway teen. So it was up to Ashley to make things right and go hunting for her lost soul sister.

She walked over to the school and stood on the steps again, as she had so many times the past week or so. She thought and thought as music from her headphones washed over her. If she were going to abduct someone, where would she take them?

Her gaze fell onto the woods. The police had combed them already, but maybe they had missed something. She walked over to them, staring at the ground for something that might have been missed. As she entered the woods, she felt a little creeped out. What if she ended up stumbling upon Alex's lifeless body? She thought she would freak right out if she did. But there would be no body. Alex had disappeared without a trace. If there was a body in the woods, it would have been found by now.

She wandered down to the edge of the water and sat staring out. She had cried a couple of times out of fear for her friend, but she hated showing weakness. Yet, as she sat there, a wave of sorrow washed over her and she found herself sobbing. Poor Alex. Just plain gone. If only Ashley hadn't skipped school that day to go hang out downtown and poke around the music and clothing stores, Alex might be here now.

As she sobbed, she noticed something shining in the mud just past her feet. She leaned over and saw a button. A tiny white button. Nothing unusual. Nothing fancy. Yet . . . she wondered, really wondered, if that was the same button that they wore on their uniform blouses. She held it in her hand, wishing she was Sylvia Brown or John Edwards, so that she could feel the vibes the button would give her. So the button could tell her the story of where it came from and what had happened here. But she wasn't Sylvia Brown or John Edwards, and her passion was music, not psychic ability. The button could not tell her.

But maybe she knew someone who could?

She turned the button over in her hand. When she went home, she would compare it to the buttons on her own uniform. If it was a match, then she just knew in her heart it was Alex's. It didn't matter that this was a popular make-out spot and girls probably got buttons ripped from their blouses all the time by tit-hungry boys. If this button matched, she knew it would belong to Alex.

And then what?

She closed her eyes and thought.

She had to find a psychic. A good one. She never paid much attention when people talked about fortune-tellers and all that stuff. She wasn't even sure if she believed in such things. But she had heard about one, over and over again, who lived in a nearby town.

If this button matched, she would find out who that psychic was and go to see her. Maybe, just maybe, there would be help.

She pulled the bandanna from her head and unfolded it, carefully placing the button inside. She rolled it up and shoved it down her shirt, into her bra.

"Don't worry, Alex. I'll find you," she whispered to the air. She crawled around the bank a while longer, wondering if there might be anything else she could find. A strand of hair. Maybe a sock! But no, there was nothing.

Nothing at all.

Except for the button, Alex had vanished without a trace.

Ashley wandered back out of the woods and set off toward the little town. She thought she had seen a flyer for that psychic on a bulletin board at the community center, and maybe it was still there. That way she could make her inquiries without anyone bothering her.

It was a long walk into town, but the day was nice and her CD player was fully charged. She wandered along, TnT blasting through her eardrums, and wondered over and over again what had happened to Alex.

The ragged flyer was right where she had remembered. A tarot reader. She tore it down and found a pay phone. Her heart beat wildly as she dialed the number. Part of her thought she must be nuts. How the hell would a total stranger find her friend when the police and parents could not?

The phone rang a few times, and she was just about to give up when she heard the "Hello" at the other end of the line.

Ashley's heart jumped into her throat. She panicked and nearly put the phone back into the cradle, but then realized that she shouldn't be such a chicken-shit and should just tell the lady what she wanted.

"Is this Vanessa?" Ashley asked, her voice sounding small and squeaky and she hated it.

"Yes. Can I help you?"

"I—uh . . . I heard that you can help people with their problems."

"Sometimes. What seems to be yours?"

"I was wondering if I could come and see you."

"Yes, I take appointments. When would you like to come?"

"Where are you? I don't drive."

When Vanessa told her the directions, Ashley's heart sank.

"I don't know how I'd get out there."

"I have a busy day today, so if you can make it out here, then I'll see you. Otherwise, we'll have to wait for another time."

"All right. I'll try." Ashley hung up the phone, her heart pounding. She could get there by a couple of buses, or maybe, if she was lucky, hitchhike. Or she could ride her bike. Might take a couple of hours by bike, but it was a nice day. Maybe that was the best plan.

Cheryl watched Vanessa's face as she turned the cards. Last time, Vanessa had alluded to something weird going on. And sure as shit, things were weirder by the minute. Her husband was more secretive than ever, yet in other ways, he was becoming more careless. Really. What married man came home night after night, later and later, for no real reason. He didn't even bother to make up a reason anymore. He'd just come in, peel off his clothes, and hit the sheets. Sometimes he'd peck her on the cheek. More often than not, he'd be snoring before his head hit the pillow.

She found herself watching every woman she saw too. Every blond woman would turn her head, and she'd stare after her, wondering . . . is that *her*?

Caring for Dina and Desmond was getting harder by the moment. All she could do was wonder where things had gone wrong. They had wanted children. What did he expect would happen?

"Well?" Cheryl asked.

Vanessa sighed. She picked up a card and fingered it, then placed it beside another. She spent a few minutes rearranging the cards and furrowing her brow.

"What is it?" Cheryl asked.

"More of the same. Be really open right now. Open to new experiences, new sensations, new people coming into your life. Your path is changing. Take some new chances and see where you go."

As Cheryl drove into town, she chewed over the reading. Again it had been vague, and she was no further ahead with the mystery of her husband than she had been before the reading. However, Vanessa was right that a change in routine might be in order. She thought maybe she should hit the little bookstore, pick up something to read before she went home to relieve the baby-sitter. She browsed the New Age section, picking up books on self-improvement and thumbing through them. As she glanced through book after book, she was aware that she was being watched.

A man stood at the end of the aisle. He wore jeans and a denim shirt. His hair was shoulder-length, sandy blond, but it was his eyes she noticed the most. Blue. Crystal-clear and glittering. And staring right at her.

She feigned a half smile and shut the book, placing it back on the shelf.

"I couldn't help but notice you," the man said.

"Me?" Cheryl blushed.

"Yes, you. You are a very beautiful woman, yet you seem so sad."

"I guess I am a bit distracted."

"You know, I run a little gathering. We're meeting in about an hour. Maybe you'd like to come and check it out?" He held out a business card. Cheryl took it and looked it over. It read SAM SNEED, GURU.

"Guru?" she asked.

"It seems as good a title as any," he said. "I help people find the way."

"The way to what?"

"To inner peace. Spiritual enlightenment."

"Oh, really?" She looked at him closely. He radiated a strange energy, one that she could not place as either good or bad.

"Come and see. I think you will fit right in."

Cheryl bought her books and went over to the local coffee shop. There she sat, turning the card in her hand, over and over.

Was this the new adventure Vanessa had seen?

At last she found her nerve. Take control, go on an adventure. She had a car. She could always leave if it seemed weird.

Cheryl drove up to the old farmhouse. She noticed a gathering of about ten people around the side of the house, and figured that must be the meeting. She parked her car and checked her face quickly in the mirror before getting out. Cautiously she approached the group. They looked as normal as she did, wearing casual clothes and everyday hairstyles.

"Hello." A red-haired woman approached Cheryl and held out her hand.

"My name is Farah."

Cheryl shook Farah's hand and felt embraced by the warmth flowing from her.

"I'm Cheryl."

"Yes. Sam told us about you. We're so pleased you could make it." Cheryl turned to the others, who were watching intently.

"Hi, Cheryl," they called to her. One by one they introduced themselves. Cheryl was amazed at how welcoming they all seemed to be.

A man who called himself Uno turned toward the house where Sam himself emerged. Sam wore a gray robe tied with a rope. The others turned toward Sam and bowed their heads in reverence.

"Cheryl. How wonderful that you could join us today." Sam walked over to her and took her hand. He led her towards the backyard and a tall tree. Beside the tree was a small table filled with glasses. The others followed behind them.

"What goes on at these things?" she asked.

"Just relax. You don't have to do anything you don't want to." Sam smiled. Cheryl felt a chill. She wondered exactly what it might be that she might not want to do.

The group circled the tree and held hands. Cheryl's hands were encircled by Uno and Farah.

Already Cheryl felt a great sense of acceptance that she hadn't experienced in years.

"Today, we welcome a visitor," Sam said, speaking from his spot in the circle. Slowly everyone began to walk in a counterclockwise direction. "Let us pray."

The people began to hum, very low in their throats. Cheryl's chest buzzed with the vibration and sang along with them. They continued to walk as they recited a simple little rhyme over and over again.

"In and out, around and through, circle of completion for me and you."

Cheryl sang along with them, her voice growing louder as everyone else's grew louder. Their singing resonated right down to her toes. A growing sense of excitement filled her. If this was what it was to be part of circle, a group of like-minded people, then she was signing up. All thoughts of her husband and children eroded from her mind as she concentrated on singing. Only singing. That same song over and over as her feet followed the feet in front of her.

The circle slowed down and the singing trickled away. Sam stepped into the center of the circle.

"We give thanks to the universe for this day and every day. We give thanks for all that we see and experience. We give thanks for the circle of completion. It is time."

Everyone dropped their hands and went over to the table. One by one they took the glasses and returned to their spots within the circle. Cheryl took a glass as well.

"What happens next?" she asked Farah.

Sèphera Girón

"Don't be afraid. It will be magical. You'll see." Farah said.

Sam returned to the center of the circle. Everyone held up their glasses.

"You may begin the ritual of purity." he said.

Cheryl stared, dumbfounded, as all around her, people peed into their glasses. Men unzipped their flies, woman were squatting or standing. The scent of urine was heavy in the air.

As people finished filling their glasses, they held them up in the circle. Sam was the last one to hold his glass of urine into the air.

"The goddess of nature, the spirit of man and woman, of the state of the universe, we ask that you bless this sacred substance of our bodies. We ask that you bring purity of thought and mind into our lives. We give thanks for your bountiful spirit. Amen."

"Amen . . ." the followers chorused.

Sam held the glass to his lips and drank. All around Cheryl, people raised their glasses to their lips and drank their own urine. It was all she could do to keep from throwing up.

"I'm not doing that," Cheryl said to Farah.

"It's all right. We never expect newcomers to do it their first time, or even their tenth time. You will do it when you are ready. Or maybe you will never be ready."

When all the urine was drunk, the glasses were placed reverently in front of each person's feet. Sam led them in another song. Cheryl wasn't following the words, though. She was still mesmerized by these people standing around drinking their own pee.

By the time the ceremony was over, her head was swimming. She walked back to her car, dazed. Sam hurried up behind her, and opened the door.

"What did you think? Not what you expected."

"Certainly not."

"Are you offended?"

"No, actually, come to think of it. Just . . . well, it seems so weird."

"There are reasons. Very ancient and practical health reasons."

"But don't we pee because we are ridding our body of toxins?"

"There is that. But there are benefits. The trick is, to use the middle of the pee. You know, like when you go to the doctor, you are supposed to pee out a bit, then go in the cup, then pee out the rest. The beginning and end part of the pee could have bacteria, but the middle part is an elixir. It can cure so many health problems, you wouldn't believe it."

"You're right. I wouldn't."

"Then there is the whole spiritual side of it. Bringing back into our body that which we eliminated. It's like eating the placenta of a baby or the symbolic meaning of the wafer at church."

"Circles . . ."

"Yes, the circle. The magic circle. How wondrous it all is."

"Do you feel different when you do it?"

"You feel cleansed and pure. You feel the energy of the god power flowing through your bones."

"Don't you feel gross?"

"I think pretty much everyone ever involved in this had to really wrap their heads around the whole idea of it. It's not an easy concept to grasp."

"No."

"But the practice has been around since Biblical times."

"Right."

"You should try it. When you are ready."

"I don't know if I could. I would feel pretty grossed out by the whole thing."

"At first you will, sure. The idea of it, as you have now. But if you study with us, you will understand it all. The knowledge will give you power. The power will give you strength. And you will want to keep building on that strength as we do."

"And then what?"

Farah joined their conversation. "Why, you will see God. You will want to be with God. You will do what it takes to be with people who see things like you do," Farah explained.

"Like a family."

"Yes, like a family. Not a cult, though. You are free to come and go. No one lives here except Sam. We meet once in a while, to share our thanks and to pray for guidance, as you saw. Nothing weird. Unless you count drinking urine weird."

"I would say it's not ordinary."

"It's not unordinary either, my dear. Go to the library and see. In the meantime, I thank you for joining us." Sam took Cheryl's hand once more and wrapped his hands around it as he kissed her once on each cheek. Cheryl watched him return to the group that was milling about and snacking on banana bread. Farah turned to Cheryl.

"You seem so lost. Are you always so sad, Cheryl?"

Cheryl rubbed her hands against her jeans. "I'm a bit bummed out. My husband. Things are just in such a mess right now."

Farah took her hand. "Ups and downs of marriage . . ."

"Yeah, seems like more downs these days."

"Don't you worry, your life is going to change for the better, you'll see."

"I wish I could believe you."

Farah held Cheryl's car door open. Cheryl stood awkwardly by the door. Farah wrapped her arms around the trembling woman.

"Look, you ever need someone to talk to, give me a call." When Farah stepped back, she was holding out a business card.

"That's my cell phone number. No one answers it but me."

Cheryl slid into her car seat and turned over the ignition. With a feeble smile and wave, she backed out of the long dirt driveway.

Chapter Five

Vanessa recognized the girl the minute she sat down. It was the friend of the dead girl.

Well, she wasn't really dead. Her blood flowed through Vanessa's veins, pumping her with life's vitality. Her flesh was woven into Vanessa's where the wrinkles and scars would bubble to the surface once more. Alex lived on in Vanessa, but of course, how could she ever tell Ashley that?

She was sorry for the girl. She could sympathize with how she had lost her friend. She thought about her own friends that she had loved and lost. But that was life. People made friends, then they drifted away. Finding new interests. People move. People die. People become bitter enemies. Or people, like Demian, just sort of lose touch.

Again she thought of Demian. He must be near or thinking of her too lately, or why else would he be constantly intruding on her thoughts?

The girl before her was crying. Such a pretty little thing if only she didn't wear those horrible rapper clothes. Talk about a fashion that never seemed to die!

Vanessa had to think of something to appease her, to stop the digging. The last thing she needed was anyone to place her with Alex.

The girl was unrolling a piece of cloth where there was a button inside.

"I think this was hers, but I'm not sure."

Vanessa took the button and a flash of Alex tingled through her. Her heart pounded and the blood within her boiled as if recognizing the object. It took all of Vanessa's strength to put the button down.

"I don't think it belonged to her. Sorry." Vanessa returned the button.

Ashley frowned. "I figured it was a long shot." She sighed and stared into her coffee cup. When she looked back up at Vanessa, her eyes were glassy with tears.

"Is there anything else you can do? Can you look at the tarot cards and see what might have happened to her?"

"Sure." Vanessa pulled her deck from her purse and shuffled the cards. She laid them out and tried to keep a poker face as the cards spilled her secrets. Looking at Ashley's face, she could see the girl knew nothing about the cards.

"I think she ran away," Vanessa said finally.

"Where?"

"Someplace warm and sunny. Maybe California."

"Why would she suddenly take off to California?

It doesn't make sense. She never talked about it."

"People do strange things," Vanessa said.

"That's a bit too strange. She had no desire to go anywhere. All she wanted was to get the hell out of high school and have a boyfriend. She wanted a boyfriend so badly, but no one was good enough for her. Or maybe it was 'cause all the guys she liked didn't like her. Typical."

"I think she had a guy and ran off with him," Vanessa said, her blue eyes steely as she held Ashley in her glare. Ashley shook her head, casting her eyes elsewhere around the little home.

"She never told me 'bout any guy."

"Maybe she thought you would be jealous. After all, it was you and her forever. Now it has all changed. She's run off with him, to California, partly to spare your feelings."

Vanessa grinned. "You love her."

"Of course I love her, she's my best friend."

"I mean, you really love her."

Ashley stood up from the table.

"No way, ma'am. I'm not queer or anything."

"Then where's your boyfriend?"

"I don't have one." Ashley noticed the witch's lip twitching, as if she was trying not to laugh. It was bugging her, this witch lady and her questions.

"A beautiful girl like you . . ."

"I don't want a boyfriend, I'm saving myself for . . ." Ashley stopped. The words would sound utterly ridiculous if spoken aloud. Even when she spoke them to Alex, she realized she sounded like the biggest geek in the universe.

But she *did* want TnT to be her first. Maybe she

could get the witch to help her with that.

"Do you have love spells?" Ashley asked.

Vanessa laughed. "Of course I do. But you are so young, what do you need with a love spell?"

"I want someone to fall in love with me."

"You should let nature take its course. Believe me, it's much better."

"Maybe I don't have time for that. Maybe I need a spell to turn his attention to me before he's married again."

"Ah . . . an older man. Is that who you're saving your precious vi . . ." Vanessa stumbled on the word. "Your virginity?"

Ashley nodded.

Vanessa shrugged. "I would never try to give advice on matters of the heart except from the cards, but I will tell you a bit about human nature. If the guy is divorced, he's probably no good for you. You are so young. You have your life ahead. Find someone with less baggage."

"I adore him. He's so talented."

"I see that."

Vanessa stood and went into another room. She returned with a small vial of oil. "He will find you irresistible with this."

Ashley shook her head. "He's far away. He'll never be close enough to smell me."

"Ah . . ."

Vanessa left the room again and returned with a tiny bag of powder. "Sprinkle this over his picture. It would be a start, at any rate."

Ashley studied the brown powder through the plastic. Might be cinnamon. Might be magic. She didn't know. But she was willing to gamble the ten bucks to find out.

"Can you get something to bring Alex back?" Ashley asked.

Vanessa shook her head.

"No. She has left on a journey that she needs to complete. Forcing her back too soon will ruin her life path."

"But everyone is worried sick. She should at least call."

"Leave it alone, Ashley." Vanessa voice was chilling, and Ashley was creeped out by the way she was staring at her. She dug in her pockets for money and put it on the table.

"Thank you, Ashley. I wish you luck on your search."

As Ashley pedaled away from Vanessa's house, she was more confused then ever. She herself was no psychic, but her gut feeling told her something wasn't quite right. She didn't believe for a minute that Alex ran off to California. It didn't make sense. Sure, Alex wasn't the happiest of campers lately, but she hadn't said anything about taking off, especially to California. In all the years she had known Alex, there had never been any talk at all about California. If anyone was going to beat feet, it would be Ashley, to start her rapping career.

She fingered the powder in her pocket. She wondered if the powder was as big a lie as the tarot reading had been. She stopped and leaned her bike against the tree. She pulled one of her CDs out of her pocket and stared at TnT. She sprinkled the powder over his face and body and stared at it. She wondered what was supposed to happen. She was a fool to think anything would happen at all. She blew the powder away and resumed her bike ride.

Alex. Alex and a boyfriend running off to California?

Not likely.

"Hey Vanessa, you slick witch bitch,
you're fulla shit could fill a ditch,
gotta get with the program dig?
Alex is just a mixed-up kid,
kids these days don't just up and go,
specially when they got no dough,
we got no dough,
we don't just blow,
we gotta dig ourselves outta our hole,
so where's this girl that's disappeared,
everyone around me acts so queer,
like I'm a retard just for trying,
don't tell me Alex is flying,
she's around I can feel her here,
she's all tied up from ear to ear,
she can't hear,
she can't see,
but she knows that Ashley will set her free,
so get it together, you crazy witch,
take your cards and magic, bitch,
climb on your broomstick and go for a ride,
'cause I can tell that you just lied,
you just lied,
you lied to me,
but that's so normal, don't you see?
No one's straight with a kid in school,

they treat me like I'm just a fool,
I'm gonna find her, yes I will,
find her, unwind her, and get her chill.
It's one of life's great mysteries,
but no one takes on a challenge like me.

Vanessa poured two glasses of wine and handed one to David as she sat back down on the sofa beside him.

"Here's to a beautiful woman."

"Here's to a wonderful man."

They clicked the glasses together, staring at each other over the rims.

"I feel like I've known you forever," David said, reaching over to take her hand.

"Me too. I've never felt so comfortable with anyone before."

"Kismet."

"Definitely."

They sat in silence for a moment.

"Did you like the movie?" David asked. Vanessa thought about the romantic comedy they had just seen at the little town's only theater. It was trite, banal. She had found the whole premise and execution saccharinely nauseating, but then again, she had never been one for romance.

"It was all right. I was more happy just spending time with you."

"I liked how despite all the obstacles those two faced, they ended up happily ever after."

"Well, they were happy for about five minutes, at the end of the movie. Who knows what time bomb awaits them in the next scene?"

"There was that whole one-obstacle-after-another schtick going on."

"I'm surprised Jim Carrey wasn't in that thing."

They both chuckled at the thought. David stopped laughing and looked at Vanessa.

"Do you believe that two people can fall in love and make it despite all odds?" David asked, squeezing her hand.

"I imagine it's possible. It just has never happened to me."

"Maybe. Just maybe it could happen."

"Maybe."

David leaned over to kiss her. Vanessa met his mouth eagerly. His lips were soft and gentle. He kissed her. Full and soft. He started to pull away, but then pulled her closer, kissing her deeply. This time she kissed back, allowing her tongue to slip out and touch his. The warmth of his mouth stirred her blood. Electric heat bubbled through her, surging. The wounds on her body pulsed, each beat throbbing a bit more painfully. It was enough to make her stop kissing David and put her hand to her throat.

"My, I'm giddy." As she looked into his soft green eyes, she felt a glow growing in the pit of her stomach and spreading throughout her body. For a moment, she thought she was going to pass out.

She stood up, holding the sofa arm as she did.

"Excuse me a moment."

Vanessa walked into the bathroom and shut the door. As she leaned against the wall, her gaze fell upon the jars.

Who was missing?

She had her suspicions now. She searched the names and saw that she was right.

Somehow she had to get her back.

She ran cold water over a washcloth and dabbed her face with it. She paused to look at her neck. There was no trace of anything out of the ordinary. All she felt had been in her head. She thought about the kiss. She had never felt so amazingly sensual from kissing someone. Maybe it had been too long since she had been naturally attracted to someone. She didn't even think that she had felt that way when she kissed Demian.

There was something special there. The idea of it made her smile.

If it was that special, it could wait. She had something more important on her mind.

Getting Alex back.

She returned to David.

"You okay?" he asked. "You look pretty pale . . ."

"More pale then usual? That's a switch."

She chuckled.

"I'm not feeling well," she said. "Maybe I'm just overtired."

"Okay. I can take a hint." David stood up.

"I really had a good time tonight," she said, walking him to the door.

"Me too." He grinned. He held her chin up and kissed her lightly on the lips. "Good night, Vanessa."

"Good night."

Vanessa stood at the door and watched until the car lights were no longer visible. She couldn't believe that yet again, she had let that handsome hunk walk out of her home without touching him. She really was changing in her old age.

Of course, this time, she knew she could wait. She had the patience to wait. If he was to love her naturally, as a mortal man loves a woman, then she needed to be patient. Not jump his bones. Not overwhelm him. Just bide her time and hope that what she had seen in his cards that day was true.

She hurried around the cabin, gathering up a flashlight, a bag, several knives, thick worker gloves, and a heavy hammer, and put them in a satchel that was slung across her shoulder. She hurried out of the house.

Vanessa walked around to the side where there was a small wooded area that led to the rocks and then the ocean. She wandered a short way in, circling the trees until she found the one she was looking for. This tree held a family of squirrels. She knew that because she often fed them and watched for where they made their home.

She put down all her supplies except the gloves, and slipped those onto her hands. She found the hammer and one of the longer knives and put them back into the satchel. She grabbed the lower branch with her hands and pulled her legs up after her. She climbed up the tree several branches until she found the hole. There was rustling inside. They had heard her coming. Several sets of eyes glowed in the moonlight. She fumbled for the knife. It glinted as she brought it down into the hole. There was a shrieking yowl as her knife pierced through a squirrel's skull. The others ran among themselves in the burrow, a few slithering down the tree from the other exit. She lifted the knife and the squirrel stayed speared to it. She smiled as it weakly twitched, then tossed it into her bag. She climbed back down the tree and lay the bag on the ground. She aimed the flashlight into the opening to see how it fared. It's breath was shallow.

"Boy, that was easy. The spirits must be with me tonight."

She returned to the house with her prey.

Once she was inside, she set to work on the final dirty deed. Within minutes, to the smell of burning incense, by the light of flickering candles, the squirrel's tail was raised in triumph, efficiently detached from the quivering body below.

As the last candle flame puffed out with a weary sigh, Vanessa stood shakily. Power sizzled through her. Circling her in golden ropes as quickly as a lightbulb popping. She shook her head.

"Enough for tonight, Katisha." The cat meowed at her.

As she headed for the bathroom, she looked down at the blood on her hands.

There was always blood on her hands, it seemed. For some reason or another. And she never meant anything by it, it was just a sort of side effect she was powerless to control.

Chapter Six

Cheryl woke to the sound of crying. She noticed that once more, her husband's side of the bed remained empty. Empty all night. Empty the night before. She didn't know if she would ever see the bastard again.

She ran down the hall to where her daughter sat up in bed, sobbing uncontrollably.

"What's wrong, sweetheart?"

The child sobbed harder, arms reaching out for a hug.

"Why did he go away, Mommy? It makes me dream bad things."

"I'm sorry, honey. I don't know why he has been gone so much and I don't know when he'll be done. He must be working pretty hard, to be gone so often." She hugged the child, smelling her soft hair and wishing that her husband was really working overtime. To buy them all pretty things. But of course, he wasn't. He was spending more and more time with that whore. Didn't even bother to cover it up anymore. Well, he never said there was another woman, but what else could it be?

The last time she saw him had not been good. It was the day before last. She was sitting at the kitchen table, staring at a glass of her own urine. She did this nearly every day since she went to the meeting. She would get up in the morning, get the kids off to school and then pee into a glass. She would then place the glass on the kitchen table and stare at it. Daring herself to drink it.

So far she hadn't. Even when she picked up the glass, held it in her hand, and swirled it around, she couldn't bring herself to even put her lips on the glass. She couldn't bear the smell. She couldn't stand the thought of what it would feel like going down her throat.

She had never been good at things involving bodily functions. She was fine with changing babies, but adults had always posed a different sensation in her. She could barely go to the bathroom in a public stall or in front of anyone. She had a shy bladder, couldn't stand the thought of someone hearing her pee tinkling into the toilet.

What would happen if they did?

Would the world come to an end?

She knew logically that of course it wouldn't. Why would the world come to an end because someone heard her peeing? She heard other people pee all the time, and it never fazed her. She didn't find it good or bad. She only knew jealousy, for she couldn't relax enough to pee in dead quiet. So how would she ever fare at this peeing cult?

Cheryl had given birth in front of a roomful of people. She could masturbate in front of her husband without blinking an eye, after a couple of glasses of wine, of course. Sometimes when they took a shower together, he would playfully pee on her foot. She found it funny, and wished that she could pee on his foot in return. But to pee in front of him . . . it was something she couldn't do. So she found it even odder that her travels had led her to a cult of people that peed in front of each other and drank it.

So there she had been. Sitting and staring at this large crystal wineglass, half filled with her own urine. She was trying to meditate on it. Trying to imagine it flowing down her throat. Spreading its nourishment to the sickly spots in her body.

All that kept flashing before her eyes was Farah's face. How bright and shiny her eyes were as she spoke to Cheryl that day. How pretty her shoulder-length red hair had been, all loose and blowing in the wind.

She wondered how Farah had gotten involved with such a cult. Several times since that day, she had pulled the phone number from her pocket and stared at it. She wanted to call Farah. To talk to her about all this weirdness. Yet, she felt she couldn't. She wasn't sure she wanted to get involved with this group of people. They must be nuts, to drink their own piss. Yet when she researched it on the Internet, it wasn't as unusual as it seemed.

A lot of important people in history had been reputed to partake of their own fluids.

She was thinking, as she stared at that glass, very seriously of giving Farah a call that day. Maybe they could go for a coffee or something.

As she sat, thinking about the red-haired woman, the door slammed open.

Tony stood there, panting.

"Tony." Cheryl turned to face him. One look at his eyes set her heart racing. He looked so angry.

"What are you doing?" he asked.

"I was just, relaxing for a moment. The kids are at school."

"So you just sit around all day. Doing nothing."

"That's not fair. You know I work." She glared at him. "As a matter of fact, I'm glad you're home."

Cheryl pushed down the anger she felt at seeing her wayward husband. He had been missing for days and all of the sudden, here he was. And daring. Just daring, to be mad at *her*?

Cheryl wrapped her arms around him. Hugging him close. Yearning to feel the strong young man she had married in what seemed like a lifetime ago.

He smelled terrible. Like he hadn't washed or changed his clothes since he left. And she supposed it could be possible that he hadn't washed or changed. That he'd been wandering around. Screwing someone or something and never washing afterward. The thought disgusted her.

He moved his hands along her back for a moment, ran his fingers through her hair. He grabbed it into a ponytail and pulled. Pulled her head hard. Yanking her back as he roughly kissed her.

Normally that would have turned her on. Made her legs jiggly. Made her feel like her he-man had come home and would throw her over his shoulder, march up to the bedroom, and make mad monkey love.

Yet he'd caught her so off guard, with his presence and his absence, with his offending odor and his even more offensive demeanor.

He kissed her roughly again. Pulling on her hair. His fingers tweaking at her nipples.

"Oh, yeah, baby. Daddy wants some sugar." He pulled her by the hair, and she followed. After all, this was a game they had once played and loved. Maybe he wanted to play again. She was angry and confused and he knew how to find her vulnerability.

"Where have you been? The kids miss you," she said as he tugged at her.

"I've been at work. Been missing you and your hot box," he said with a leer. He spoke slowly, as if his tongue was too big for his mouth. "Whatever happened to us, baby? Whatever happened to my rock'n'roll chick?"

"I had two babies for you, Tony. That's what happened. Two babies that we made and now must make decent citizens of the world."

"We used to have such fun." Tony pushed open the bedroom door and threw her in. She was amazed at how strong he was. He had never really pushed her before. Not with the force that he had just used. The way she nearly flew across the room and landed on the bed was not a normal thing for them.

She scrambled back on the bed, growing alarmed at what was going on. He stood before her, his hair askew. His clothes smelling even worse as he pulled them away. He had great clumps of dirt and grease smeared across his body. His arms. His legs.

She thought for a way to buy time.

"Tony, honey . . . let's play in the shower first, huh? We haven't done that in a long time."

He looked at her, his eyes glassy and unfocused. "Shower?"

Cheryl sat up and took his hand.

"Remember how much fun we'd have with the soap, honey? We'd draw nasty pictures on each other?"

They went into the bathroom. She opened the shower-stall door and turned on the spray. Slowly, she peeled away her clothes. He stood watching her, his arms hanging limply at his sides as if he were a marionette whose puppeteer had suddenly lost interest in the strings. His dick was rock-hard as if it had no connection to the rest of the man.

What was up with him? Maybe he had hit his head and had amnesia. Maybe he was on drugs. Was he smoking crack?

Tony had never been one for drugs, though. He would puff the odd joint at a party, but that was about the extent of his dabblings. He liked his beer. Especially when a game was on. But he'd rather die than drink a martini.

There was something wrong with him. No question. She just couldn't put her finger on exactly what it was. She rubbed lather along her breasts. Her torso. Her legs. She batted her eyelashes as she made a show of lathering herself up. She had to diffuse his anger.

"Come on in, honey . . ."

He stood staring. His head cocked, as if he were a child who had never seen a woman washing.

She leaned out and grabbed his hand. Her anger toward the way he had treated her the past few months was ebbing away as it grew more apparent that something was really wrong with him. She forgot about the strange woman the cards told her about. She forgot about how he had been neglecting her, how he had been impatient with her, how he had disappeared with no explanation.

Her fingers traced his sunken cheekbones, while she gazed at the eyes she had loved and adored for so many years. Her hands traced his chest, circling nipples she could identify in her sleep. She ran her hands along his torso. Every bump and line, the smooth sensation of soapy flesh. Remembering how much smaller he had been before they were married. How he'd had a temporary weight problem during her second pregnancy, and now he was back to normal. Not thin, not fat. A man. Her man. Her man that was not himself at all.

His hair was coarse to the touch. She poured shampoo on it while he twiddled with her breasts, as if he were a child with a new toy. His breath was rancid, worse then coming home from a party where there was chain-smoking and beer.

"Where have you been the past few days?" she asked very quietly, rubbing his scalp into a full lather.

"I—" He looked at her. Looked her straight in the eye. She saw fear there. Pure fear. These eyes didn't belong to her husband. Not these frightened childlike eyes. Her husband had proud eyes.

Tony's hands stopped playing with her breasts and hung limply at his sides. He narrowed his eyes.

"I don't know where I've been," he whispered. "I don't know. . . ."

His eyes filled with tears. Cheryl wrapped her arms around him.

"You've found someone else, and now you don't know how to tell me," she said.

"No . . ." he sighed, raising his hands to cup her face. He looked deeply into her eyes and this time, she saw what she had seen long ago. Love. Hidden way back behind the pain.

"I don't know what's been going on. But I love you. I miss you. That's why I'm here now. Touching you. Wanting you." He pressed his lips against hers. She had been aching for him so much that she didn't care how he smelled. Her primal senses took over. He was her man. Her man was here. Wanting her.

Whatever had happened with the blonde, wherever it was he had been, she was ready to forgive him everything. They could be a family again. They could try again, and not fall down the same path. They could rise above statistics and be happy and successful.

They embraced in the shower for a long time. All the soap foam slipped down the drain. Soon the shower ran cold.

"Come on, honey," Cheryl said, taking his hand. He stood as still as a statue, his head down. He was shivering.

Cheryl wrapped a towel around him and led him to the bed. He moved as if he were sleepwalking.

"Are you tired? Are you sick? Should I call the doctor?"

Tony lay back for a moment, his eyes staring at the ceiling. Suddenly, as if someone had punched him, he sat up. His eyes were blazing again. Forceful and angry. He reached over to her and grabbed her hair.

"Trying to distract me, were you?" he roared.

"Not at all . . . I thought . . ." Cheryl couldn't finish speaking because he rammed her face right down onto his throbbing erection.

"Please your husband, you filthy whore."

Cheryl tried to pleasure him, but he kept ramming her head down too far and too fast for her to get any decent sucking or tongue action working. She was gagging on his enormity. He was growing larger by the moment.

He pulled out and rubbed himself, looking at her. Looking past her. His eyes were far away now, as if he were peering into another world.

"Tony?" Cheryl gasped, wiping spittle from her chin.

"Get on the bed," he said. She climbed onto the bed and lay on her back.

"No, turn over." She braced herself on her hands and knees and caught a glimpse of herself in the mirror. She looked pale and frightened, not at all like someone eagerly waiting for her husband to make love to her.

He squatted behind her and thrust himself in to the hilt. Tears sprang to her eyes as he impaled her. He had always been a bit big for her, but he was usually cautious of that. Now, he didn't care as he thrust into her. A sharp jab twinged inside of her as he plunged. She wondered if the blonde could take his length better than her and that's why he was oblivious to her discomfort. She put her hand between her legs and felt their connection. She played with herself, and ignored the sharp tearing sensation.

There was no way to talk to him. No way to keep his anger at check. Men were strange creatures at the best of times, and to stop him from fucking her because he was too rough, because he had run away, because of all the reasons that she shouldn't want to fuck him at all—this was not the time to complain. She was small and he was big. She didn't know what he was on, if he could hurt her or even kill her. That was the bottom line.

Instead, she focused on the fact that she hadn't been fucked in weeks, and rough could be . . . well, it could be exciting. This was her husband even if he was screwed up. She had loved fucking him these past few years; she would look at the pleasure instead of her anger. If she tensed up, it would only hurt more, and infuriate him.

She let him fuck her. Hard and slow. Deep and fast. She let her brain turn off for a moment, letting her body enjoy the sensations washing through and around her. It was hard for her, for any woman, to not be thinking a million thoughts during sex. But she forced herself. The kids weren't home. This was her husband. She had been so horny earlier that she was considering how pretty Farah was! What was wrong with her?

So Tony was being weird. So Tony had a helluva

lot of explaining to do. So Tony was being rough . . . she let him ride her like they were the Pony Express on the highway to hell.

Orgasm slipped up and caught her by surprise. Time and again. She was raw energy. Raw power. She was a rushing cascade of the most exquisite sensation in the world that kept creeping back. Every time she thought she could come no more, a new climax would shudder through her.

Tony lasted longer than she had ever known him to last. She took full advantage of his endurance. As she finally was able to catch her breath and her senses once more, she caught a glimpse of them in the mirror.

It was kind of sexy, really. In a porn-movie kind of way. Tony grabbing her hips. She hugging the pillows for leverage. He must be getting ready for the home stretch. He was harder and bigger than earlier and his moves were faster and jerky. She could tell he was going to blow. After all, she was his wife.

"Come on, baby." She called out for encouragement. For a moment, she flashed on what the blonde might say to him.

How did she talk to him? She probably talked totally nasty. She probably had huge tits and a big round ass. She was probably stretch-mark-free and childless. So easy to be a sex goddess with no kids hanging off your tits.

Tony cried out as he came. Cheryl tried to pull away from his harsh grip as a cold burning gushed inside of her. He held her tightly to him until he was finished.

He shuddered and sighed. He pushed her away with a groan. She rolled onto her back, simultaneously spent and frightened.

As he leaned against the wall, gasping, she put her hands between her legs. She wasn't surprised to see blood. It had been rough and deep. And it had been a long time. But the other substance on her hand made her sit up. She looked down between her legs and saw, mixing in with the smattering of blood, a greenish gel. She looked over at Tony. At his cock that was still pretty hard. A glob of something that looked like pus was dangling from his dick, like a raindrop ready to fall.

And the smell.

The smell was putrid.

Unbelievably disgusting.

She ran into the bathroom, not knowing whether to puke or wash or pee. She opted for the shower, where she pointed the nozzle into her mouth and then took the hand attachment to wash her dripping crotch.

He must be sick. Must have some sort of infection.

She lathered soap, lots of soap, all over her. Anything to get that smell of . . . what was it? It smelled like dead things. Or what she imagined dead things smelled like. She wasn't too sure what dead things smelled like.

"Tony . . ." she called out to him. She was half afraid to see him again, yet she needed to understand what was going on. What was wrong with him?

"Tony!"

She finished washing and wrapped the towel around her. When she went into the bedroom, Tony was nowhere to be found. She searched the entire house, and there was no Tony.

The glass of urine on the kitchen table was empty. He must have drunk it on his way out. Her lip curled a little as she wondered what the hell it was he thought he was drinking. She wondered if he just chugged it down, thinking it was another one of her weird-ass health drinks.

Yet that didn't solve the immediate problem. Where had he gone now?

Bastard.

Came home for a quickie and took off again.

She ran for the phone and called the police. She explained to them that he had come home for a little while, and was acting very strange. He was dirty and sickly. She didn't know what was wrong with him, but there was something going on.

As usual, there was no real response for her. They said they'd make notes, that they'd try to find him should he be roaming around hurt or lost. But for the most part, there wasn't much they could do.

She found herself jumpy for a long time after that. Even now, she wasn't sure if he was going to come bursting through the door at any moment and take her once more.

Cheryl had gotten Dina back to sleep. Then woke her up again to catch the school bus with her brother. Cheryl was supposed to go see Vanessa this afternoon. She took her glass, went into the bathroom, and filled it. Once more, she placed it on the kitchen table, where the sun shone brightly on it.

She figured, if she really felt that she had to drink urine, she could throw it in the blender with some fruit juice and Slimfast and kill the taste. She wondered if actually tasting it was part of the weirdness of the ritual. She didn't know. All she knew was here she was again, sitting alone, staring at a glass of urine. Wishing her husband was back, that they could have wild monkey sex again, and that everything was normal.

But it would never be normal again.

She sat and stared at that yellow liquid. Would she see god if she drank it? Would she feel better about all the shit that had been going down?

Would drinking it bring her husband back?

No. Of course not. Nothing was going to bring him back. He was obsessed or drugged or something.

She sat, too lethargic to cope. She was tired from being up with Dina. She was sad from thinking maybe, just maybe, Tony had returned to her. But all he had wanted was a quick nasty fuck. She hadn't seen him since.

Why did he even want to fuck her? He had that blonde . . . that woman that he was throwing away his marriage for. So what was the point. Obviously blondie was better at sinking the pink than she was, or else he would be here. Right now. Wouldn't he?

He was sick. That color on him. That smell. That . . . whatever the hell it was that had leaked out of his dick. What the fuck was that all about? To think she'd had his dick in her mouth. The thought made her retch, and again her gaze fell onto the glass of urine.

Well, there was all sorts of bizarre bodily fluid stuff going on around here, wasn't there?

She put her hand around the glass. Felt the warmth of the urine through the glass and against her skin. She shivered.

She picked up the glass and stared into it from above. There it was. Dark yellow morning urine. Full of nature's melatonin they say. Yummmmy.

The smell of it made her want to hurl, and she put the glass back down. How would she ever get something like that on her tongue, against her teeth. She wondered if they ever had people drinking their own piss on *Fear Factor*? God knows they ate and drank every other disgusting thing in the universe.

As she stared at the liquid, she thought again of Farah. Maybe she should call her. Maybe talking to someone would help.

Of course, there was Vanessa. Her reading was today. She wondered what was in the cards, if it was more of the same, or something new.

Cheryl watched Vanessa as she flipped over the cards. Vanessa frowned.

"My, but the cards are odd today." she said. "You've seen him recently."

"Oh, yes. We even had sex. But he's disappeared again."

"He's not well."

"You can say that again."

"And you . . . you are looking to another."

"Wouldn't you if your husband was screwing around and wouldn't talk about it?"

Vanessa looked up from the cards. Her gaze was

steely. "I don't know if I'd ever trust a man, after all the things I see in other people's marriages."

Cheryl sighed. "I know there are good men. I'm sure of it. I'm sure there are men that never cheat, would never even consider it. I thought I had one of those. But I guess, that's what we all think. For the record, I have never cheated."

"When he came home, did he say anything?"

"No. He was really weird. If I didn't know any better, I'd say he'd been on a bender."

"It's not that. . . ." Vanessa stared at the cards. Cheryl wished she could understand the deck being used. It wasn't the easy-to-figure-out Rider-Waite. It was some other deck that had only pictures of sticks or cups or coins or swords. They meant nothing to her.

Cheryl fidgeted with her purse strap.

Vanessa sighed. "You have a long, odd journey ahead of you. Be very careful—things are not what they seem."

"You already told me that."

"But it's more so now."

"I know that too. Tony was fucked up when he came in. He hadn't washed in days, I don't think, he looked weird, we had really rough sex, and then he took off. What was that all about?"

Vanessa flipped some more cards over. "He's torn. He loves you, but he's also following the wishes of another." Vanessa shook her head. "Be careful. Leave him alone for now."

"But he's my husband."

"I'm sorry, that's all I can say. That's all I can see."

"Is there anything I can do? Some spell? Some curse? Can you do something for me?"

Vanessa stood up. "I don't think you want to mess around with spells right now. Your resistance is weak. There are things that I don't quite understand just yet about your case for me to know what kind of spell I would use."

"Why not a 'love me like you used to' spell?"

"Every time you manipulate someone's free will, there is a ricochet in the universe. At this point, I suggest you let things play out, because there is no way to know what the fallout of a spell would be."

Cheryl realized that Vanessa was showing her the door. She put her money on the table, more confused than ever.

"You know, Cheryl, it won't be long before everything becomes clear. Really clear."

"Do you think?"

Vanessa nodded. "When we hit the peak, we can then decide which way to proceed. He may even come back to you on his own. But at this point, we can't see that. Tarot is not an exact science. Nothing is, really."

Cheryl returned to her car. She drove into town and found a pay phone. As luck would have it, Farah answered on the first ring, and even luckier, was already in town. They decided to meet at a coffee shop.

Cheryl waited nervously. What would become clear? That Tony would return? Or would she realize she could live without him? Could she live without him? She thought they had such a good thing. She thought they could work through all that

119

they had been through. When Tony had appeared that day, she'd thought it was possible. Seeing him, making love . . . well, it was more like pure sex, with him, reminded her of the good times. Of the times when things used to be okay. Of a life still filled with possibility. Would it be possible to go back to that?

Cheryl sipped on her coffee and looked out the window. The roads were quiet today. The occasional car rolled past. There were three crows perched in the tree just by the window. She could hear them bickering through the glass. They flapped their wings and danced along the branches. They flew up suddenly as a man walked a lumbering mastiff. The dog huffed and puffed, sniffing at every post, piece of garbage, rolling pop can. The crows hovered above, nattering and screeching at the dog, until it was out of sight. They fluttered back to their perch, observing the traffic with unblinking eyes.

"Hello." Farah slipped into the chair across from Cheryl.

"Oh, my. I didn't see you come in." Cheryl said.

"No? I walked through the door."

"I was watching the birds. I think birds are kind of neat." Cheryl said.

"Crows. Good thing we don't live in Ontario. They have that West Nile plague going on up there."

"Yeah, between that and that SARS scare a while back, they've got it pretty rough. Sounds like a dangerous place."

"I'm sure it's no worse then many other places in the world. At least they don't have terrorist threats."

"It's all so unnerving. That's why having a good support group like Sam's is a comfort. At least you feel like you have a little bit of control of life, of peace."

"Is it about peace?"

"I would say it is. Finding inner peace and then trying to share the idea of it with others."

Cheryl leaned forward and whispered, "What does drinking pee have to do with it? Couldn't you just pray for peace without that?"

"I suppose. It's a ritual. One that we've come to accept. I wouldn't say enjoy, I've never really enjoyed it."

"I can't imagine enjoying it."

Farah went over to the counter and ordered a coffee. Cheryl watched her. She seemed so confident and happy. Her red hair was up in a ponytail and she had on only a trace of makeup.

"So what did you want to talk about?" Farah asked when she returned.

"I guess I just wanted to talk. I have to get my kids soon."

"Do you have many friends?"

"Not really. We moved here a couple of years ago from a nearby town. With the kids and living in the boonies, it's hard to meet people. Seems like I just live in a whirlwind of activity sometimes and the days just fly by. Next thing I know, I've lived here for ages and still know no one."

"The isolation of the small town. Well, our group is a friendly one. And there are some like you too. Just never get a chance to meet other people."

"And now that my husband is being so weird . . ."

121

"Are you getting a divorce?"

Cheryl put down her cup and stared at Farah. "Divorce?"

"Well, you said you thought he was fooling around."

"Yeah . . . but . . . never really occurred to me to get a divorce."

Farah nodded. "I'm divorced. Sometimes things just don't work out, that's all. We are lucky to live in a society where we can get out of a marriage that doesn't work."

"But my kids are so young."

Farah put her hand over Cheryl's. "I'm sorry. I didn't mean to scare you."

Farah's hand was warm and calming. Cheryl stared into her eyes and saw a peace there that she hadn't felt in herself in years.

She could get lost in those eyes. Her fingers tickled. It was getting annoying, and she broke Farah's gaze to look down. She screamed. On her hands were tiny red spiders. They were all over the table.

"Oh, my God." Cheryl jumped up, swatting at her hands.

Farah jumped up too, also rubbing her hands to rid them of the spiders.

"What the hell?"

She ran over to the counter.

"What kind of friggin' establishment are you running here anyway?" Farah said to the stunned clerk behind the counter.

Farah stormed off out the door.

"Come on, Cheryl. We don't need anything they have."

Cheryl was still trying to rid her hands of the horrible feeling the spiders had left on her. She rubbed them against her legs as she followed Farah out the door.

"I'm so freaked out by spiders," Cheryl gasped. "I can't believe I didn't have a heart attack."

"It's okay." Farah slipped an arm around her. "See, you are getting stronger already."

Farah cupped her hand under Cheryl's chin and looked into her eyes. "You're okay, aren't you?"

Cheryl fell back into Farah's hypnotic gaze. "Yes, I'm fine. Just fine."

"Good." Farah touched her lightly on the nose. "The power of the group flows through you. It gives you courage where before you had none."

"Stop." Cheryl laughed. "They were just spiders. I know they aren't going to kill me. Would they?"

"I don't know much about spiders. And I don't want to find out."

They stood awkwardly outside.

"Why don't we go for a drive?" Farah said. "You don't have to leave just yet, do you?"

"No." Cheryl looked at her watch. "Well, I guess I could for a tiny bit."

They went to Farah's convertible, and soon were speeding along the highway. The wind felt great in Cheryl's hair, and she realized it had been a long time since she was just the passenger. Farah turned on the radio, and "Highway to Hell" was playing. The women laughed and sang along to the AC/DC anthem.

Farah turned off the highway and the car bumped along a dirt road. Cheryl turned down the radio.

"Hey, I recognize this road."

"I thought you would."

Cheryl turned to Farah. "I don't have time to visit anyone, you know."

"It's all right, I won't take long."

As they wove up the driveway, Sam and the others were waiting for them.

"I'm glad you could make it after all," Sam said to Cheryl as he hurried her from the car.

"I-I can't stay. I told Farah that."

"Nonsense."

"I have kids at home. They'll be getting off the bus. . . ."

"You have a sitter that meets them, don't you?"

"But I really . . ."

Farah took her other hand, and Cheryl reluctantly followed them to the circle.

"Today, we welcome back Cheryl. She graces us with her beauty." Sam smiled at Cheryl. Cheryl looked down to the ground. Her stomach was beginning to rumble. She had to get back to the kids.

"Look, guys. I don't want to be a drag, but I don't have time to do this today. I really need to go home."

"It's okay, Cheryl. We'll get you home."

"Promise?"

"Promise."

Day stretched into early evening before Cheryl was released back into Farah's care. As they drove back, Cheryl's eyes were bright.

"I can't believe the power I felt there. It was incredible."

"I told you that it was what you needed."

"I know. I'm sorry I didn't believe you."

By the time Cheryl hugged Farah good-bye, she sensed that the next morning, she wouldn't be staring remorsefully at the glass of golden nectar. She would be able to partake once and for all. If going to the meetings felt this good without it, she could only imagine reaching the next threshold of ecstasy that she saw echoed in Farah's eyes.

Chapter Seven

It was night. A lovely fall night when it wasn't too hot or too cold. Vanessa loved this time of year, where the leaves crunched under her feet. She had spent the evening gathering acorns and wildflowers, smelling the damp air and enjoying the colorful trees. She had sat on the rocks over the ocean, watching the sun set. Thinking about so much, yet trying to clear her mind at the same time. She kept having the sensation that she was being watched, yet whenever she looked around, there was nothing there.

She had thought about David. She wondered what he was doing. She sensed that he would like nothing more than to sit and watch the sunset with her, but she had work to do. Very important work. There would be other sunsets to watch with David. This was not one of them.

The sunset revitalized her. The ocean lulled her

mind into patterns of rhythms. When the sun and the moon were both clearly visible in the red sky, she knew the time was right.

She returned to her home, put the flowers in a vase, and set the acorns on the counter for later use. The next hour was spent organizing her altar in the center of the room and pushing furniture out of the way.

At last she was ready to organize the articles on the altar.

A vial of virgin's blood, courtesy of Alex.

Eye of cat.

Nose of dog.

Tail of a squirrel.

Vanessa lit several white candles and three kinds of incense as she raised the cone of power around her. The vibration was high and strong today. She placed a pinch of salt, then poured springwater into a clay dish that she herself had made over the cold winter months. With her anthame, she stirred the water three times while chanting a few simple words. She poured the water from the dish into a larger cauldron that hung over the fire in the fireplace. One by one, she added the other ingredients, stirring and chanting as it boiled and smoked. To finish off the potion, she threw in a handful of herbs.

First things first.

Find Alex.

Vanessa placed a glass jar in front of her. She sat, feeling the energy of the cone of power.

Where was Alex?

She closed her eyes, trying to feel where the elusive spirit had gone.

"Alex, come back to me.
We are not done.
We have more to see.
Alex, you must return.
Together we will seek what we yearn."

She waited, hoping to feel the girl's spirit return. She felt something flickering and wavering in the circle. Before her a misty gloam formed and then dissipated again.

"Alex?"

There was only silence except for the sound of the cauldron boiling.

"Alex, return to your home.
You won't be happy being all alone."

Vanessa sat and meditated a while longer, but the mist didn't return.

She stood up and walked around for a while, touching her crystals, fingering her anthame. Alex wasn't going to return to her so easily.

She realized she was going to have to put thoughts of getting Alex back aside for now and continue on with the other part of her ritual.

While the brew steamed, she sat on the floor with a large crystal ball. She thought about what she needed to do.

Her clients' mates were disappearing.

There was something going on. Something terrible and dark. It was beyond the disappearing men. It had something to do with her, but what, she wasn't sure.

She peered into the crystal ball, hoping to see images that might mean something to her. Anything!

Clairvoyance, second sight, divination.

It was all such a crapshoot. She wasn't sure how she was able to read the cards for people. Half the time she looked at them and they meant nothing to her on a conscious level, yet her mouth would start babbling on and somehow put them into an order that the client could relate to. Yet she wasn't even sure what she had said. Sometimes she didn't even remember the question when she was finished. Tarot cards were her strongest tool; it all went downhill from there.

She looked into the crystal ball, wondering if a little movie would pop out at her like she had seen before, or if it would be a bunch of nothing.

She concentrated on Larry, wondering if he had left Betty for another woman, finally, or if something else was going on.

Steam rose from the cauldron, carrying with it a foul smell. Still, nothing was as disgusting as the spell for eternal life had been. She still shuddered when she thought about how awful that potion had tasted.

Nothing was coming for her in the ball.

She went over to the cauldron and scooped out a cupful of the liquid into the clay bowl. She set it on the altar to cool.

She shuffled the tarot cards and tossed a few

spreads. Nothing was making sense to her.

She tried another deck, but still, she was unable to see anything she didn't already know.

At last, the potion was cool enough to drink. She waved her hands over it, blessing it with a few words, and then raised the foul substance to her lips. It didn't taste that bad. There had been far worse over the years. She chugged it down quickly and wiped her lips.

She closed her eyes, saying a few words of a spell, chanting.

A chill rushed through her, and suddenly she was very aware of everything. Her senses sharpened and she looked again at the crystal ball.

A red neon light glowed from within the ball. She lay down, trying to see it better. Red pulsing light, like a sign.

Yes, it was a sign.

She could see movement, like people walking around under the sign.

She squinted. She blinked. She stood up, walking around the ball, observing the red blinking sign from every angle. Suddenly, the sign filled the crystal ball, DECADANCE. Vanessa blinked.

Decadence?

What did that mean?

Was that the name of a place?

She figured it must be, by the glowing neon.

What was the link?

Her hands were hot, and she rubbed them on her legs as she thought.

Of course, the phone book!

She flipped through the pages and yes, there it was.

Decadance.

A gentleman's club.

Yeah . . . a gentleman's club for pigs!

Strip joint.

Was the common denominator really a strip joint? Larry was known for frequenting strip joints, but that seemed so obvious. That a stripper would whisk him away . . . Vanessa watched the ball for a moment longer. The Decadance sign was fading, rippling into other images.

For a split second she saw Demian, as she had first seen him. At the university in the music studio, playing his guitar, his long dark hair falling over his pale oval face. Music twinkled into the room for a moment. She recognized snatches of the song he had written for her so long ago. It danced along her skin, stirring her blood. Warmth spread through her. His music was like no other. She ached to hear him play one more time.

The music stopped. His image faded. Then it was gone.

Vanessa stared into the ball for any more messages.

Why had it shown her Demian when it was David she was losing her heart to? Maybe it was telling her that she would never stop adoring Demian, or the idea of Demian, no matter who else came along.

The crystal ball grew dark. A swirling black and gray mass whirled inside; little red flashes glinted. Heat was radiating from the ball, and Vanessa stood back. The swirling grew more frantic. A face pressed against the glass as if trying to break out. It was a horrible face. Red glaring eyes, cruel mouth, crooked nose.

Vanessa wanted to turn away from the monstrosity, yet she was captivated at the same time.

The ball exploded into a shower of sparks and smoke.

Vanessa half-expected to see the demon, the club, Demian, all in her living room. But of course, there was nothing.

"Betty." Vanessa held her hand out to the surprised woman as the door swung open.

"Vanessa, I didn't know you were coming." Betty pulled her robe closer around herself. Her eyes were swollen and puffy, her hair seemingly uncombed for days.

"May I come in?" Vanessa peered into the house. Betty nodded.

"Of course. I'm sorry. I'm so distracted."

"It's a terrible time for you, I know. But I think I may have something to go on."

"Please. Anything. Anything to help."

"You went to the club he goes to, right?"

"Yes."

"And they claim to know nothing."

"They said he'd come in to watch, but he hadn't been there in a while. Like a few weeks."

"What's the name of the club?"

"Wait . . ." Betty retrieved the book of matches she had found. She handed them over to Vanessa.

"The Hot Box." Vanessa frowned. She held the

matches in her hand, but she knew they weren't what she was looking for.

"Were there any other clubs?"

"I really don't know. I think that's the only one in this town."

"Have you ever heard of a club called Decadance?"

Betty thought for a moment. "No. Why?"

"I had a vision. But I don't know."

"Would it help if I gave you something of his?"

"It might."

Betty brought out some clothes and a ring.

Vanessa touched them, but they didn't speak to her.

"There's something else. . . ." Betty said. "I don't know if it means anything."

Betty went over to the bookcase and reached up to the highest shelf. She brought down a little straw doll wrapped in material like it was wearing pants and a shirt.

"I found this under the car seat yesterday."

"Oh, my . . ."

"I mean, I don't believe in voodoo, but it sure looks like a voodoo doll. And it was in Larry's car. And now . . . he's gone." Betty's eyes filled with tears.

"Weird." Vanessa held the doll, feeling a burning heat rush through her fingertips. "It certainly looks like a voodoo doll. I wonder . . ."

"Do you think he's in a cult or something?" Betty asked.

"He might be. It's more like he was lured away.

You said he didn't have any enemies that you know about."

"No. Not that I know about, but who knows? Maybe he messed with the wrong girl and a boy-friend got mad or something."

"It happens."

Vanessa touched the clothes of the doll. The heat was suffocating her, and finally she had to put the doll down. "There is power in the doll. That much is certain."

"It's real?"

"Well, I tend to believe that certain things about voodoo are as real as you want them to be. Yet there are other aspects that are certainly out of our control. Maybe it was a gift. Maybe it is why he disappeared? I don't know that just yet."

"Have you been able to find out anything at all? The cards?"

"It's a mystery. It's almost like there is a fog cast over my eyes whenever I'm trying to figure out where he is. I'm wondering what we're really dealing with here."

Vanessa sat and thought for a while.

"Have you ever been to a strip club?"

"A couple of times, to please Larry, of course. I myself . . ."

"I don't need explanations. I say that tonight we go find Decadance and see if there's anything we can unearth. You need to change your appearance, and so do I."

Vanessa and Betty sat at a table in Decadance. It was a medium-sized club, with two golden poles set up on either side of the raised stage. The place was packed with mostly men and a few women. On the stage a lovely blond girl with enormous breasts was baring all to AC/DC's "Shook Me All Night Long." Vanessa had tucked her hair into a bun under a toque and wore baggy rapper gear. She had been careful to choose different colors and a different style of pants than the outfit she had abducted Alex in. Betty also wore rapper gear, and a headband over a short blond wig.

"You actually look pretty good like that." Vanessa grinned as she raised her beer glass to Betty's.

"I feel like a freak."

"Better to feel like a freak than have anyone recognize you."

"I don't think my own mother would recognize me with these clothes and purple lipstick."

"Good."

Betty nervously looked around.

"Betty, no. Don't look around like that. Watch the stripper and let your glance wander lightly. Smile at people and whatever you do, look like you're into it."

Vanessa continued to watch the girl gyrating on stage. It must be fun, dancing around naked like a taunting serpent for all these horny guys. Yet on the other hand, it was easy to see how it could all get tired real fast.

As she turned to talk to Betty, she realized a leggy blonde had seated herself down with them and was talking Betty's ear off. Betty shrugged as Vanessa looked over. Vanessa smiled, sizing the woman up.

"This is Millie." Betty introduced Vanessa to the stripper. "Millie, this is Candy."

"Pleased to meet you, Candy." Vanessa shook Candy's hand. A chill surged up her arm. Candy's eyes were large and her smile too wide.

"I was asking your friend here what brings you ladies out tonight."

"Just felt like going for a beer and looking at all the pretty ladies." Vanessa winked.

"I see." Candy grinned and placed her hand on Vanessa's thigh.

"Maybe you would like to see more?"

"I really don't. . . ." Betty started to protest, but then stopped as Vanessa shot her a nasty look.

"What are you proposing?"

"A private dance . . ."

"Here?"

Candy smiled, running her hands along Vanessa's breasts.

"Oh, no . . . we have a private room. Downstairs." Candy pointed to a stairwell.

"And how much is that going to cost us?"

Candy started mentioning prices while Vanessa raised an eyebrow at Betty.

"We'll come down for one drink and one dance." They followed Candy down the darkened stairs, where they were stopped by two large bouncers.

"Ten bucks each."

The women looked at each other.

"I'll get it." Vanessa put down a twenty in disgust. Already she was feeling cheated, but she was curious to see where this game would go.

Candy led them into a large room that had a bar

with many chairs and tables and then little rooms, curtained off. Two of the curtained rooms were closed. There was no one sitting in the bar or at the bar tables.

"What's the difference? Where we sit?"

"You can sit wherever you desire." Candy rubbed up against Vanessa, stroking her arm with long warm fingers.

"Maybe one of the little lounges?" Vanessa pointed. "Is that extra?"

Candy smiled. "This lounge is free." The women followed her into the little room, where she was joined by a tall, voluptuous woman, Ginjer, who made Vanessa's breasts look like pancakes.

Vanessa sank into one of the soft couches. Betty did the same, clutching her purse, trying not to look inexperienced. The two strippers wasted no time in peeling off their clothes and dancing.

"Um . . . how much does this cost?" Vanessa said.

"Don't worry. You are beautiful women, you will enjoy our services."

The strippers undulated along each other, kissing for the women. The tall one nestled herself into Vanessa's lap. A waitress came into the room with shots of something dark on a tray.

"Oh, you must buy drinks! It will be more fun," Candy said.

"I don't know . . . we've spent enough already."

Candy took two shot glasses and before Vanessa could say anything, had poured the liquid down the throats of Betty and Vanessa. Betty shivered. Vanessa closed her eyes, trying to see what Candy was really up to. All she could tell was that there was blackness everywhere. The women appeared to her like jackals with their ready grins and high-pitched laughter. The sambucca or whatever it had been had been too sweet, too thick, and now burned strongly in her stomach.

"I need to use the bathroom," Vanessa said. Candy pointed to a door a few feet away.

She looked at Betty and hoped that if she left her for a moment, she'd be okay.

Vanessa hurried to the bathroom. It was a disaster. None of the doors closed right and the floors were disgusting. She rinsed her hands off and stuck a finger down her throat. She needed to get the booze out so she could think better.

But this was more than booze.

Already she was growing dizzy and her perspective seemed off. She stood over the toilet, tickling the back of her throat, hoping that one of the gags would be successful.

At last, she emptied black bile from her gut into the toilet with a splash. She stared at the mixture as it went down. This was no sambucca shot. Her intuition had been right. They were trying to drug them.

She opened the door, intending to return to Betty as fast as she could. Yet now the door didn't lead back to the club. She shut the door and opened it again.

This was not the club she had just come from.

She had to get back to Betty.

She shut the door again.

This time the hallway was bright and white. She walked out into it. Confusion roared through her senses. She didn't know where she was; the drug was distorting her perspective.

She walked into the room and saw curtains blowing. She knew instinctively that even though things looked odd, she was in the right spot.

She peered into the first booth. An obese man sat naked on a couch. Rolls of flab spilled from his breasts to the hanging saggy thighs. A woman was kneeling between his legs, ostensibly giving him a blow job. Another woman was rubbing her breasts along his back. His face was one of stupefied pleasure. Drool hung from his mouth. On the wall, Vanessa saw something that looked like a dream-catcher. An odd shape with feathers stuck into it. If it was art, it was the ugliest thing she'd ever seen.

She withdrew and peered into the next booth. A man was lying flat on the couch while a young petite girl straddled him. Another stripper stood leering, holding a shooter of the black stuff. As the man grunted and thrust, the stripper holding the shooters sauntered over and touched the drink to his lips. He lapped at the liquid while awkwardly thrusting into the bored girl, who was staring off into space.

There was a stinging on her shoulder, and as Vanessa turned around, she realized that Candy had pinched her.

"You aren't allowed to watch others, you know."

"I'm sorry, I was lost. . . ."

"I'll show you back. . . ."

Vanessa's head was throbbing, and she realized it

was partly because of the techno crap that passed for music being spun down here.

She breathed a sigh of relief to see Betty still sitting on the couch with the other stripper. Betty's head lolled back as Ginjer gyrated in front of her, rubbing her own nipples. Betty wasn't even watching, as the drug started to take effect. Vanessa noticed that their booth too had the weird wall hanging that the other two booths did. Also, every single stripper wore the same type of red gem necklace.

"I think we're done now. . . ." Vanessa said. "What do we owe you?"

"Three hundred dollars." Candy said without blinking.

Vanessa stared at her. "Excuse me?"

"Two strippers, drinks, we danced. It's three hundred."

"We don't have that kind of money," Betty said.

"You have a lot of nerve. I'll give you fifty. Christ, we've only been here not even half an hour and we paid to get in."

"That's the house rule. Three hundred."

"Fuck that," Vanessa gave Candy fifty dollars. "This is more than enough. It's not like you fucked us or anything."

Vanessa took Betty's hand and led her out of the room. Betty was wobbling, her eyes glazed. As they tried to leave, the bouncers took them by the arms.

"You owe the ladies money."

"We paid them fifty bucks. It was more then they deserved."

"They say you owe three hundred."

"For what? It's not like they ate our pussies or anything."

"Pay the ladies or you'll be sorry."

Vanessa narrowed her eyes. She really hated to use her powers unless absolutely necessary, for whatever she used she had to recharge, and that took longer the older she got. However, she wasn't paying any three hundred dollars for a couple of girls to dance around for a few minutes and feed them drugs.

She turned around to face the bouncer, who easily stood a foot taller then her. He was young, dark, had a strong jaw and dark brown eyes. She put her hand on his, feeling the strength of his fingers beneath her.

"You know that nothing happened. That we are just two ladies who wanted to sit and have a drink. We didn't ask for anything to happen."

Her fingers grew hot as she willed a surge of energy into the young man. He jumped.

"What the hell . . . ?"

"We will be on our way," Vanessa said.

"Not until you settle your bill."

Vanessa raised her hands and aimed them at the young man's face. Blue streams of electricity bolted out and slashed him across his cheek like a handful of fingernails.

"Jesus Christ," he cried.

Two other bouncers ran in, and Vanessa assumed that he had pressed some sort of button to call them. She waved her hands, slashing the other men too. Terrified at bleeding from an unseen presence, they stood back and let her go.

Candy and Ginjer watched, hands on hips, shrieking for their money. Their friendly happy faces now revealed the true heartless shrews that they really were.

"Why don't you get out of my face before you piss me off even more," Vanessa said to them, cutting the air near their faces. A shimmer of sparks popped in the air and there was the smell of burning flesh. The girls stared at the marked faces of the bouncers. Still disbelieving.

"Come on," Vanessa said as she took Betty's hand. Betty was delirious and staggered willingly after Vanessa.

"Larry?" she muttered.

Vanessa tucked Betty into her room. She stayed by her side, giving her sips of an herbal antidote she created from spices she found in the cupboard. She hoped the drug wouldn't affect Betty too much before the herbs had a chance to work their way through her system. While Betty thrashed around in her bed, Vanessa went into the living room and looked around the house. She wondered if Larry had gone to Decadance. Had he been lured into the den and then whisked away somewhere for something?

She wondered as well about the two men she saw being pleasured. Somehow, she knew, she just knew, that they wouldn't be going home.

What did it all mean?

Vanessa returned home just as the sun was peeking up over the horizon. Betty was sleeping peacefully, the drug gone from her system. Vanessa took the voodoo doll, some feathers, and a man's shirt that she had found and tucked them into her purse. As she walked out into the sunshine, she noticed red drops glistening on the porch. Looking up, she saw a blackbird had been spiked over the doorway with a cryptic symbol painted around it.

She pulled the bird off and held it gently in her hands. She could feel the terror it must have felt in its last few moments of life. She placed the bird in the hedge and tossed some dirt over it, muttering a blessing as she did. She kicked more dirt over the blood drops on the step.

She raised her hands to the door and made symbols in the air while muttering a prayer. When she was done, she bowed her head for a moment, and then looked around to see if there was any indication of things being odd.

Satisfied that there was no real evidence of this latest thing, she went to her car.

As she drove, her fingers felt funny, like there was something wrong with the way the car was driving. She attributed it to exhaustion, or maybe her powers were wonky since she'd had to use some at the club. She looked in the rearview mirror and saw that there were bags under her eyes, a couple of crow's feet dancing near her temples. How she hoped that all she needed was a good night's sleep and not another virgin-blood bath.

The car seemed to steer itself as she headed along the winding ocean-view roads. Her mind was overloaded with what she thought might be going on. Playing out a thousand different scenarios. It was making her mental. So she decided to mull over more pleasant thoughts.

Thoughts of David.

They had known each other a while now. She really liked what she saw. She wondered if it was possible, even remotely, that she could be falling in love. She laughed. He was so different from anyone she had ever known before.

Love was such a weird thing.

Was it emotion? Lust? Was it just something to clog the loneliness of day-to-day existence?

What did love even matter?

Her heart pounded.

When she thought of David, a warm calm flooded her. It was like he somehow completed her. His presence made her own more real. It was more than a sexual chemistry. For what was sex, really, than just flesh rubbing against flesh? Anyone could get off with almost anyone if they really truly wanted to. It was the whole package deal that was getting under her skin. Maybe that was why she kept waiting to make love with him. She didn't want it to be just sex. She didn't want sex to get in the way.

What if they had crappy sex?

She didn't think that was likely from how they looked at each other, but what if it was? She had had crappy sex many times. Her fault. The man's fault. The bodies just not fitting as well as they might.

She couldn't worry about that now.

She didn't think sex would be a problem anyway. She loved every inch of him.

Sèphera Girón

He was a manly man. That was how she thought of him.

In that singsong way like the old Irish Spring commercials. "Manly, yes!"

Demian was a delicate flower compared to the strong muscular countenance of David. David had a deep voice, large powerful hands, broad shoulders, and all those wonderful muscles in the arms. Biceps. Triceps. He was blunt and purposeful, didn't take shit from anyone. She loved to watch him when he didn't know she was watching. To see that man's face transform into a boy's as he studied the ocean or a bird. That place of vulnerability that every woman adored in a man.

She wondered how David thought of her. Had he gone out with another woman last night? Did he only want to be with her?

She thought that he might only be with her, but of course, she knew better than to believe it. The world was full of liars and cheaters. Why wouldn't he be another one? He could be lying in bed with another woman right this very minute. He could be touching another woman in ways that Vanessa had yet to taste.

She figured she would enjoy things with him one day at a time. She couldn't hope for more, the world had become too crazy.

No expectations equal no disappointment.

She pulled into her driveway, and Katisha shot up the path to greet her.

"You out all night, poor baby?" Vanessa soothed as she scooped up the cat. She unlocked her door and went inside. Something seemed . . . odd. But

146

she couldn't put her finger on it. It was like someone had been here, yet, upon looking around, she could find nothing moved or disturbed in any way. She hurried over to her shelf where she kept her most obscure powders and herbs, but everything appeared to be intact.

Nerves.

Just nerves.

Especially after the disturbing bird creation at Betty's.

Someone definitely had it in for either Betty or Larry or both.

She couldn't sit around baby-sitting her, though, she had her own stuff to do.

She checked her answering machine. Another hysterical wife wondering where her husband had been for the past three days. Two of her regulars wanting early appointments.

A hi from David, who probably called on the off chance that she had canceled her appointment.

She stripped off her hip-hop clothes, relieved to feel air against her flesh once more.

Naked, she lay down on the couch and drifted off into sleep.

Chapter Eight

Vanessa stood on the rocks. It was a weird twilight sky. Magenta and violet clouds swirled like the strokes from a mad artist's brush. The ocean was an odd crystal clear, where she could see seaweed dancing and schools of fish darting.

Someone was coming toward her. At once she recognized that shuffling gait. Once the person drew close enough to see, she laughed.

"Well, well. Look who it is."

"Not much to do to amuse ourselves around here." Sophie said. "Waiting for dreams or consciousness slips."

"That bored, are you?"

"I guess I must be."

"So what dire message do you have for me now?"

"I'm to bring a dire message, am I?"

"Well, you are the harbinger of doom and gloom. The wet blanket of fun."

"Are you having fun yet?"

"Life has certainly taken a turn. Never a dull moment."

"Do you ever wonder if I'm just a dream? A portion of your consciousness?"

"No. I know what's going on."

"So you can't make me tell you."

"I already know."

"I don't think you know this particular angle."

"What. You're going to keep Alex from me?"

"It's nothing to do with Alex, but since you are so eager to see her, I'll let you talk to her for a moment."

"Oh, you'll let me."

"Well, you did kill her . . . poor virgin. Where did you think she'd go?"

"Now I know this is really a dream."

"Believe what you like. She's right over there."

Vanessa looked to where Sophie was pointing and saw the shadow of a figure standing alone on a rock. She ran over to her. It was Alex. Her face was full of fear.

"Why did you kill me?' Alex's eyes glistened with tears, bright like diamonds.

"I had to. I have no choice."

"There is always choice. You should just learn to grow old like everyone else," Alex said.

"It's beyond growing old, Alex. I have scars. Horrible scars that pus and burn like pokers stabbing me. Believe me, I put it off as long as I can."

"You should accept your fate. Everyone does. You don't like your looks, go to a plastic surgeon," Alex said.

"You don't think I have? I spent thousands of dollars and dealt with hundreds more questions of how I got the way I got. No sooner than the wounds healed, they split wide open. It's a never-ending battle."

"Then just die and leave the innocent alone."

Vanessa reached for Alex, but she turned away.

"You don't understand. I can't die. And I can't bear the pain of living."

"Everyone dies. Just accept your turn," Alex said.

"I can't die." Vanessa's eyes filled with tears. "I did this to myself and there's no reversing it. I have barely begun my journey and already I am so full of despair that a mere mortal would have had a stroke long ago."

"You're a selfish bitch."

"No, you live through me. Don't you understand?"

Vanessa reached again for Alex, but she was gone. Behind Vanessa, Sophie snorted. "Pathetic."

"Oh, fuck off. I want a better dream."

"Oh, you will dream, won't you? There are hundreds of years of dreams awaiting you, and I will be there."

"You will move on."

"We'll see. I may hang around just to torment you."

"So was that my big message? You getting Alex to tease me?"

"No." Sophie smirked. "Your message is that you are treading on very dangerous ground. You have angered someone."

"So what else is new? Get in line."

Sèphera Girón

"It's more than that. You are sabotaging someone else and they know it."

"Hey. With the exception of the virgin-blood thing, I've been playing by the rules. I even do my own housework and earn a living."

"I'm not the one who judges."

"Could have fooled me."

Sophie walked away.

Vanessa turned her back on her and stared out toward the water. She was whisked into a montage of dreams. Of falling. Of strippers. Of rock bands and stoned groupies. Of high school students running up the stairs as the bell rang. Of grassy meadows and fetid swamps. Her dreams ran her through a roller coaster of emotions, and she lay screaming and crying on the couch as day turned into night turned into day.

The doorbell ringing jerked her awake. Startled, she realized that she was butt naked.

She reached around on the floor for the baggy hip-hop sweater, then realized that she couldn't wear her disguise for anyone who might be at the door. Then it wouldn't be a disguise anymore. And there was the matter of that missing teen from the next town.

"Just a minute" she cried out, gathering up her clothes and running into her bedroom. She pulled a long baggy black dress from the closet and tossed it on. She tried to smooth down the rat's nest of hair that was a disaster from being under the disguise all night and then a restless sleep on the couch.

She pulled open the door and there was David,

with a large coffee and a box of donuts.

"Oh, my!" she cried out. "You scared the crap out of me."

"Aren't you a vision of loveliness?" he joked. She blushed as she pulled at her hair.

"I'm glad it's you. You won't mind if I suddenly need to take a shower." Vanessa grinned as she took the coffee from him.

"Did I catch you at a bad time?"

"Just sleeping late. Got in so late."

"Was it successful?" David asked. Vanessa pulled his arm.

"Let's go inside where there's less chance of anyone hearing."

They parked on the couch. Vanessa drank the coffee and nibbled on a donut.

"I'm not at all sure what happened to Betty's husband. I had a vision to go to Decadance, but my visions aren't necessarily clairvoyant or helpful. Divination is such a weird thing. Of course, if we could control it, psychics would be winning the lotteries instead of listening to desperate people ramble on!"

"What happened?"

"Not much. A couple of strippers tried to drug us and rip us off. Typical."

"You should have zapped them," David joked, waving his hands around. "Hocus-pocus, you are locus!"

"Yeah, I'd love to curse people. But I have to be careful. What we put out comes back, and you never know what it will be. I fooled around with curses before and it was a big mistake."

"Does magic really work?" David asked.

"Sure it does."

"Have you cast a spell on me?"

"I keep telling you, I don't and I won't cast a spell on any man. I trust nature to bring me what I need."

"I hope you're right, because you are so beautiful." He wrapped his arms around her and squeezed her. He was trembling. Vanessa pushed him gently back.

"What's wrong?" she asked.

David looked out the window at nothing for a while. He hummed and sighed. Vanessa wanted to touch him, to nuzzle him into comfort, but he was deep in thought. At last, he was able to speak.

"I had a weird dream last night," David said. "I dreamed about . . . her."

"Your ex?"

David nodded.

"What was the dream about?"

"I feel odd talking about it, but I think I should."

"Then do."

"She was . . . walking on a beach. Her hair was so long and golden. She really is a pretty woman."

Here we go, Vanessa thought.

No man will ever truly love me. Just me. He's still hung up on the ex. The walking wounded never recover from loving those that abandoned them.

"She was walking. She wore a bikini, but just the bottoms, not the top. She had on these big sunglasses, but I could tell it was her. I watched her, from the bushes, or maybe I was invisible. I don't know what it was. I realized, like, all of the sudden, that she was pregnant, though I don't think she was a minute before. It was like one minute she had a beautiful flat stomach, the next, she was bulging with a baby ready to be born any minute."

"Any chance of her being pregnant in real life?"

David shrugged. "Haven't seen her in a few weeks. Not since . . . well, I guess it was the day after you and I met, she dropped in at the store."

"Oh . . . she did?" Vanessa pushed down the pang of jealousy that was creeping into her gut. She had spells, oh, yes she did. She could put a curse on this woman who threatened her new relationship.

But she couldn't.

No.

A curse would be wrong. Then David wouldn't love her for her. She would never know if he loved her for her if she did such a thing.

"What did she want? When she came to see you."

"I'm not sure, actually. I think she just came by to say hi. She didn't buy anything. Maybe it was to rub my face in her presence."

"I see."

David stared out the window for a while. Vanessa fiddled with some candle wax that stained the tablecloth. She could feel his pain, his unrequited love, ebbing from him in waves. She closed her eyes, wishing the pain away, wanting to plant herself in his vision instead.

"Your dream?"

"Oh . . . yeah . . . the dream. So she was walking down the beach, belly big with baby. Then this bird comes swooping down, like it wants to dive-bomb her. It does this three times. A big black bird. I don't think it could see me. I don't know . . ." He shrugged. "So this bird swoops down yet again. And wouldn't you know, it rips her belly open and flies off again, never missing a beat. It was like a dancer or something."

"That's gross."

"Yeah. And get this. What falls out of her belly?"

"What?"

"Me . . . yet I'm watching this. But there I am, full-grown man dropping out of her ripped-open belly in a big bag of water. I stand up and there I am. A man. I can watch this while I'm living it."

"Then what?"

"Well, then she turns to me, and she's all back to normal, like her belly was never big or torn. She looks me over and puts her hand on crotch. And she says, 'Come to Momma.' Next thing I know, we're at an orgy with all these people that have big red eyes and huge appendages. Everyone is having their way with me. I'm enjoying it, but I'm scared at the same time."

"And?"

"Then I woke up." David stared out the window again.

"Were you having sex with her?"

"Sure. I was doing it with everyone. I was doing things I never thought I'd do. I really was enjoying myself."

Vanessa nodded, feeling even more jealousy flood her. She had to cool it. Be careful or she'd freak him out.

"So . . . tell me . . . why do you think you were dreaming about her? Do you miss her?"

David blushed. "I can't lie . . . I do miss her. I

don't want to be with her anymore, I don't like the way she treated me, but I do miss her. I miss the good times we had."

"It's always hard when someone leaves us with unfinished business."

"Oh, we were finished all right. She left me for someone else, remember? There isn't a bigger done deal than that."

"Maybe she realizes what she lost. That's why she came to the store that day?"

"Maybe. But you know, she did that to me a couple of times. Cheated on me. Left me, then came back. I may be trusting. I may be an optimist. But it seems to me that I'd just better move on, even if she does want me back."

"Well, I'm sort of not the person you should be talking about that with, you know. I like the fact we are building something between us, and there's no place for exes."

"Oh . . . am I bothering you?"

"Yes and no. It's good to talk things through a bit, yet at the same time, it's hard to hear that someone has feelings for an ex. It makes me wonder if it's too soon for you right now. For us."

"I think my dream has a bigger message. It felt big. It didn't really seem like it was about *her*. Although I woke up missing her. It was something more. Symbols."

"I can see the dream full to bursting with symbols. I have to think about it for a while 'cause there are so many things the dream can mean."

Vanessa cupped her hands around his hands. She couldn't help it, her mind was already commanding thoughts of Lizzie to be gone before she consciously realized it. Vanessa was seething with jealousy, though she knew it wasn't productive. She looked into David's green eyes. She remembered a scene from *Gone With the Wind* where Rhett Butler has his hands around Scarlett O'Hara's head, massaging it roughly while saying that he wished he could remove all thoughts of Ashley from her mind, knowing that *he*, Rhett, was the perfect match for her, not milquetoast Ashley. She wondered if this was how it would be with David. If he would grow more obsessed with his ex the longer they were apart, and not appreciate the good energy he could share with Vanessa.

Everyone needed time to grieve over a broken relationship. How much time was enough? She hadn't seen Demian in years. Was she grieving? Did they even have a relationship? They had never talked marriage or future. They'd just felt like they had been together forever and would continue along that way. They'd had an odd sexual energy, a pull that was hard to deny.

With David there was comfort. He was strong and masculine. When he hugged her, she felt safe though she knew she never really needed anyone. Yet even *she* was lured into that primitive sense of man protecting woman when he wrapped those muscular arms around her.

Was this her fate, though? To be dealing with a man hobbled by longing for the past instead of focusing on what the future might bring?

She had to snap him out of it. She had to snap herself out of it.

"David. You and Lizzie. What did you really think would happen between you?"

"What do you mean?"

"Well, you said it had been turbulent. So you intended to tread water the rest of your life, or did you think you would land on shore at some point?"

"It started off fantastic. She was the best thing that ever happened to me. Blond and beautiful, a good sense of humor. Everything was perfect."

"Nothing is perfect. It's all smoke and mirrors."

"Well, I know that now, don't I?"

"If it seems too good to be true, it probably is."

"You've never made mistakes?"

"Oh, I've made plenty. That's why I don't want to make any more. But how naive to think that it would have worked out for you two."

"We had really good times. We had some really shitty times."

"The good was good enough to outshine the bad."

"Most of the time. We had an amazing sex life." David blushed and looked down at his hands. "Maybe that was all it was, though . . . sex."

"Sex isn't everything. It's not even close to everything. There is so much more to life. So much to see and taste and feel."

"Sex is pretty important."

"Is it?"

"Well . . . yeah."

Vanessa nodded her head. "But sex can come from anywhere. If you closed your eyes you could be doing anyone. It doesn't matter." Vanessa stared directly into David's eyes. She waited for him to think for a moment.

"Men don't care who they are fucking, do they? Really?" she asked, trying to read his face.

"I care."

"I think that as long as there's something about them that is pleasing, they don't care if it's a different girl every night, as long as she is willing to perform the necessary deeds to get him off."

"You sure are bitter," David said. "I won't pretend that sex is sacred, that it is an act only for two people pledged together for life, but I won't perpetrate the myth that men just want to fuck anything. Some of us actually care."

"So what was it about this Lizzie that made you care? She have a beautiful body?"

"I loved her body. But it was familiar. I knew where to touch, what to do."

"That's how it is with any relationship."

"No . . . not really. Sometimes you just don't click at all."

Vanessa swallowed.

"So what else was it?" she asked.

"We just seemed to understand each other. That was the biggest thing. Like minds and all."

"I can see the benefit to that. But there is also the whole idea of opposites attract."

"Of course there is. You asked what there was to her. I'm just trying to answer." His voice had an edge to it.

"Right. So you had like minds, about what?"

"Well . . ." David sat and thought for a long time. He seemed about to speak a couple of times, and then said nothing.

"Just about stuff. It's not important. What is important is right now. You and I."

"I agree."

They kissed. Vanessa put her arms around him. He hugged her back. Their lips met and parted eagerly, their hands roaming along each other's bodies. When they finally stepped apart, they were breathless.

"I wish . . ." Vanessa started to say.

"What?"

"Nothing . . ." Vanessa looked at him a moment longer. She looked at the clock. "Oh, my, it's getting late."

"It sure is. I have to get to work."

He kissed her once more. "I love you, Vanessa. I'm really falling in love with you."

Vanessa smiled and touched his cheek.

"I'm falling in love with you too, David."

Chapter Nine

She was old again. It never lasted. Life was a cruel and dirty joke. She looked over at the young man sleeping beside her. Such a sweet young man. Newly wed. She grinned. What would his darling wife think? Not three days after their wedding he had been at the strip club. Judging by what she had been able to discern, and she had to admit that she hadn't been terribly interested, he was already worried he had made a mistake. Sure his wife was a beauty. Eager to please and ready to make their home his private palace. But he had cold feet. Was this really the only woman he would ever see naked again? Would ever sleep with again?

It had been so easy to lure him down to the VIP room at Decadance. How she had danced for him. It took three songs to lead him back to her lair.

Now, he lay sleeping and she had returned to her original form. She had to work fast while he slept.

She slipped out of the bed and went into the living room, where she grabbed a vial of liquid. A few men were back on the hooks, others were still out and about. She smiled. They were no doubt returning home to bewildered wives. Only to pretend they were sorry and then disappear once more.

She stood over the handsome young groom. Chris. His name was Chris.

She sprinkled a few drops from the vial over him. The sensation woke him up. He groggily opened his eyes. When his gaze fell upon the old woman before him, he jerked upright.

"What the hell?" She threw the contents of the vial at his face. It burned his eyes.

"Who are you?" he cried, rubbing his eyes in pain.

"I am your mistress, that's who," she croaked.

"I think you've made a mistake, lady."

"No mistake here." She raised her hands.

"Follow my bidding,
follow my spell.
Whatever I want,
you will do well!"

The man stopped rubbing his eyes and stood silently.

"Go on then!" she commanded.

The man walked slowly toward the dark room, the woman walking behind him. When he reached an empty hook, he turned around so that his back was to it. He reached behind himself with strong hands and lifted himself onto the hook. His face didn't change expression as his flesh was pierced and he was hung. She snapped her fingers and he closed his eyes, waiting, like the others.

Cheryl tossed and turned in her bed. Her dreams had been outlandish. Swimming in golden streams. Dancing and laughing with Farah and the children. She could fly. She could jump. Her body throbbed with joy and bliss.

When she woke, the happiness ebbed away. She lay alone in her queen-sized bed. Her husband nowhere to be found. Down the hall, she could hear the beeping of a video game.

She stretched her arms out and yawned.

If Tony didn't want her anymore, what was she going to do?

She couldn't bear the thought of a life without him, yet this had gone on so long, what more could she think? Tears filled her eyes as she remembered the last time she had seen him. Where had he gone?

Her hands strayed to her breasts as she thought about him. About their rough lovemaking. Her body ached for him, hungered for him once more. Why couldn't he see that she still loved him?

Yet every day he stayed away led her thoughts down stranger paths.

She thought about Farah a lot. She found reasons to call her, to meet with her, nearly every day. Farah filled the gap that she missed with her husband. Adult companionship.

"Mommy! Look what I found!" Dina ran into the room, clutching a little doll.

"What's that?" Cheryl examined the doll. "Where did you get it?"

"I was letting the cat out and it was there on the step." Dina said.

"It's a voodoo doll," Cheryl said, half to herself.

"What's that?"

Cheryl studied her daughter's face. "Nothing, dear. Just a special type of doll. Here, Mommy better take care of it."

"I like it."

"It's not for kids, honey." Cheryl took the doll and put it on the fridge. She would definitely have to take this to Vanessa.

As Vanessa entered the store, she had an odd sense about her. Something wasn't quite right. She touched the pile of apples, and was amazed at the cloud of fruit flies that swarmed up. The bananas were brown, the lettuce was wilted. It wasn't like this store to have produce that wasn't up to par. It was the main reason she shopped here. The fresh food. The reasonable prices.

She looked around, but didn't see either of the usual produce men. Maybe they were sick.

The store was humming with fluorescent lights as several shoppers pushed their carts up and down the aisles. She hated fluorescent lights, but usually she didn't notice the ones in here. Why could she hear them buzzing so loudly today? She looked up at their flickering glow, at the flies circling and slamming into them. The odd bird swooped and dived along the rafters. The humming was so loud because there was no annoying elevator music piped in to-day.

The woman next to her studied the bin of tuna. Vanessa recognized her as someone she had read the cards for once or twice many months ago.

"Hello." Vanessa said. The woman startled and dropped the tins she held.

"Oh, my!"

"I'm sorry." Vanessa helped the woman gather up the rolling cans.

"Just feeling jumpy lately, I guess."

Vanessa felt waves of sorrow flowing from the woman.

"What's wrong?"

"I know you," the woman said, staring more closely at Vanessa. "I went to you for help once."

"Yes. Did I help?"

"In a way. I mean. You didn't give me any con-crete solutions, but I guess some stuff we have to figure out on our own."

"We all have free will. . . ."

"I guess. At the time, I was upset that you didn't solve my problem for me. But now, I can see what you were doing. I have to live my own life. I have to do what is realistic for me."

"So things are going much better then?"

"No . . . actually. They aren't."

The women returned to browsing the aisles, filling their carts while talking.

"I left my husband. I know you can't remember every person you talk to. But I did leave my hus-band. I was single for a few months. I didn't know if I ever wanted to even look at another man again

167

after that. It's devastating, you know. No matter who is leaving who. You have all these hopes and dreams. You marry in such happiness, looking forward to a whole new life, and then it's all over."

"I know. I've heard it all before."

"At any rate, I thought I'd found happiness. Thought I found a new man. And now . . . well, I guess it's all falling apart too."

"Why?"

"He stopped calling. I haven't seen or heard from him in a couple of weeks."

"Really?"

"I guess he just lost interest. Not the first. Not the last, I'm sure. But Christ, I hate it when guys do that."

"Yeah, I know. So do I." Vanessa looked into the woman's eyes. "I don't think he lost interest, though."

"No?"

"I think . . . well, it doesn't matter what I think. But be patient."

"Do you think he's coming back?"

"He might."

Tears sprang into the woman's eyes. "You've given me hope."

"I think there's something he had to do, but he'll be back."

The woman grabbed Vanessa's hand. "Thank you."

"It's all right."

The lights were buzzing loudly now. Vanessa had an odd sensation of being watched. By who or by what, she wasn't sure. In the rafters, the birds had all gathered along one beam, and sat quietly looking down on her.

Vanessa noticed the shelves were half empty, as if they had been picked over. Maybe the store was going out of business. Yet it was the only real grocery store for many miles, and there were always people in it.

The people today wandered along as if lost, barely looking as they tossed products into their carts. Mostly women and children. She wondered what it meant. How could it mean anything? Were they all having marital problems too?

By the time she got to the car, she was more then a little freaked out. She decided to go over to the hardware store to see if David could soothe her nerves.

Ashley lay on her bed, staring at a large poster of TnT. It was one of the ones where his eyes looked so large and blue and lost. As if he were shocked and shamed by his sudden meteoric rise to the top. She knew that if she met the real TnT, all would be right in her world. He was so smart. So clever. He would have figured out how to find Alex. He would have told that witch to her face that she was full of shit.

Something in the pit of her stomach told her that whatever had happened to Alex was over. Somehow, she knew, she just knew, she wouldn't be seeing her friend again in this world. Alive. It had been too long, with no clues.

That wasn't totally true. There was one clue. The blurry video camera images of Alex walking with a rapper. No rapper that Ashley recognized. Someone new. Someone that had a liking for the latest TnT fashion.

Ashley had asked the school for copies of the security video. Demanded every copy they had with Alex and the stranger. Since the school and the cops felt that she might be able to help, they had made her copies of everything they had on Alex. She watched them over and over again.

Sometimes there were videos of her with Alex, standing a ways from the school yard, sharing a butt and yapping about God knows what. Tears would run down her face as she'd see her friend, walking along like the loneliest soul in the universe. She had always known Alex was a loner and lonely, but to see it played out on video, endlessly, day after day, was heartbreaking for her.

Why hadn't she been more sensitive to Alex?

Ashley was a loner herself. But with her it was for artistic reasons. It took a lot of time and energy to write rap songs, and she couldn't always be hanging out everywhere and write at the same time.

Alex walked slowly along the road, then stopped to talk to the rapper. Ashley hit the remote, freeze-framing on that rapper.

Funny. She had always thought that she was Alex's best friend. Yet, on the tapes, Alex had made a new friend.

A friend she had never told Ashley about. Ever. Not even hinted about. Nothing at all.

Ashley wondered if Alex had fucked this new guy. Maybe that's why she hadn't mentioned him to her. She knew they had a pact and if Alex had broken the pact, Ashley would have been hurt. Ashley wondered if that was the dude that had spirited Alex away. Or if that witch was involved somehow.

Her gut feeling over and over again was that the witch had something to do with all of this. Maybe the man worked for the witch?

What did the witch have to do with Alex? Why on earth would she even *want* Alex? There were lots of more beautiful people around. There were people with talent, with money, with connections. Alex had none of that. Her family was modest, typical blue-collar.

Murder for sport?

Why did she keep coming back to murder?

Maybe Alex had run away as the witch said. Maybe that's just how it was. Alex had just up and left. Sick of the loneliness. Sick of school. Sick of all the wanna-bes hanging around.

Yet Alex had no dreams that she knew about. Not like Ashley had. So where would she go? Why would she bother?

Maybe her parents beat her?

Ashley didn't think so. She'd known Alex forever and there had never been anything like that going on, she didn't think. She would have known.

Sure Alex's parents didn't understand her. What parents did understand their teenage children? Life was full of misunderstanding. Ashley had figured that one out long ago.

Ashley sat up. Lying around would accomplish nothing. She had to keep moving. Keep her brain and body moving.

She rolled off the lumpy mattress and crawled

around on the floor, until her fingers reached the edge of a box she had hidden under the bed. She pulled it out.

It was a Ouija board.

Ashley stared at the garish picture on top of the box. Some weirdo with a turban on his head raised his hands to crudely drawn kids that looked like they were out of the fifties.

Amaze and astound your friends.

Yeah, right.

She knew about Ouija boards. She knew good and bad things about Ouija boards.

Ashley was pretty certain that she could never trust anyone not to cheat on her if she did the Ouija with someone else. Except for when she and Alex had played.

It had been a couple of years ago when they bought the board at a garage sale. It had been Alex's idea. She loved that damn board, was forever wanting to play with it. Yet she wouldn't take it home. She was afraid her parents would take it away from her and burn it or something.

Ashley and Alex spent many a Friday night fooling around with the thing.

Until the night they decided never to play with it again.

They had gone to the park first, smoking a joint and teasing each other about boys and whatnot.

"Why don't we try to call TnT?" Alex said with a wicked gleam in her eyes.

"He's not dead." Ashley pointed out. "You're supposed to call dead people with a Ouija board."

"Maybe we can force him to say hi, though. Like

a phone call to his unconscious!" Alex mused.

"No. I don't think so. Besides, don't you think he'd be pretty pissed to be called away from whatever important work he's doing to talk to two giggling teenagers? No way. I'd rather meet him when I've done my CD."

Alex hauled on the joint and passed it back to Ashley. She batted her eyelashes innocently.

"I just thought it'd be fun, is all."

"No biggie. I think we'd better stick to dead people."

Ashley watched the smoke waft from her lips.

"Who should we call today?"

"I don't know, maybe just see who comes to us?"

They returned to Ashley's house and set up the board and two pillar candles. They lit the candles and turned off the lights. They put their hands together on the planchette. Ashley was always astounded by how strong the energy from Alex was during these sessions. She positively hummed like some sort of homing device.

Within minutes, the planchette was circling the board. Round and round. Ashley saw Alex peeking at her, to see if she was moving it. They both opened their eyes and watched in awe as the planchette roamed from letter to letter, too quickly for them to realize what it was spelling.

One of the candles fell over. The flame danced along Ashley's bookcase. As the girls hurried to pour their bottled water over it, they heard a sound like muffled struggling coming from the closet. There was banging on the door and someone trying to call out, but they sounded mute, as if they were gagged.

"Oh, my God!" Alex said, dabbing up water from where they had poured it.

Ashley crept over to the closet. The door shuddered with every knock against it from the inside. The moaning and pleading grew louder. Ashley gathered all her courage and opened the door.

There was nothing in there.

In the distance, there was a woman screaming.

They looked back at the Ouija board and watched as a puff of smoke was emitted from the planchette that had flipped over on its side. The smoke swirled into a gray fog. In the fog glowed two red dots. The dots grew larger until they formed the shape of cat eyes. A leering face grew visible for a second and then swooshed back into the planchette.

Alex flicked on the lights. The girls stared at each other and then looked back at the board. They tossed the planchette and board back into the box and shoved it under the bed. The girls ran out of the room and back to the park, where they sat on the swings, silently chain-smoking cigarettes until their nerves stopped trembling.

The next day in the paper, they discovered that a local college girl had been raped and murdered not far from where they lived.

After that, Alex didn't ask to play with the board, and Ashley kept it out of sight, out of mind, under her bed.

Now, here she was, looking to the Ouija board for answers.

How else could she talk to the dead, if Alex was dead?

Or even if Alex wasn't dead, maybe someone who

was dead could tell her what was going on.

It was worth a try. Not that much to lose. Well, except for getting freaked out.

Pulling out the board and the planchette, she realized she was trembling. Her hands were icy cold and she fumbled trying to open the board.

Well, if she was going to do this, she might as well do it right.

She gathered up a dozen or so tea lights that were scattered around the room and put them all on her dresser. One by one, she lit them all. They flickered, little orange flames licking tentatively at the air. A couple of them kept going out, so she had to keep relighting them. At last they were strong enough that she turned out the electric lights.

She hopped onto the bed and sat crossed-legged, her fingers lightly touching the planchette.

"Alex, wherever you are,
come to me,
bring me messages,
let me see the truth . . .
Alex . . . Alex . . . Alex . . ."

Ashley closed her eyes, chanting Alex's name over and over again. The candlelights flickered. Hot wax spit and sizzled. A chill trembled along her arms, as if an unseen hand were stroking the fine hairs.

The planchette vibrated and then slowly, shifted beneath her fingers. Ashley stifled the urge to cry out.

"Alex? Is that you?"

The planchette crept hesitantly along the smooth board until it stopped. Ashley opened her eyes.

Yes.

Her heart slammed and she fought the urge to burst into tears. Instead, she fueled her energy back into the task at hand.

"How do I know? How do I know if it's you?
How can I be sure the words you speak are true?
How do I know it's you, not someone who talks like you,
who wants to be like you,
who acts like you,
who is coming through you but who is who?
You are you and you gotta prove it,
you gotta move it, you gotta do it,
show it, move it, groove it, prove it,
fall on your knees and let me walk you through it.
Do it."

Ashley put her hands back on the planchette and watched as it wandered over to new letters.

A TO A
T N T

"Oh, my God." Ashley nodded. "It's you. I know it."

Her joy was short-lived as she realized that Alex's ghost was speaking to her.

"So you *are* dead."

The planchette streaked across the board until it revealed another answer.

Yes.

Tears rolled down Ashley's face as a host of memories flooded her.

She saw Alex as she had the very first day they met. They were five years old. In kindergarten. Ashley had been the new girl. Well, they were all new to school, but most of the kids knew each other from the playground, local pool, and library story hour. Ashley had just moved into the neighborhood over the summer. Ashley had known Alex was different from the others from the moment she laid eyes on her. Alex was dressed in the pinafore uniform all the girls wore. Her clear blue eyes were wide with apprehension. Ashley ran over to her, in the manner that five-year-olds have, before they become censored and Stepford cautious, and took her hand.

"Come. I'll show you the fish." She dragged Alex over to the aquarium and they spent the next few minutes admiring the colorful guppies.

From that moment on, they had been friends.

Theirs had been an odd friendship. Twisting in and out like two trees growing side by side. Roots entangled, the odd branch poking toward the other one. Sometimes, they were inseparable, spending all their time at each other's houses. Sometimes, they went weeks without seeing each other, preferring the company of new and interesting people.

But the one thing they had shared the most was the idea of sex.

How badly they wanted to taste the forbidden fruit.

How badly they wanted to be "bad," yet on the other hand, they wanted to be special.

They had made a pact, back when they were eleven, that they would remain virgins until they met the man they were going to marry. Or a rock star!

They had crushes on lots of people. Giggling over boys in class. There were always cute boys to giggle over. There were always big-busted girls who never spent Saturday nights alone to wonder about. There were always people to watch and learn from, whether their behavior was considered good or bad, moral or sleazy.

Ashley's arms tingled and she imagined Alex running her hands along them, like she used to do when she thought Ashley was upset. Alex would lean against her, rubbing her arms, and Ashley would feel her already large breasts pressing into her back. Alex always smelled nice. Freshly scrubbed nice, like herbal shampoo and Clearasil.

There had been a couple of times, when they were smoking dope, when sometimes they would explore each other a little further. After all, they wanted to be ready for when a man came. Spurred on by preadolescent books by Judy Blume and others, they experimented with kissing each other. They learned how to pucker their lips. How to dance their tongues around each other. How to tilt their heads to avoid noses and hair and teeth clicking. They didn't make a habit of necking. But the few times it had happened, Ashley had loved it and she was sure Alex had too. She loved to feel the swell of Alex's bosom beneath her fingers, and even more so, she loved the tentative touching and pinching of her own nipples by Alex's curious fingers. Sometimes, they were so stoned and horny, they would lie down on the bed. Kissing and playing with each other's breasts, pulling flesh from underneath shirts, and wrapping their legs around each other. Dry-humping their passion to the latest album by TnT or whoever was hot at the time.

Tears rolled down Ashley's face.

Was she a lesbian?

Why did her heart break so, knowing she would never taste Alex's sweet lips again?

No, she wasn't a lesbian.

She loved her friend, but she loved the idea of having a cock of her own one day. To gobble or lick or shove between her legs whenever she wanted.

Alex had no cock.

"What happened, Alex?" she asked the air. Her nipples were hard and throbbed achingly against her shirt.

She wondered how the spirit would spell out the whole story. But she needn't have worried, Alex wasn't so talkative.

dead

"I understand you are dead. How did you die? Were you murdered?"

The door slammed open and the candles nearly went out with a gust. Meredith stood in the doorway, long blond hair wild, her eyes wide as she surveyed what her daughter was doing now.

"Ashley."

"Yes."

"What did I tell you about lighting candles?"

"I know. But I wanted to call Alex. I just know she's dead. She spoke to me!"

"Oh, you poor dear. You're losing your mind." Meredith wrapped her arms around her daughter and kissed her on the top of her head.

"I know you miss her terribly. And I know most of us think that she must be dead. It's been too long now. But of course, they did find that Elizabeth Smart girl after many months. I guess all we have is hope."

"And a Ouija board. She is talking to me, Momma. She really is."

"You know, those things only work by how you push them around. If you don't believe you are pushing it around, then your unconscious is even more powerful than you imagine. I don't like you playing with that thing, though. They're dangerous. You never know who you're going to call."

"I read *The Exorcist,* Mom. And a million other horror books. I'm not going to call the devil with a Ouija board. He has bigger fish to fry than me."

"Devil or not, you can't have all those candles burning in the house. It's a fire hazard."

Meredith leaned over to blow out the tea lights. Flames shot up in a furious gust, igniting her hair.

"Mom!" Ashley ran to her mother, grabbing a towel from where it lay on the floor from her last shower. Burning hair fell in a clump to the floor. The smokey essence left a lingering stink hanging in the air. Ashley hurriedly put out the candles with the snuffer as Meredith ran to the bathroom and jumped into the shower, clothes and all. When the candles were out, Ashley went to see her mother. Her mother was peeling off her clothes, her hair soapy with shampoo. Ashley stuck her head through the curtain.

"Are you okay?"

"Yes. Just burned a clump of hair, is all." Meredith rinsed the hair out and showed Ashley the burnt part.

Ashley stared at the charred section of hair.

"How did that happen? There was no wind in there or anything," Ashley said.

"I told you. Candles are dangerous. Now leave me alone. And throw out that Ouija board."

Ashley watched her mother pull at her hair with trembling fingers. Meredith's face was white despite the cold front she put up. Ashley figured her own was probably pretty pale too. It never mattered what the deal was. Play with a Ouija board and something's gonna happen. Nearly one hundred percent guaranteed.

Amaze and astound your friends.

Ashley returned to her bedroom. The smell of candles and burnt hair permeated her room. She opened the window to air it out.

"Are you still here, Alex?" she called to the air.

She felt like there was nothing there. That heaviness in the air. That buzzing of electricity. All were gone now.

But if it had been Alex, maybe there was a way to call her that didn't involve a Ouija board.

"Alex?"

Ashley folded the Ouija board back into the box

and shoved it back under her bed. She put a TnT CD case into her pocket, along with her Walkman and headphones.

Ashley poked her head back into the bathroom.

"I'm going for a walk, Mom. I'm too freaked out."

"Be careful and don't be late," Meredith said. "And no more fooling around with the spirits. Nothing good ever comes of such things."

Ashley walked through the subdivision until she came to the neighborhood playground. She sat on a swing and slowly rode it back and forth. She often came here at night. Not too late, when the older kids were hanging around drinking. But at the time between little kids playing and older kids partying.

It was her time.

And it used to be Alex's time too.

She pumped her legs on the swing, going higher and higher.

She missed Alex so much. Maybe Alex's parents could cling to the hope that their daughter had just run off, but Ashley knew the truth. Whether anyone believed in ghosts or not, the truth was Alex was dead.

She pumped the air harder. She couldn't believe Alex was dead. TnT wouldn't have let her die. No way. TnT might want a lot of people to die, but not her Alex.

Ashley imagined TnT in front of her, dressed in a glittering baby-blue jogging suit, waving his hands in the air, pointing toward the woods. She squinted her eyes. It was like he was really there, only transparent, like a film movie without a back screen.

"Weird America.
come this way.
Wacked-out Ashley,
it will be OK.
Touch it, you know it, you feel it, you grow it,
it's all here, it's all queer, it's in the air,
you know where,
it's all clear, so clear, plastic wrap and plastic
fear,
put it in your pocket and take it home,
blow away the bullshitters,
don't let those bastards say no.
Weird America,
it's Alex and you.
Weird America,
it's Alex and who . . . ?
Weird America: We'd know what you say.
Weird America: It's never your way."

The TnT ghost disappeared, although his song still rattled around her head.

Ashley jumped off the swing and went over to a picnic table. She pulled the CD case out of her pocket and put it on the table in front of her. There was no one around except a man in the distance walking a dog. She pulled out the little plastic bag of love dust and sprinkled it over the CD. Maybe TnT would come back and tell her more. Maybe she just imagined him and she was just singing to herself.

She looked toward the woods.

"Alex? Do I need the Ouija board?"

183

There was nothing. Not a sound except for the crickets chirping.

"What happened to you, where did you go, who
did you screw?
Why did you leave, who did you meet, why
didn't you tell me your fear?
Why did you run away, trying to hide, what
darkness met you on the path?
Why did you lie?
Who did this to you, who do I need to pursue?
Alex, I want to touch you,
want to taste you.
I want to save you, be brave for you.
Whatever I can't save, give to you, forgive, re-
lieve you.
It was always yours, it was mine to give.
Alex, what did it mean to live?"

Ashley stood up, wiping her hands on her pants.
She paced around the table, continuing her rap.

"So if you are dead, Alex, when did death come
for you?
Was it dressed like a man or a bitter old shrew?
Were you lured with false promises, deceitful
wishes, and lies?
Why couldn't you stop it? Just open your eyes!
I hope that person comes and tries to steal me
away.
I'll give them a run and they'll find the price
to pay.
If there's a man or witch to destroy,

I'll run them off faster than a cheap-ass toy.
I'm much stronger than that.
I'm much smarter than that.
I read Anne Rice's books.
Could kill that whiner Lestat.
Saw the *Wizard of Oz*,
know how to melt down the witches,
fool the Cat from the Hat,
kill him with Thing One's broom switches."

Ashley walked around the table again, friction building as she grew more agitated. Golden sparks flew from her sneakers as she marched and skipped. She watched the sparks bouncing, wishing that she had a friend to share it with. But of course she didn't. The only friend she had ever had was Alex and Alex wasn't here anymore. Alex wasn't even here to play on the swings.

She could almost hear Alex singing along with her and TnT in her head. Alex's voice was weaker in her mind. It was more like it was Ashley's wishful thinking. She returned to the swing and started to pump herself in the air again.

Alex.

A couple of boys were wandering along the far path and Ashley could nearly sense them without even seeing them.

The boys' voices were deep and vibrating, distracting her from her rap.

She closed her eyes.

Before her was the ghostly figure of TnT. He jumped in front of her, trees shining right through him. He pointed his finger at her.

"What was forgotten,
what was before,
is all irrelevant, it's all a bore.
All we know is that all the fucking grownups
are blind.
All we know is Alex was wrongly taken before
her time.
And we think we know who knows, but how
can we get her to confess?
Everything is confusing, it's a fucked-up mess.
You keep to it.
It's time to be reborn.
Grade school was such a drag, but you're past
that scorn.
High school is practice for dealing with dicks.
Don't let them get to you, don't let them feed
you their shit."

Ashley opened her eyes again. The figment of
TnT was gone.

The boys were gone. The park was silent save for
Ashley once more.

"If only there were a way that no one had to
lose,
but of course there are no winners if there is
nothing to choose.
Whatever path things take, we will find a way.
It's inevitable things are messed up today."

Ashley jumped off the swing. She dug her feet in
the sand. She sank down, digging her fingers
through it. The sand ran through her fingers. She

scraped it into mounds. She built little mountains and then kicked them down. She returned to the swing once more.

"Weird America, solve my mystery.
Wacked America, make it clear to me."

Ashley pumped the swing hard.
She listened to the sounds of the night. The wind.
A distant dog barking. Rapping in her head.

"How much more can it be?
How much more can I fly?
Did the universe expand so that I'd under-stand?
Would there be enough dope
to cope with the mope,
set it off, buzz it off, sleep it off?
There's no hope."

Ashley jumped off the swing again and lay down in the sand. She closed her eyes, letting the glow of the moon wash over her. Alex had to be here. She just had to be here somewhere. Ashley almost felt ready now to try to call her again.

She lay, listening to the sound of her own breath. So loud and jagged in the darkness. Finally, she sat up and wandered over to the picnic tables.

She knew Alex was there. Somewhere. Somewhere in the ripple of the air. Watching. Waiting. She hoped Alex was there, watching and waiting and ready to tell her what she needed to know.

She put her fingers on the CD case and closed

her eyes. Her head swam with the sound of TnT rapping. Images of that witch Vanessa flashed through her mind.

"Come and stand by my side.
Feel the tension, feel the torment.
Hear my battle cry.
We'll get that bitch, we'll find a way.
Somehow or another, we'll make her pay."

Ashley's fingers trembled as the CD case grew hotter. She could almost see TnT behind her closed eyes, beckoning to her. He was waving his arms and again, pointing toward the little woods. This time she felt braver. His image grew stronger, and he glowed white, his blue eyes burning like laser fire. She wanted to follow him. He would take her to Alex. She stood up from the table, slowly walking toward him. He moved along to the grove of trees. She hesitated only for a moment before entering the woods. Branches snapped beneath her feet as she continued deeper along the path. She smiled, following him. His figure flickered as if he were rippling between shadow and something else. It was like someone was wearing TnT's skin. She followed him quickly, wishing she could get close enough to touch him. The ripple flickered faster. She was so close to him now, yet she couldn't smell him. She put her hand out, reaching for his shoulder.

Suddenly, she was in a throng of people. Above her, the sky flickered with colored lights. She realized that ahead of her was an orb of glowing white light. Standing on her tiptoes, she was able to see over the man in front of her. It was a stage, filled with lights and a few people. A short-haired blond man with muscular chest and arms adorned with tattoos was ranting at the crowd. Yet she couldn't hear him. All she heard was a steady crunching sound. She looked ahead again, being pushed forward by a crowd of people from behind. Over to her right, she recognized a profile.

"Alex!" she cried out. She frantically pushed her way through people jumping and swaying to unheard music. She fought mightily, using her elbows and hands to shove her way through oblivious people. Her vision was blocked by so many that were taller, and she had to jump up and down herself to try to spot her missing friend.

"Alex!" Her voice echoed. In the distance was a croaking and then a splash. There was rustling.

She looked toward the stage again. The band was jumping around, the singer running back and forth, waving his arms in a primal fashion. It looked so much like him, yet how was he here?

Remembering her mission, she looked over to the spot where she had spied Alex. She was there no longer. She jumped up and down again in a circle, trying to find her, but she was gone.

Maybe Alex was trying to make her way toward the stage. Ashley pushed her way forward. Several times she was met with resistance and had to change her path. She grew closer to the stage, to him, yet still there was no sound.

It was like having a bell jar around her head save for the constant chirping of crickets.

She was so close to the stage that she could now

see the sweat on his face. A scream started to build
in her throat. As he turned to look at her, she saw
half his face was eaten away, white bones gleaming
with chunks of rotting flesh swinging in strands. She
put her hands to her mouth, trying to choke back
sudden vomit.

Squeezing her eyes tightly shut, she felt a great
sense of aloneness. She opened her eyes again.

He was gone. Everyone was gone. Blinked off like
a light.

She was in darkness. Even the moon couldn't
penetrate the trees. Her heart beat rapidly against
her chest as she realized she was truly alone. Alone
in the woods at night.

"Alex?" she asked. She waited hopefully. Maybe
Alex would be a dull glow, or maybe she'd feel her
arms around her.

"Alex? I'm here."

There was no answer. A chill swept through Ashley. In the distance, a stick snapped.

"Who's there?" she cried out.

There was nothing, and then the sudden scurry-
ing of an animal. A mosquito hummed loudly by her
ear.

Ashley pressed her fingers to her mouth.

"Alex?"

Something brushed her head. She bolted, not
stopping to wonder if it was a stick or an animal or
something else.

She ran blindly in the dark, stumbling along the
fallen leaves until at last, she saw a dull glow that
indicated a way out.

She ran toward the gleam. As she grew closer,

she realized it was a patch of fog, lit up by hundreds of fireflies in a small clearing in the woods. The bugs swarmed toward her. She screamed, trying to bat them away. They crawled along her, in her hair, down her shirt, their tiny wings fluttering, their little legs creeping around her.

"Get off of me!"

She stumbled through the darkness once more. Her foot hit a branch and she fell face-forward, sliding through a pile of leaves. As she sat up, she realized she had bit her lip. More mosquitoes buzzed around as she ran. They were sticking her. Searching for a snack. In despair, she sat with her knees curled up to her chest and rocked quietly. How was she going to find her way out?

Her mom was going to give her so much shit when she got home.

Tears ran down her face and before long, she couldn't help how loud her sobs were getting. She cried. Cried out of fear of being lost in the woods at night. Cried at her failed attempt to talk to Alex. Cried even harder at the fact that she would probably never see Alex again.

A hand patted her head. Softly. Gently.

"What is wrong, little girl?" Ashley lifted her head and saw a woman standing before her. Ashley thought she was the most beautiful woman she had ever seen in her life. She reminded her of the Blue Fairy in *Pinocchio*. The woman held a flashlight that she kept aimed at the ground so that she wouldn't hurt Ashley's eyes.

"I'm lost," Ashley said.

"No, you aren't."

"I've been walking forever and I can't find my way out."

"Take my hand." The woman held her hand out to Ashley. The girl took it and pulled herself up. As she saw the woman's face she thought she had never seen anyone more beautiful in her entire life.

The woman's hand was soft, and instantly Ashley felt a peace swell through her like a warm-water bath.

"Who are you?" Ashley asked.

"Some people call me Molly. You can call me Molly if you like."

Ashley nodded. They walked a short ways and Molly aimed her flashlight out of the woods.

"See how close you were to the edge?" she asked.

"I was close. But which side am I on? Where am I?" she asked.

"You are where you started." Molly shone the beam on the distant picnic table.

"So I am." Ashley could even see the reflection of the CD cover on the table.

"Hey . . . how do you know where I started?" Ashley asked.

"I saw you when I went into the woods. Then I heard you crying so I went looking for you."

Ashley nodded again, not daring to ask what business this woman might have in the woods at night. As if in response, the woman held up a burlap bag.

"I was gathering herbs and stuff. You have to pick them at a certain time or they aren't as potent."

"Herbs . . . like to eat?"

The woman smiled and nodded. "Herbs have many uses. But you should go now."

"I guess I should."

Ashley started toward the picnic table to get her CD. She turned back to Molly. Ashley noticed her odd clothes. A big black cloak hung over a long dress. It could have been some sort of brown, but it was hard to tell. Ashley started to speak and then swallowed. Molly looked at her quizzically. Ashley took a deep breath and then spoke.

"Are you a witch?" she asked.

"What would you say if I said yes?"

"I would ask you a big favor."

"And what would that be?"

Ashley paused and looked hard at the woman, who was waiting patiently with a smile on her face.

"I need to talk to the dead. Is there some way you can help me?"

Molly grinned at Ashley. "Now why would a young thing like you want to do something as morbid as talking to the dead?"

"I need to ask someone something." Ashley resisted the urge to reach out to the woman. Her nerves were as taut as an overtuned E string on a violin.

"Maybe I can help you."

Molly sat down at the picnic table. Ashley breathed a sigh of relief so loud that it startled the older woman.

"Sit across from me." Molly indicated the bench. Ashley sat down and watched while Molly rummaged through her bag. She pulled out a few leaves with the roots and mud still on them. She ran them along her face in a circle, watching Ashley intently as she created a symbol. When she was finished, she handed the clump to Ashley.

"Do what I did." she guided. Ashley rubbed her face as Molly had done. When she was finished, she gave the herbs back to the woman, who put them in the bag.

"Hold my hands." Molly said. Ashley clasped the woman's hands and felt a surge of energy pulsing through them. She had a strong urge to let go, but she didn't.

"Who are you calling?" Molly asked.

"My friend, Alex. I don't know where she's gone. I think she's dead, but I don't know."

Molly closed her eyes. She cocked her head as if listening to something unseen. She nodded her head and opened her eyes.

"Yes, she's dead, I'm afraid. She's near but she's frightened."

Ashley grabbed Molly's arm. "I want to talk to her."

"She wants to talk to you too, but right now, she's being pulled in other directions. It's very hard for her to get to you."

"She was trying to tell me something on the Ouija board but then my mom came in. I was hoping she would finish what she started."

Ashley sighed. "Do you even believe me?" she asked.

Molly nodded solemnly. "Yes. I do believe you. I know a lot about the talking boards. Even without them, I know she's here and she just needs more time."

"More time for what?"

"To learn how to ripple back and forth. When you're newly dead, it takes a while to get the hang of everything."

"How can you even believe in this stuff? What proof do you have?"

"I've talked to a few dead people in my time."

"Like who?"

Molly laughed. "Well, for starters, that bastard ex-husband of mine. He likes to come around and complain. It's through a lot of his bitching that I've managed to figure out how to talk to the spirits and what to expect."

"Ask Alex what happened."

"I don't think she could tell you if she wanted to. I see lots of water and pain. There is a sense of another, a struggle. But that's it."

Molly closed her eyes and raised one of her hands. "Slow down. I can't hear you."

She opened her eyes and looked at Ashley. "She's speaking so fast I can't make it out. It's like there's this big wind spinning round and she's calling into it instead of standing on the edge, talking to me."

Molly closed her eyes again. "She wants revenge. I can feel it. She wants whoever did this to her to pay."

"Did she say who?"

"I can't tell. But I can tell you that she thinks it's who you think it is." Molly raised an eyebrow.

"Bitch." Ashley sat up straighter, fingering the CD case. She turned it over and over, slapping the table.

"Can you help me?" Ashley asked, putting down the CD case.

"Help you with what?"

"I need a curse. For this bitch that killed Alex. I want something that will make her feel as terrible about her loss as I feel about mine."

"Curses are easy. Just hope for the worst. It usually happens without anyone helping at all. Humans are makers of their own misery."

"No. I want something more." Ashley grabbed Molly's hands tight. "I want her to hurt, to ache, to throb with pain. Heartache. Death would not be a release. Death would only take her further into a downward spiral."

"Your passion rings through strong," Molly said, reaching into her bag again. She pulled out a different plant this time and broke off a piece. She ran it along Ashley's face and then set it on her tongue. "You don't need me. You will do fine on your own."

"I hope you are right."

Ashley walked home, her stride confident. Whether she had contacted Alex or not didn't matter anymore. The woman was a sign and a godsend. With her help, Ashley would get to the bottom of everything.

Vanessa would pay.

Chapter Ten

A car rumbled up the gravel driveway. Vanessa peered out her living room window. She recognized the face of the woman, but couldn't quite place her. The woman cautiously looked around as she hurried up the walkway. Vanessa opened the door before the stranger could knock. The woman jumped.

"Oh, my . . ."

"What can I do for you?" Vanessa asked.

"I . . . Can I come in?"

Vanessa led the woman into the living room. The woman was trembling.

"Can I get you some coffee or tea?"

The woman shook her head, clutching her purse to her chest. "I'm sorry to bother you. And I didn't want to call because, well, I just don't know how to describe this."

She pulled something out of her purse and laid it on the coffee table. Vanessa immediately recognized it. It was a poppet like the one she had seen on Betty's doorstep.

"Where was it?"

"I was getting the paper and there it was." The woman sighed. "I'm Grace, by the way. I don't know if you remember me. I came to you a couple of times, long ago."

Vanessa studied the woman. "Yes, I remember your face, Grace."

Vanessa picked up the doll, turning it over in her hand. It gave off an unpleasant energy, like crackling static. She put it down again. "Has anything been going on at your house? Strange things?"

Grace began to cry. "Yes. All sorts of strange things have been going on. Nothing magic. Just human strange."

"Your husband?"

"Yes, my husband. He is barely around anymore."

"Do you think he's having an affair?"

"I'm sure of it."

"Has he been home the past couple of days?"

Grace sobbed, reaching for the tissue box. "No."

Vanessa let her cry. It was epidemic, all these wandering husbands. Who could have such a hold on them? When Grace finished her crying jag, she looked up sheepishly and forced a grin.

"A forty-five-year-old woman sobbing like a baby over her cheating bastard husband. You must think I'm crazy."

"Not at all. I would cry too if my husband cheated on me."

"But you know . . . I never expected it of him in

a million years. Not in a billion years. We used to be so happy. We did everything together. We had an amazing sex life. We raised children together. I thought we were a success story."

"When did it fall apart?"

"You know, I can't exactly put my finger on it. However . . ."

Grace took a deep breath. "I think it all started when his company was taken over. He had to answer to a new boss. There were new coworkers. The pressure grew. And that was fine. I didn't give him cause for any stress. Together, we were still fine. But his boss, well, there was a party one night. For the men. I still don't really understand why only men could go, no spouses. But he took them to some strip club. And I swear, he wasn't the same since."

"Maybe he was disturbed at going to a strip club?"

Grace looked down at the tissue she was knotting into shreds between her fingers. "No. He wasn't disturbed at going to a strip club. Sometimes we went together for fun. Get all dressed up and watch the girls, then we'd go home, and well, I'd do a little dance . . . you understand." Grace blushed.

"I've known people who do that. It's not as bizarre as you might think."

"I know. I've seen other couples. I know we're not total freaks. But our friends don't know about some of our habits."

"Your secret is safe with me."

"So, if I'm open-minded and all, why . . . why is he cheating on me?" Grace's lips trembled as she fought back tears.

Vanessa looked at the woman before her. She sure didn't know. Although Grace was in her forties, she could have passed for someone in her thirties. She had stylish hair, stylish clothes. Her figure was trim except for her large bosom. Vanessa suspected it was fake.

If Vanessa were a man, she would have no problem going home to that package every night.

Vanessa took the woman's hands. Soft hands with nicely manicured nails. Not long, bright claws like most manicured women, but a friendly nail with a gleam.

"You're not the first person in recent days to come to me with such a story. But I don't know the connection. The problem with magic, psychic ability, even witchcraft, is that you can only find out so much. You can only manipulate so much. There is always what I call that wild-card thing. And if you are dealing with people who don't want you to know what they are up to, it can be very hard to find out, no matter if you can use telepathy like a phone."

"So what is going on?"

"I don't know. Tell me . . . what has been different?"

"Besides keeping odd hours after a lifetime of clockwork?"

"What about how he's dressing?"

"Not much has changed with regard to that sort of thing. He's just always distracted when he's around. Mumbling in his sleep. He's disturbed. And now, he hasn't been home in a couple of days. Then I find this damn thing."

They both looked at the poppet.

"That's why I came to you. I figure you know about this voodoo stuff."

"I don't know a huge amount about voodoo. I guess you were meant to find it."

"Do you believe?"

"I don't know what to believe in anymore."

Vanessa picked up the poppet. "Can I hang on to this?"

"Yes. please do. Maybe it will help you. Maybe you will see something."

"Maybe."

"I'm so sorry to bother you like this. Here, let me pay you." Grace dug into her purse.

Vanessa put her hand over top. "Please don't do that. I want to help. Like I said, you're not the only one."

After Grace left, Vanessa retrieved Betty's poppet and put it beside Grace's. She couldn't understand it. The obvious things were true. Some kind of voodoo was at play here. But why? How?

Why were men leaving? Where were they going? And what did the poppets have to do with anything?

She phoned Betty, but there was no answer. She hung up as the answering machine started.

She decided to go into town.

Ashley walked along the sidewalk, her headset blaring. She had heard a bunch of the kids were going to be hanging at the local recreation center club. Everything was so confusing lately, she needed to get out and be with other kids. Sometimes only geeks and nerds went to the rec center, but then there were other times that some hot rapper guys showed up. They'd get talking and rapping and once in a while they would hold impromptu rap contests.

She didn't know if it was just her, but everything seemed so weird lately. In school, people were subdued and odd. She couldn't quite put her finger on it. She expected a huge part of it was the missing girl, although Alex hadn't been popular. She guessed most people hadn't even know Alex existed until she was gone.

Now, as Ashley walked through town, she still had that strange sense of surrealism. Maybe it was just her, though. Maybe that woman in the woods that night had given her some drug or done something to her. Who knows what she really rubbed on her face?

In front of the fudge shop, a large brown dog lazily lay in the sun. Ashley had been stopping to pet old Jacob for years. She knelt down and put her hand on his head. Jacob jumped to his feet, lips rolled back to reveal sharp pointed teeth. The hair on his hackles raised up in tufts, like a clean-shaven porcupine. Ashley stepped back.

"Oh my . . ." cried Ashley. The dog barked at her and Ashley stepped back farther. "It's me, Jacob. Don't you remember me?"

The dog limped over to the fudge shop door and stood in the entryway, barking and yelping, as if it couldn't decide whether to come or go. Whether to leave her alone or rip her head off.

Ashley knew better than to run. She slowly crept back away from the beast until she was well down the street.

In one way, the dog didn't surprise her a bit.

More proof that the universe was tilted on its side. Yet in her whole life, she'd never seen that dog bark at anyone or anything.

She continued on toward the rec center, thinking about horror movies and how animals usually hated evil people. But she wasn't evil. Was she? She loved rap and dressed in baggy clothes, but she wasn't evil. She didn't wish harm to people unless they brought her harm. She wasn't even a slut, and barely did drugs. So what the hell was the animal freaking out at her for?

Maybe she still stank from the herbs.

Or maybe Jacob had seen a ghost.

Alex?

Alex, are you here?

Ashley stopped walking. She closed her eyes. She tried to hear, the way she had seen Molly doing. She cocked her head first left and then right, wondering if she was supposed to act like a radio receiver to the other world.

It didn't matter. There was nothing to hear that she could detect.

She opened her eyes and continued on until she reached her destination.

The rec center was busy. Lots of rappers were hanging around wearing baggy clothes and donning Walkmans. A few bounced a basketball around with other kids attired in more appropriate gym wear. Ashley followed the sound of a boom box over to the pool tables. Riz and Scorch were shooting a game, while Jerry, Lana, and Marie watched. The girls were as androgynously dressed as the boys. Hats lowered down over eyebrows. Earrings and neck chains swinging.

"Hey, Ash." Riz waved. Ashley nodded.

"Riz."

"Ash." A few more called out greetings. Ashley waved nonchalantly.

"You gonna do the contest?" Riz asked as she handed her pool cue over to Scorch.

"What contest?"

"Five o'clock. Gonna do a battle."

"No shit?" Ashley smiled.

"Yeah, man. Jerry and Scorch are in. You?"

"Fucking right."

Ashley smiled. She looked over at the clock on the wall. There was time to compose herself. There was time to think of something killer.

"Where you been lately?" Riz asked.

"Just hanging."

"Bummed about Alex, eh?"

Ashley nodded, fighting back sudden tears that ebbed to the surface.

"We're all bummed. Man, I hope she turns up soon."

"She's dead, man. You know it."

Riz stared at Ashley. "Dead?"

"Of course she's dead. Where else would she be?"

"Run away. Maybe found some cool dude and got the hell away from her parents."

"She never said anything to me about having some new guy, or even wanting to run away. It's all very weird in my eyes," Ashley said.

Lana and Marie wandered over, catching snippets of the conversation.

"Everyone talks about running away. Few get the balls to do it, though."

"It's not even about balls. It's about reality. She didn't even have a part-time job. What would she use for money?"

"Maybe that guy . . ." Lana said.

"Does anyone know who that guy is?"

"I've watched that tape a thousand times and I can't figure it out," Ashley said.

"I can't figure it out either. It's no one I've ever seen before," Marie said.

"I hope they find her. . . ."

"I don't know if they'll ever find her."

"The whole thing makes me nervous," Lana fiddled with her necklace, wrapping it around her fingers.

"Really?"

"What if it's another Bernardo or Bundy or something? Just someone that comes along and mysteriously entices people away? How would you know till it's too late?" Scorch said.

"Just have to be extra careful, I guess," Marie said.

"You can't even trust people you think you know, when you get right down to it. How are you going to trust anyone?"

"Super-paranoia. Just live in the moment. Nothing you can do anyway," said Riz, shrugging.

"Yeah, man. When your number's up, you can't exactly run away from it."

"Hey, if she's dead, why don't we have a seance and find out what happened to her?" Marie said.

Ashley stared at her. "Seance. As if they work," Ashley said.

"You never know. Wouldn't it be cool if we called her and she came?"

"I've never done a seance," Lana said. "I don't know if I want to."

"What can it hurt?" Marie said. "She either comes to us or she doesn't."

"What if something else comes?" Scorch said.

"As if," Marie said. "You watch too many movies."

"Well, you do too if you're talking about seances."

"I watch John Edwards every day and he doesn't even need a special place. He just goes on TV and talks to the dead."

"He's a phony."

"Then how does he know stuff?"

"It's all bullshit. Sheesh . . . you'd have learned from Miss Cleo," Scorch said.

"I think there's something to that stuff. I saw James Van Praagh freak people out."

"Good God, you guys know shit. You gonna rap about God and ghosts, or you gonna get real. Battle's on in a few," Riz said.

"Shit, yeah. I gotta get a drink before this starts."

The teens dispersed to get ready for the battle. Several wandered over to the pop machines. Others went out for a smoke. Still more went to the bathrooms. When they had performed their rituals, they started to filter back through the doors and down the hall. It didn't take long till they were congregated in the auditorium. The hall was noisy with nearly a hundred teenagers mumbling and catcalling.

One of the rec leaders took the stage. He raised his hands until the crowd settled.

"Okay, kids. We gotta great lineup today." The crowd burst into cheers before the announcer could even finish reading the list. Ashley's heart pounded so hard against her chest, she thought that everyone around her could hear it over the microphones. The contest passed in a blur.

One by one, teenagers took the stage. They did their rap and sat down again. Ashley clapped and whooped with her peers, her mind chanting snippets of verse in a nonsensical fashion.

At last, it was Ashley's turn. She looked over at her friends. They cheered her on, even though they too were in the contest.

Ashley took to the stage and awkwardly stood before the crowd. They hollered her name. She smiled and stared up to the ceiling.

Nerves. Be calm.
Calm. Blue. Ocean.
I can do this.
This is what I want to be.
Ashley. Ashley.

Ashley opened her mouth and words tumbled out. Her feet stomped, her fingers pointed, her arms waved. She was a giant puppet. A giant deaf puppet. Again she had that sense of being trapped in a bell jar, only this time, she couldn't hear herself. She knew she was rapping; her lips were going a mile a minute and her throat was getting sore.

The audience was clapping along to her, but she

didn't see them. In the distance, above the exit light, she watched a mist form. A vague mist that hung in the air like cigarette smoke. It fluttered to the beat of the clapping.

Ashley came to the end of her patter and stopped, arms folded. Suddenly, the sound broke through and she was amazed to hear applause.

Ashley returned to her seat, where her friends high-fived her. People screamed and cheered.

There were only two more rappers after her. She sat on her hands through the performances, her mind wandering once more. Turning through the odd events that had recently transpired.

When everyone had a turn, the announcer returned to the mike.

"Judging from the audience-participation poll, I'd say it's hands down that Ashley is our winner here today."

The kids cheered and chanted as Ashley returned to the stage. How she wished Alex and TnT could see her now. She stood staring out at her peers, tears in her eyes. The mist was still there over the exit sign. Pulsing. Glowing. Throbbing larger as the applause continued.

"Thanks everyone. Be cool." She managed a grin and waved her hand. She hurried off the stage and down the hall. She had worked so hard to be the best and now, in her moment of triumph, she could only think about Alex.

Marie and Lana found her crying in the bathroom.

"Hey, sister. You won."

"I know. I'm just missing Alex is all."

Lana hugged her, wiping Ashley's eyes with a piece of tissue.

"I know, sweetie. It's always hard when someone goes away. I think about my brother all the time."

"I know . . . I just wish something official would be done, ya know? Like, why the hell haven't the cops got on this already?"

"I guess they have no clues. They gotta get that John Edwards on it."

"Sylvia Brown. She's great at that shit."

"Who the hell can afford anyone?" Ashley said. "And I'm sure as shit they're not gonna do any charity work for a teenager."

"It's a big case, though. Missing girl . . ." Marie said. "Wouldn't it be cool if Sylvia Brown came to town!" Marie giggled at the rhyme.

"Stop with the pipe dreams. This is serious stuff. There are missing kids every day. Sylvia or anyone else will just say she ran away. That's what they said on the news last night."

"That's 'cause they don't know what else to say," Ashley said. "They have to say *something* when they're on TV. What else are they gonna say?"

"Well, they do show that stupid sketch of the dude in the rapper gear."

"Yeah, love the funky sunglasses they drew on. Don't look anything like the videos." Lana laughed.

"Stupid artists."

"Stupid people telling the artists what to do!"

"True."

"Then I guess it's up to us to figure it out," Ashley said.

"What say we go have that seance tonight?" Marie said.

"I don't know, man," Lana said.

"Aw, c'mon. Now's the perfect time. What if we find out something that's been overlooked and break the case! We'd be friggin heroes!" Marie said. "I've heard of that. A psychic breaking a twenty-year-old case."

"Yes, we know. We've heard it before."

"Jeeze, Marie, you're obsessed. Surprised you haven't been to get your tarot cards read."

"How do you know that I haven't?"

"Have you?" Ashley asked. "By a professional?"

"Yeah. I went to see that Vanessa witch chick over by the cove. Mom and I went."

"Really?"

"Shit, yeah. She's been freaking 'cause Dad hasn't been around much lately. To which I say, good fucking riddance. Nothing pleases him anyway. But she is worried or mad or something. Maybe all of it. So she went to get her cards done."

"What did she say?"

"He's screwing around. *Duh*. But she said some other shit too that was freaky. Hit the nail on the head. Gave me the chills."

"And what did she say to you?"

Marie frowned. "Kind of bummed me out. Said that things looked difficult the next while. And it has been, hasn't it?" Marie said.

Lana put her other arm around Marie as she held Ashley.

"Nothing has been easy, that's for sure," Lana said.

"Well, if we're gonna go, we should go before cur-fews hit," Marie said.

"Yeah."

The girls marched out of the hall, focused on their mission.

Chapter Eleven

The day was hot, even for fall. Vanessa was sweating by the time she found parking near the hardware store. As she walked toward the entrance, she noticed an old man shuffling along the other side of the road. Something about him seemed odd, and she followed him for a little while. He would take a step or two and then weave a bit, first to one side and then the other.

It was most peculiar. Maybe the poor guy had missed his medication. Or maybe he was drunk. As he stumbled into Joe's Tavern, she realized he must be drunk.

She turned back toward the hardware store. There were several people out this beautiful day. She had a sensation of being in a parallel universe. People walking oddly. Nothing she could really put her finger on. And when she smiled at them, it was like she was invisible. Their eyes were focused on some faraway place.

Weird.

But maybe the sun was so bright and people were just preoccupied. Maybe there was some sort of new rumor going around about her. Over the years she found most people were friendly to her, yet there were others that were either frightened of her, or just didn't want to deal with her.

The hardware store door jingled as it always did when she went in. It was dim inside. A cold clamminess hung in the air. Musty. Damp. There were only two other customers in there. Two men, probably not together. Standing and staring at the hanging tools.

Vanessa headed toward the back, where she figured David might be. On her way, she turned to look at the men again. They hadn't moved at all. It was like they were hypnotized by the gleaming of metal objects.

"Hi!" David startled her as he gave her a hug.

"Hi," she said. "How's business?"

"Slow." he said. "But that's okay 'cause that means I can talk to you."

Vanessa grinned. She saw that his shirt wasn't tucked into his jeans as it usually was. He had greasy smudges streaked along his chest. His hair wasn't even combed.

"Rough night?" she asked.

"Huh?"

"Your clothes . . ."

He looked down at himself.

"Oh . . . no, just was working on something in the

back." He tucked in his shirt. She caught a whiff of sweat. He wasn't wearing his usual aftershave. He must have been working pretty hard.

Between him and the general reek of the shop, her stomach lurched.

"I just thought I'd stop in for a minute. I have to go, though," she said. An urgency filled her. The men still hadn't moved.

David was staring at her with a quizzical expression. "That's too bad. I always like to see you."

"I like to see you too. Maybe we can have dinner."

"Sure."

Vanessa kissed him lightly on the cheek, and left.

Once out in the sunlight, she realized she had been holding her breath. Now she took deep gulps of sweet air. Had the place been that stagnant?

She was so agitated, she thought she would crawl right out of her own skin.

Maybe she should go pay Betty a visit. Helping someone else solve a mystery might put her mind at ease.

When she got to Betty's house, the car was in the driveway, yet no one answered the door when she knocked. A wave of uneasiness filled her. She went around to the back, hoping the woman was there puttering in the garden, but there was nothing. She toyed with the idea of going into the house. But why? She barely knew Betty. Maybe Betty was finally getting some sleep. All Vanessa could do was get back into her car and try to figure out why things seemed so off kilter today.

As she opened her car door, she had the distinct feeling of being watched. She turned around, toward the bushes. There was nothing there that she could tell. She looked back to the house, wondering if the woman was watching her from behind the curtains. There were no shadows. No movement.

Vanessa got into her car and drove off.

Marie stopped the car in a little dirt parking lot, adjacent to a popular park and picnic area. Since it was fall, there was no one around. Tourist season was over. Colored leaves skipped along the ground in a gentle wind. The grass was brown in patches. Once-well-groomed flowers were beginning to wilt and droop, in anticipation of the coming winter.

The ocean air was thick with salt. There was a dampness coming in with the tide. The roaring pulse of the waves echoed against the rocks. Seagulls screamed as they circled high above, no doubt hoping for a messy picnic.

Ashley and Lana stepped out. Ashley clutched the Ouija board box, half-hoping, half-dreading that with the other two girls, they could get a connection with Alex.

They walked along the edge of the beach, climbing along giant rocks that were slick with seaweed and barnacles.

"There's a perfect spot, just beyond those trees." Marie pointed. Ashley nodded. She knew what was there.

It didn't take long to make their way across the rocks and through the trees. The late afternoon sky had shifted. The sun was glowing orange as it began its descent toward evening.

Marie pointed. "See?"

There was a small overgrown graveyard. Crumbling stones, decapitated angels, creeping ivy, and looming granite markers fuzzy with moss decorated the little area. The girls stood staring in from behind the iron gate.

"Well . . . ?" Marie asked.

"Well, what?" Lana said.

"If we're going to do it, let's just fucking do it then."

Ashley rattled the gate. "Man, it's locked."

"No, way." Marie wrapped her hands around the iron bars and rattled them.

"Shh," Lana said.

"We'll have to climb over." Marie looked at the tall spindle-pointed fence.

"I'm not so sure about that," Ashley said.

As the girls paced in front of the fence, there was a shrieking noise as the gate slowly opened.

"Oh . . ." Ashley gasped. She strained to see who was there.

Nothing.

No Alex.

No demons.

No ghosts.

"C'mon, guys. Let's go." Ashley waved the girls over.

"But that was locked solid," Lana said.

"Maybe we loosened it somehow."

Ashley marched through the wrought-iron gate

and stood facing the others with her hands on her hips.

"Coming?" she asked.

"Of course we're coming." Marie walked through next. She rubbed her arms as she stood beside Ashley and the crumbling graves.

"Here goes nothing!" Lana said, walking into the graveyard. She looked around wide-eyed. "Is it just me, or did the temperature just drop ten degrees."

"It's all part of that good old-fashioned graveyard fun."

"Yeah, well, let's hope we don't get any good old-fashioned creepy-ass ghosts coming around."

"What is this place anyway? Like, it's so small and forgotten," Lana said.

"It's a witches' graveyard. From when they used to do the hangings," Marie said.

"Bullshit."

"Yeah, no shit. Look on any of the tombstones and read about it at the library. That's why there's no church around here. What church would want a witch in its cemetery?"

"Too freaky."

The girls found a stone bench overgrown with weeds. They set to work clearing it away. Ashley pulled the Ouija board from the box and laid it out.

"Now what?" Ashley asked.

Marie looked at the bench. "I guess two people should sit on the bench and one can kneel on the ground."

"Does the Ouija work with three people?" Lana asked.

"I don't see why not. The more power the better I would think."

Ashley and Lana sat on the bench while Marie kneeled on the ground. The sun was merely a blip on the horizon. Long shadows stretched from the battered gravestones, while waves slapped nearby rocks.

The girls looked at each other solemnly. They put their hands on the planchette.

Marie took control.

"We call upon the spirit of Alex to send us a message. Send us a message."

The other girls took up the chant.

"Send us a message. Send us a message."

They closed their eyes, saying the words over and over again. The planchette trembled. It shook and wearily began to move.

Ashley opened her eyes, trying to ascertain if either of the other girls were moving it. They both had expressions of deep concentration on their faces.

The planchette moved violently, jetting around the board, not stopping anywhere. Ashley felt a terrible presence emerging. She looked at the other girls, who popped their eyelids open.

"Do you feel that?" Lana asked. Her face was pale.

"There's something."

"Look."

The sun was nearly gone and the moon was glowing in the sky. There were a few distant street lamps but for the most part, it was darker than it was light.

The girls watched as a dark fog wafted up from

several of the gravestones. It undulated, gathering together as it expanded. The sensation was tangible. Darkness and foreboding.

The planchette moved around in circles. Faster and faster. Ashley was the first to take her hands away. Then Lana. Then Marie.

"Alex?" Marie called, taking Ashley's hand. Ashley slipped her hand into Lana's and as Lana touched Marie, the circle was complete. The planchette continued to move.

"It's not Alex," said Ashley.

"What is it?" asked Lana.

"I don't know."

The fog grew into a dark cloud. Red shards sprayed from it in flashes. A low, rumbling, growling noise was heard.

"Who are you?" asked Marie.

The rumbling grew louder. It was deep terrible noise. A screeching whine. The grumble of a large beast.

Lana tried to shake her hand loose, but there was a current shooting from one person to the next so rapidly that she couldn't.

"I can't stand it."

The cloud swirled faster and darker. The planchette continued to circle rapidly. A glowering face emerged from the cloud. Red eyes flashing, cruel mouth taunting loudly in gibberish. The sound was deafening.

"Where is Alex?"

The face leered.

"Alex is dead," it said.

The girls all looked at each other.

"We know she's dead. Where is she?" Ashley said.

"I have her." The face laughed.

"No!" Ashley screamed. "You're lying."

The face scowled.

"Who's next?" it roared. Lana stood up, her fingers clenching and unclenching as she stared at the monster. It roared and screeched, billowing larger as vapors from the graves entwined within it.

Lana stumbled toward the gates of the graveyard.

A large clawed hand swiped out at her as she ran, barely brushing her back. Lana screamed and pushed herself to run faster.

Ashley scrambled to her feet and ran. She didn't care what this thing was, or if it had Alex or not, she just wanted to get the hell out of there.

Without looking back, she slipped and slid in the dark. Bursting from the graveyard, scampering along the beach rocks, she ran, gasping gulps of air, until all she heard was Marie's distant screams.

Chapter Twelve

Betty sat in a rented car outside Decadance. The emotions running through her ranged from helpless to hopeless. She wasn't even sure why she had come here.

It was barely dusk. The sky was in eerie transformation from daylight to starlight. She sank her head down on the steering wheel. Her eyes had been getting weary on her of late. Certainly lying awake at night mourning her lost love didn't help any.

But even at that, signs of age were quickly making themselves known. While Larry was gone, she'd had a lot of time to think. To discover things about herself that she hadn't noticed. She had been so busy tending to the house, to her man, to all the little life things, that she hadn't taken the time to realize what was going on in her body. In her mind.

Her countenance had changed dramatically over

the past few years. What had bothered her in her younger days no longer held such importance.

The realization had struck that morning as she wandered around her empty house. Ghosts of things that had once been, haunted her exceptionally so today. She saw phantom images of her children running through the living room. The kitchen, bright and sunny with women bouncing babies in their arms. Sit-downs around the dinner table, laughter in the air. And always, the rooms were spotless. Floors gleamed. Dishes sparkled. There were cloth napkins and candlelight. The coffee table glowed with a weekly polish and no matter where baby dropped a bottle, milk stains were quickly rubbed up.

Now, those images were there no longer. Since Larry had left, housework had become meaningless. Hours she had spent scrubbing and cleaning to please her man were now spent wondering and worrying.

It was human nature to stray. She had already been well aware that now and again, her husband had stepped out on her. But she had always felt in her heart that Larry would come back to her when he grew bored of his dalliances. In all their years, he had never actually left her overnight. He had always been careful about covering his tracks, about not rubbing her nose in what he did. She never harped and complained, she just tried harder. How she always tried harder. She wanted nothing more than a beautiful home and an adoring husband. If she created a palace for him, he had to adore her, didn't he? If she was his very own madonna-whore, why would he look elsewhere? No matter, though. He would settle down for a while, but then, once more, his patterns would tell her that he was sleeping around again.

Her marriage vows had truly meant till death us do part. Whatever that involved, she had planned on being married to Larry until they died. She thought he enjoyed going through life secure in the knowledge that she would always be there for him. How naive she had been to think that her man was different from any other. Like a dog running with a pack, he had gone off sniffing for new scents. The more she let him off his leash, the farther he roamed. She should never have been so accommodating. She should have put her foot down, as her sister had done, when she caught her husband cheating. She could see that now.

Human nature was human nature. Who was she to stop his primal urges? Man had strayed since the dawn of time. The human species wasn't meant for monogamy. At least not males that live past twenty-five. Maybe even females.

She herself enjoyed the look of a well-dressed man. Now and again she wondered what it would be like to be in another's arms. But she had self-control. She didn't want to throw away what she had spent years building.

She should have insisted her husband use the same self-control.

Hindsight was always 20/20.

Her father had left her mother when he was in his late fifties. Betty was already a new bride when it had happened. It had been a shocker for her, because she had always thought her parents had a comfortable relationship. They understood each other's idiosyncrasies, and they had a weird compatibility as they tended to the mundane aspects of life. She figured that the excitement of family-raising had been part of the glue that held them together and when Betty was married off, that was the end of an era. Maybe they just grew bored with each other as they were faced with endless days alone. Betty never really knew. She had been so caught up with Larry that she hadn't been visiting her parents as often, and didn't really take notice of anything odd when she did.

But it must have been so.

One day, her father just up and left. Her mother made believe nothing happened for the longest time. She'd just make vague references to him being away. Betty discovered the truth months after he had left. At the time, she figured her mother was in denial. And now, she wondered if she was doing the same by trying to find Larry. She hadn't even told the kids that there was something wrong.

Her father had announced his departure, and even taken his belongings with him. In Betty's case, nothing had been disturbed. That was what was so worrisome. That was what she kept coming back to when she replayed the past few weeks.

Nothing was gone.

Today she had a new attitude. Maybe he just was too chicken-shit to come home. Maybe he wasn't hurt at all. Or maybe he was drugged, like she had been, and was continuing to be drugged.

They had been married for nearly thirty years.

She knew him inside and out. As much as she toyed with the idea of him being just a dog sowing his wild oats without a thought for her, the other part of her remembered how so recently he had hugged her out of the blue and told her that he was so lucky to have found such a wonderful person to travel with through life's grand adventure.

She had laughed and kissed him, telling him how much she loved him. He was so much older than the young smiling groom at the altar, yet she could still see the handsome young man among the age lines.

What about her own face?

Had he looked at her face and not seen the young girl for the first time? Had whatever he had fallen in love with somehow faded over the years? Maybe she had grown too neurotic? Too concerned with perfection? Maybe, somehow, she had driven him out with requests?

So many times in her life she'd wished that she was being taped on one of those reality TV shows. Then she could play back the tape and see where it was she went wrong. What behavior had it been that made him look somewhere else?

Or maybe it wasn't her behavior at all.

Maybe it was the fact that it was getting harder to get out of bed every morning without her bones feeling heavy and her muscles aching. Her teeth often hurt from grinding all night, even though she was fanatical about wearing her night guard. Her eyes still sparkled with life, but my God, the crow's feet were coming in fast and furious. She had always worn her hair long, but as it thinned and broke through the years, she had cut it.

Her energy during the day was beginning to suffer too. Sometimes she was astonished to find herself waking up from a nap when the last thing she remembered was polishing a knickknack.

Yet so many of her friends would ask her where she got her energy. How did she manage to juggle a million chores, do volunteer work, go to her part-time job, keep the children organized and dinner on the table? How was she able to please her husband in bed and still find time for laundry and toilet-scrubbing and groceries?

She had done it because she believed in the dream.

That dream of holding her marriage together at all costs.

If there was a problem in the marriage, if there was a reason that Larry kept having affairs, then she would fix it. She would keep trying different tactics, until one day he would realize that she was good enough. That she really did deserve all of him, and him alone.

But now, she was just tired. She lifted her head from the steering wheel, running her fingers along her forehead, wondering if she had a mark there now. She pulled at some of her bangs, hoping that she didn't look too crazy.

The Decadance sign buzzed and blinked in the night sky. Daring her. Taunting her. It was the key.

Her mind raced as she sat staring at the neon sign. What would she find here? She was dreading whatever it might be. Even discovering nothing would leave her no further behind than she was this afternoon. Now that she had finally had the nerve to rent a car and come here on her own, she had to see whatever it was she would see.

As the sky grew darker, there was a flurry of activity. There must be some sort of shift change as a steady parade of women marched in and out the side door. Most of them wore long coats over street clothes, but some of them wore very skimpy outfits, as if embracing the last of the warm weather.

Betty recognized many of the women from the night she had come here with Vanessa. She had been so nervous that day and dreading what she might see. There had been much out of the ordinary, she still couldn't decipher what had really happened that night. The fact that she had been drugged gave her hazy memories and that sense of not being able to distinguish reality from a dream.

She couldn't decide if she was more nervous now that she had already been here before or not. She still had no idea what to expect, if anything. She should have brought Vanessa with her. She had wanted to bring Vanessa with her. But of course, Vanessa had a life and didn't need to be wasting it with Betty's own paranoia and crumbling marriage. Betty would have offered to pay her, but she wasn't sure how long she might have to make the money in the bank account last. If Larry just disappeared, she would have to make the money stretch for years.

Was there insurance for people that just disappeared?

She wouldn't be able to support herself on her part-time job.

He would come home.

She knew he would.

He always did.

She wouldn't think about him being gone forever. That was the whole reason why she was here. She needed to discover the truth. What was he really up to and what did he want?

He wasn't dead. She could feel it in her bones.

On the other side of the club, there was growing activity as more people, mostly men, headed for the door. Most arrived by car, but now and again, someone would come shuffling along by foot. She thought some of the pedestrians were walking in a peculiar manner.

It appeared the first two strange men were drunk or stoned or maybe a bit of both. They weaved a jagged line along the parking lot, leaning into each other for a few steps, then bobbing apart. They didn't speak. They didn't look around. They continued their weird dance of bumping together and swinging apart all the way along the parking lot. They continued slowly toward the entrance and stumbled up the stairs. She caught a glimpse of the muscular black arm of a bouncer holding the door open to let them in.

As a couple more of the odd men appeared across the parking lot and wandered toward the door, she grew suspicious. There was something weird about how they stumbled and bobbed, almost exactly like the previous two men. For a moment she wondered if it was the previous men, if she hadn't noticed them coming out and going back in again. But they weren't. These men were definitely not the same men. They were different in build and wore different-colored clothing.

A fifth man lurched along in the distance.

Betty studied him as he loomed forward. Her hands began to sweat, and she wiped them on her legs.

There was something about his gait, his build, that was familiar.

Yet that odd lurching stagger was not familiar at all.

Betty got out of her car and crept along the side of the building to get a better look. He had the appearance of Larry, no question. That was Larry's build. The shape of his head. The dip of his hips. The Larry she knew wouldn't be caught dead the way this man was dressed. The clothes were disheveled and dirty, even ripped in places. His hair was askew. Obviously she knew nothing about this man called Larry who she had shared her life with for so many years.

Betty nearly burst into tears. She didn't know whether to be relieved that he was alive or angry as hell.

She was torn between flinging herself at him in a fist-flailing rage, or leaping onto him with arms wrapped around his big strong shoulders, her hungry lips sucking on his with blissful relief.

She decided to wait and see what happened as she crouched in the hedges. He painstakingly made his way up the stairs to the entrance. The bright glare of the outside veranda light illuminated his face briefly. Her breath caught in her throat.

His eyes.

There was something wrong with his eyes.

It was instantly recognizable. He couldn't see or wasn't seeing or it was like he was sleepwalking. They were milky, glassy, unfocused.

No one else was around as Betty raced up the stairs. She pulled him by the arm.

"Larry."

Larry turned his head toward her. He tried to focus on her face. His mouth moved, but nothing came out.

"Larry. Come with me."

She grabbed his sleeve with her hands, but he stood firm. He turned his face back toward the door, reeling toward it.

"Larry!"

He looked at her again, seeing but not seeing, then brushed her away as if she were an annoying insect. With great effort, he pulled the door open and walked into the club. Betty followed him.

Once they were inside, there were two large male bouncers at the door. They stood grimly, arms crossed, bulging biceps framing ample bare chests. Larry bumbled past them and careened down a set of stairs. Betty started to follow. The tall black man she had glimpsed earlier stood in front of her.

"Sorry, lady. Private party." He grinned as he blocked her way.

"That's my husband. Larry!" Betty shouted and waved down the stairs, but Larry had already disappeared down the hallway.

The bouncers looked at each other and shrugged.

"He doesn't seem to know you, lady."

Betty held up her hand with the wedding band.

"He's my husband. He's not well."

She attempted to push her way past them again. They were as impossible to maneuver around as a brick wall.

"Do you have an invitation?" the black bouncer asked. The blond one chuckled.

"Invitation?"

"To the party."

"No."

"Then you can't go in."

Betty sighed. She looked toward the stairs going up. There were only three, and then it was the strip club.

"Can I go in there and maybe one of you can go get him and tell him I'm here?"

"You can go into the club, but we can't leave our posts. Maybe he'll come out to see the girls."

The bouncers laughed.

"Hysterical." Betty turned from their arrogant jeers and marched up the three steps into the club. It was loud and already getting busy, but she found a table near the back by the wall. TV sets set in the walls flickered with hard-core porn movies and a baseball game. Betty sat down and looked toward the stage. A small brunette was dancing to "Thunderstruck" by AC/DC, wearing nothing but a thong and a smile.

Nervously Betty clutched her purse, looking back toward the door. She could barely see the bouncers, but she could tell by how they were laughing and waving their arms that they thought she was a big joke.

In front of her were several men seated by the stage. They sat watching in fascination as the girl danced and slinked against the tall brass pole. Betty sighed as she turned her attention back to the girl. She was so young and pretty. Firm flesh, curves, and legs.

Time was a cruel joke.

One day that lovely woman would be as old as Betty, and no doubt lamenting the loss of her looks. There was no way to stop time. To freeze-frame a point in one's life where you could just live forever. She wondered when she would pick. Maybe her wedding night, when everything lay at her fingertips. A woman on the brink of discovery, of her new life.

She remembered that moment with clarity.

It had been a whirlwind of a day. Things had gone fairly smoothly, just the odd glitch here and there, but nothing for "America's Most Disastrous Weddings." They had danced and feasted. They drank champagne and did all the little rituals one does at a wedding. Garters and bouquets, cake-feasting and kissing toasts.

At one o'clock, she and Larry had climbed into their limousine and drunk champagne until they arrived at their hotel room. There, they had giddily stumbled through the halls to their room.

He'd surprised her by suddenly lifting her into his arms as he unlocked the door. He'd carried her across the threshold into their room, where he gently laid her down on the bed. They had made sweet passionate love. Afterwards, she remembered lying in the dark, grinning from ear to ear. She was no virgin, not even with him, yet something about the day, their pledge to each other, the whole idea of them battling life together now in a sacred bond, had made their lovemaking one of the most joyous experiences she would ever taste. How wonderful she had felt that night. Her handsome husband had played her body like a violin. He had lain beside her in the dark, content and breathless. They'd held sweat-slicked hands and whispered about their future together. Their hopes and dreams and desires. It felt like anything had been possible in that moment.

That was the moment she wished to freeze-frame for all eternity.

But life goes on.

Now, here she was, sitting in a strip club, trying not to cry, as her husband was doing God knows what downstairs in the private lounges.

"What will it be?"

A waitress stood before her. Betty looked up at her, a bit startled. The waitress adjusted the strap of her black lace bra and waited, tray loose in her hand, idly staring around the club.

"Rye and ginger," Betty said.

"Okay."

The waitress left. Betty studied the club. The stage, the poles, the huge speakers, the multitude of TVs. All the little tables and cubbyholes. Pockets of perversion, she thought. Decadance was aptly named. In one of the booths, she saw a stripper gyrating on a client's lap. The way her legs were straddling the chair, Betty was pretty sure that there was more than a dance going on. She decided to check out the bathrooms. From what she remembered, there was a hallway leading away from them, and maybe, just maybe, there would be another way to get downstairs.

She made her way around the club and down the hallway. She passed the grotty little room where the strippers changed their outfits. Beyond that spot, there was another exit to the outside and right beside it, a darkened stairway.

Betty's heart raced as she crept down the stairs. It was very dimly lit, and she dreaded the idea of what might be scuttling around in the dark. She walked along the dreary hallway until she came to a door. Her heart raced as she stood before it.

This had to be the other entrance to the private lounge.

She took a deep breath, wrapped trembling fingers around the knob, and pushed the door.

It was locked.

Frustrated, she felt tears well in her eyes. She jiggled the knob, first lightly, then furiously.

It wasn't fair.

Larry was on the other side of this door and there was nothing she could do. Tears burned in her eyes, hotly streaming down her face.

Or was there?

There were always options. There were always choices. She could call the police.

Yet, even though she had reported him missing, the idea of sending the cops into the strip joint for her husband was not what she wanted to do. She could already see the looks they would give each other. Could just imagine the stories they told when they went for their after-work beer. It was bad enough the bouncers had made her feel about an inch tall and pure psycho. She had to handle this in a different way.

She made her way back through the hall and up the stairs. She hurried out the side exit door before anyone could see her coming up the stairs. As the door banged behind her, she stared up at the moon. There were stars dotting the sky and she made a wish.

She felt like she was going to have a nervous breakdown as she crept back to her car. Opening the glove box, she fumbled around until she found her cell phone. She dialed Vanessa's number.

Please be home.

On the second ring, Vanessa picked up.

"Vanessa. It's Betty." The words were barely a whisper as she struggled to regain composure.

"What's wrong?"

"I found him. I found Larry." Betty began to cry.

"Where?"

"Decadance."

"Really?"

"Vanessa, you have to come. Now."

"I already have plans."

"Please."

There was silence on the other end.

"Vanessa?"

"All right. I'll be there as soon as I can."

"Thank you." Betty clicked off the phone and

slumped into her seat. She closed her eyes and prayed that Vanessa wouldn't be very long.

Vanessa hung up the phone. She was supposed to be meeting David in a few minutes, but maybe she could see Betty and meet up with him later.

She dialed David.

"I hate to do this, but something really important has come up."

"Oh, you're canceling on me." David's voice was light, but there was hurt in it.

"No, I'm not canceling. But I have to move our date. Have dinner without me. I'll come by your place when I'm done."

"How long will you be?"

"I'm not sure. A couple of hours."

"Okay. I'll miss you."

"Believe me, I'd rather be having dinner with you than going where I'm going."

Vanessa hung up the phone and thought for a moment. She honestly would rather be with David any time, but poor Betty sounded like a mess.

Larry at Decadance.

Her hunch had been right after all. Somehow Decadance was involved.

It didn't take her long to arrive at Decadance. Betty ran over to her car when she arrived.

"I'm pretty sure he's still in there," Betty said.

"Did you talk to him?"

"I tried. But he wasn't himself."

"Well, what do you want to do?"

Betty swallowed. "I'm not really sure. But you see, he's downstairs, and they won't let me down.

They say there's some sort of private party going on. So I found another way in, but the door is locked. I was wondering . . . well . . . maybe you could unlock it somehow."

Vanessa nodded. "All we can do is try."

Betty showed her the side door that the strippers used, and they went inside. Immediately Betty pulled her down the stairs.

"This way."

"Christ, it's creepy down here."

They wandered along the dim hallway until they came to the door.

"This is it."

Vanessa rattled it. It was locked. On the other side, there was noise, like drumming and music.

Vanessa closed her eyes. She summoned her power to sear through the door. She turned the handle again, and this time, it opened.

The drumming was very loud now. The women stepped into a dark hallway that led into the cavernous room they had been in previously.

Tonight, it was set up differently. The curtained sections were gone. Everything was opened up. The women saw what looked like some sort of tribal meeting. People danced around like they were in a trance. Several other people played drums, recorders, and other primitive instruments.

It didn't take long to spot Larry swaying by himself.

"Look." Vanessa guided Betty's gaze around the room. "He's not the only one."

Many of the men were in the same state as Larry.

Disheveled and bleary-eyed. Swaying hypnotically to the music.

Suddenly, the music stopped. A beautiful blond woman in a leather outfit commanded the floor. Her leather bra strapped together a large bosom, while her exquisite torso was adorned with a cross-patch of leather straps and dangling chains. She raised her arms to greet the people in the room.

"Welcome. Tonight, we celebrate bringing prosperity to this sacred place. Tonight, we give thanks to the forces that allow us to keep living how we love to live."

There were several cries and sporadic clapping from the crowd.

"To show our thanks to the Dark One, we must give sacrifice."

A red-haired stripper stepped forward, carrying a squirming, clucking rooster.

"Thank you."

The blond woman took the chicken and held it in her hands. She stared into its eyes. It squawked at first, struggling to get away. It flapped its wings and pushed with its legs. The woman kept staring at it and before long, the squawking dimmed to sporadic clucking. As the chicken lowered its head, the woman bent over it, licking its feathers. Then she sank her teeth into the neck, gnawing at it until she was able to release its head from its body. A flurry of feathers shot into the air as the headless torso struggled. The woman didn't relinquish her grip. She held the neck with the head in her teeth triumphantly. She showed the others by walking around the room. They cheered and clapped. When she had completed the circle, she spat it onto the ground. She took the chicken and held it over her head, letting the blood run down on her. She opened her mouth to catch it, laughing and speaking softly.

When she was finished, she placed the rooster down on the floor.

"Thank you, oh, dark forces."

The drumming began with a frenzy. Again, the dancing started.

Betty turned to Vanessa. "Jesus Christ."

"Voodoo, maybe," Vanessa said.

"What are they doing and why is Larry here?"

"I don't know. But one thing I do know. We should get out of here before they see us."

"What about Larry?"

"We'll have to just let him be for now. We have to let him find his own way."

"I can't leave him."

"Shhh."

Vanessa nodded toward the blond woman, who had stopped dancing. She was looking around, her hands up as if she was feeling the air.

"Shit. She senses us."

"How do you know?" Betty swallowed. "Of course you know."

"We have to leave. Now. Quietly. Don't panic, she'll smell your fear."

The women carefully backed down the hallway, and when they reached the door, they shut it. Hearts racing, they ran back up the stairs and then paused. There was no one nearby, so they ran out the side door.

"I can't leave him there," Betty said as Vanessa hurried her to their cars.

"You don't want to mess around with people like that. Believe me. We'll figure out a way."

"Maybe we should call the cops."

"And tell them what? You know all the evidence would be gone. . . ."

"Not if we go right now, while they are still doing it. We can get Larry out."

"I know you want to, but it's so risky. We are dealing with ruthless people. You remember how those strippers scammed us the other night. That was nothing. Think of what they could do to us if they knew we were spying on some secret ceremony of theirs."

"There are laws."

"Not for the lawless."

"You could stop them."

"I'm not that powerful. I'm one. They're many."

"Who says any of them have power?"

"You may be right, I've battled before, but I'd rather wait. I have a lot to lose."

Betty sighed.

"You're right. I'm being selfish."

Vanessa touched her shoulder. "No, you're not selfish. You want your husband back. We'll get him, don't worry."

"Maybe we should wait until he comes out."

"It's too risky. They may be looking for us now if she thinks someone was spying."

Betty looked longingly at the club.

"Go home. I'll think of something to do," Vanessa said.

Betty reluctantly got into her car. Vanessa waved her on. Betty frowned as she shifted the car into gear.

Vanessa watched as she drove away.

With a sigh, she climbed into her own car. She stared at the blinking neon of Decadance for a moment, then sped off into the night.

Chapter Thirteen

Ashley ran blindly for what seemed like miles. The sight, that feeling, had been so terrifying that she barely opened her eyes except for a tiny squint to make sure she wouldn't smash into anything. She didn't know where she was or where she was going.

Exhausted, she slowed down to a jog, and then to a quick walk. Shin splints stabbed her legs, and she stopped to rub them. Sweat dripped from her forehead and into her eyes, and she wiped it away with the back of her hand. She gasped and sobbed, still trembling and now, possibly lost.

She stood up and looked around. Little beacons of light dotted the trees through the evening fog. As she walked a little farther down the gravel road, she recognized the street winding down to the cottages along the cove.

She had really gone a long way.

And why had she come to this particular road?

She knew this road.

She knew the road veering off from it too.

She had been here before.

That witch bitch lived around here somewhere.

Was she meant to come here?

Had Alex led her here somehow?

Now that she was this close, she had to see for herself. Anything that witch could do was nothing compared to the scare she just went through.

Ashley walked quietly down the road, peering at the houses, careful not to stumble over loose pieces of driftwood littering the road. It wasn't hard to find Vanessa's house again.

There was no car in the driveway. Ashley skulked along the driveway and around to the side of the house. She peered in several windows.

No one was home.

In the distance, she could hear the waves crashing against the rocks. The sound was powerful, yet soothing. It was a familiarity, like the heartbeat in the womb.

She listened. Drawing strength from the night, from the water. So much had happened to her. So much had frightened and confused her that it was a relief to feel grounded for a moment.

She crept to the back door. From inside, she could hear a cat meowing. The door handle jiggled, then the door swung open. Ashley stood frozen as she stared into the witch's kitchen. There was very little light, and all she could make out were a few pots and pans. The cat was just inside, eyes glowing in the darkness. It growled. Beyond the cat was a shimmering light.

Ashley.

Ashley dared to breathe. The cat backstepped as she walked through the doorway. Her hands were her eyes as she weaved her way through the kitchen and into the living room, where a table lamp cast a dull glow that barely reached the sofa.

Ashley.

The voice was coming from the shimmering light that hovered just above the altar. Ashley spotted three dolls laid upon it and hurried over to them. She picked up one that wore a makeshift business suit and a tuft of gray hair. She fingered the clothes while surveying the rest of the items. Candles, incense, feathers, bones. An endless array of colored stones and little statues of animals.

She put the doll down as the glow shifted around the room. She watched it as it seemingly disappeared. As she walked a little farther, she realized that it had only gone down the hall and into the bedroom.

Ashley flicked on the light and saw the Jacuzzi. The light was now a glass bubble as it floated over to the shelf of jars.

She put her hand to her mouth as the glass jars jiggled and shook. Little puffs of smoke appeared to roll around in each of them. She picked out a pale blue jar and held it up to the light. Inside, the mist circled and spun like a miniature hurricane. The glass grew hot in her hand, and just as she found a spot to put it down, it exploded. The mist screamed out like a firecracker and shattered into the air. For a moment, she was filled with a dreamy kind of peace, where the sun was shining and she was sit-

Sèphera Girón

ting on a swing in the park while her parents took turns pushing her and laughed and flirted while she tried to touch the sky.

The lightbulb exploded, plunging the room into total darkness. The sound of clattering jars filled her ears. She wanted to scream, but couldn't. She ran out of the room just as headlights illuminated the living room.

Vanessa was home.

Ashley dropped to the floor and crawled frantically toward the kitchen. The cat tried to block her path, frantically hissing, but Ashley kept swatting it away. The car door slammed, there was laughter, then the key was in the lock. Ashley's hand hit the partially open closet door. She felt around in the dark. Yes, she could make it.

She crawled into the closet and pulled the door shut just as the front door opened.

Vanessa entered the living room with David. She was laughing at a joke he'd made in the car, but she suddenly stopped. She cocked her head as if trying to hear or see something that wasn't there. She flicked on the light and stood with her hands outstretched.

"What is it?" David asked.

Vanessa wriggled her fingers. Whatever odd energy was in the room, she couldn't figure it out. She dropped her arms.

"Nothing. Nothing at all."

She put down her purse and glanced at the answering machine. She was relieved that there were no new messages. For now.

248

"Would you like a glass of wine?" she asked.

"Sure." David lit a cigarette while Vanessa retrieved the wine. Once she poured the wine into large silver goblets, she retired to the couch with David.

She raised her cup.

"Here's to what's left of the night and hoping there'll be no more surprises." She touched her goblet to David's.

"No more nasty surprises," David said. They drank to their toast.

Vanessa tried to push the night's events from her mind, but it was difficult. The ceremony. The dancing. Those weird men. The sacrifice. Each thing in its own right was freaky enough, and then to top it off, there was the leader. There was something about that blond woman that she couldn't put her finger on. Something familiar. Something about her energy.

"What are you thinking?" David asked.

"Just trying to unwind."

"You look so far away."

"I'm sorry." Vanessa smiled as she saw the concern in David's eyes. "I'm here now."

"There's always something going on, isn't there?"

"It certainly seems that way. At least life isn't boring."

"No. It isn't." They drank their wine in silence.

"Do you believe in voodoo?" Vanessa asked, startling David from his thoughts.

David frowned as he considered the question. "I don't know. I've never really experienced it, seen it or anything." He shrugged. "I've seen stuff on TV about it, but that's about it."

"I wish I knew more about it. I just thought of it as another religious system and didn't really pay attention to it. Now I'm wondering if I need to know more about it."

"You really think there's voodoo going on around here?"

Vanessa went over to her altar where the dolls lay. Her arms were full of goose bumps. She frowned. Something was amiss. She touched the dolls, tucking their tiny clothes back around them. She fiddled with them as she looked at how the patterns had been disturbed. She couldn't remember how she had lain the dolls, but now they looked thrown onto the altar instead of placed. She looked over to Katisha, who was watching her, tail twitching. Maybe Katisha had disturbed them.

She gathered up the dolls and returned to David.

"Do these mean anything to you?" she asked him as she held out the poppets.

David took them and examined them. He shrugged. "Look like voodoo dolls. Like the kind people bring back from New Orleans or Haiti. Hell, you can even order the things off the Internet."

"These are from women who are having marital problems."

"Well . . ." He looked at the dolls. "If these are the men, can't they just make the doll be good?"

Vanessa laughed. "Jesus. That seems so obvious now that you say it."

Vanessa put her hand over David's and squeezed it. "Maybe I can make the men come home again."

She set the poppets on her altar. She lit several candles and some incense. She smiled at David. "What would I do without you?"

She kneeled down before the altar and closed her eyes. David watched as she made several symbols with her hands and quietly muttered words he couldn't hear.

A golden glow surrounded her. Her long hair lifted and shifted as if it were a nest of snakes. Candles flickered. Flames danced wildly. She stayed like that for a while, the electricity in the air so thick that it seemed like a haze was settling in the room.

She stopped praying and put out the candles with a snuffer. Her hair calmed to a twitching and then was still. The golden glow was gone. The haze in the room dissipated.

Vanessa turned to him with a smile. "There. Maybe that will help. Maybe not. I have no idea if I'm strong enough to override what is going on with these guys."

"At least you tried."

Vanessa went over to David and sat on the couch. She was exhausted. "Knowing you are here makes me feel so much better. You have no idea."

"I know that when I'm with you, nothing else matters."

David leaned over to kiss her. She met his lips hungrily. Her hands stroked his broad shoulders. Her breasts pressed against his chest as she savored his warmth. His calming energy.

They kissed for a while, hands roaming over each other's bodies. Touching. Teasing. Caressing. Vanessa pulled back and stroked David's face with her fingers. She looked into his eyes. Eyes so green, so attentive, that all the magic in the world couldn't equal the power he held over her in that moment.

"Would you like to go into the bedroom?" she asked breathlessly.

David grinned, kissing her juicily before he spoke. "I would like nothing more."

Vanessa stood up and took his hand. They stood kissing once more, Vanessa wrapping her leg around him as she savored his body against hers. She ran her hands along his chest, kissing exposed flesh as she unbuttoned his shirt. She ran her tongue along his nipples, nibbling playfully.

"Okay, let's go," she sighed. She led him into the bedroom and shut the door.

Darkness settled over the room.

There was the sound of a door opening.

Ashley stepped out of the closet and looked around. Satisfied that the coast was clear, she went over to the altar. She touched the dolls. They felt warm. From the bedroom, she could hear the sounds of Vanessa and David giggling and kissing.

She went over to the couch and looked at David's coat.

Carefully, watching the bedroom door, she slipped her hand into his pockets. She pulled out a lighter, some used tissue, some receipts, a comb, and a pack of gum. She held up the comb, and was pleased to see that there was some hair in it. She crammed everything into her pocket.

From the bedroom, there were moans and laughter. Ashley frowned. It wasn't fair for that bitch to be making love when everything was so wrong.

She went back over to the altar and took the dolls. Without stopping, she hurried out of the house.

Her dreams made no sense. She was falling. Drowning. Flung against rocks. Through it all, she was gasping for air.

Vanessa burst awake, feeling as if she were suffocating. David's arm was wrapped tightly around her throat. She pulled at it, but it was locked as if it were a vise. She kicked her legs in the air, and finally she was able to loosen his grip. She rolled off the bed, panting. Her movement disturbed David, who burst awake.

"What?" he asked.

"You were trying to strangle me," she said rubbing her neck. Her precious neck. It felt rough, and she hoped that he hadn't pulled away the new skin.

"Strangle you?" He sat up.

"Yes. You had your arm wrapped around me and I couldn't breathe."

He reached over to her.

"Oh, honey. I'm so sorry. I must have been having a nightmare."

"I'll say."

"Come back to bed. I promise I won't do it again."

"I don't know if you can help it. Sleep behavior is so strange sometimes. You know, some people do kill people in their sleep."

"But that's not me," he said. He reached over and took her hand. "Come back to bed."

Reluctantly, Vanessa clasped her fingers around

his and slid back into bed. He wrapped his big strong arms around her and she nestled into them, spooning. His heart was beating a mile a minute.

"I would never hurt you, Vanessa." he said sleepily, kissing her head. "I'm falling in love with you."

Vanessa smiled.

"I'm falling in love with you too, David. So don't kill me, Okay?"

"Okay."

Vanessa slept fitfully the rest of the night. In sleepless bursts, her mind raced. They had made love and it had been wonderful. She had never felt so complete. So fulfilled. It was like he knew everywhere she needed to be touched. Her hunger for him had finally been satiated, and she was glad she had finally succumbed to him.

Yet, while she reveled in the afterglow of lovemaking, she worried about Betty and Cheryl and Grace and the other women who were losing their men. She hoped that the spell she had cast would help somehow. It was hard to know what to do for them, for she didn't know what powers she was working against.

A shudder passed through her. She looked toward the window, and again had that sensation that someone was looking in. It agitated her so much that she had to get up and look. There was nothing there.

Vanessa wandered into the bathroom and took a shower. Sometimes that helped her when she had too much on her mind. As the spray fell onto her, she gasped. It hurt. She turned the shower head to a softer setting, but still, the water hitting her stung like a thousand poison nettles. She looked down at her arms and saw that her skin was flaking. Not a lot. At this point, it only appeared like a red rash with a bit of peeling. She put her hands to her neck. It was happening there as well. She quickly turned off the shower and ran to the mirror. It was happening again. It took all of her self-control not to scratch. It took even more self-control not to scream and throw things in a fit of rage.

She paced angrily around in a tiny circle, going around herself thirteen times until she finally felt able to think clearly.

She took a deep breath.

Focus.

Focus on the task at hand.

First things first.

She opened the cupboard and found the concoction she had created over the years. A soft gentle lotion that took away the sting and helped the flesh to stop deteriorating rapidly. With any luck, she could keep her skin intact for a few more weeks. She rubbed the lotion gently into every part of her body. It felt good, and she could see the redness starting to ebb.

When she was finished, she put the lotion back.

She returned to the bed and David's arms, passing the rest of the night listening to him breathe, hoping that he would never find out her terrible secret.

Tony had never returned since that day. The children were at school and here Cheryl sat once more staring at a damnable glass of urine. She had to do it. She needed strength. She needed insight. She needed a way to stop hurting.

She wrapped her fingers around the glass. It was warm as it always was. She raised it to her lips. The smell of it made her gag.

She put the glass down again.

She would never be able to do it.

She knew that now.

Whatever she needed in life, drinking urine was not the answer.

She missed her husband. Even though things had been so difficult, she still missed him.

She thought about Farah. Who was she kidding? A temporary infatuation with a woman who seemed to have it all together. Sure Farah was bright and fun and seemed to know all the answers. But Cheryl needed real answers. Answers about her marriage. Answers about how to talk to the children. Pretending there was nothing wrong wasn't fair to anyone. Farah couldn't help her with that.

As good as the gathering felt, as wonderful as things were in Sam's presence, in the end, all she wanted was her family back together again. The energy of joy that she experienced at the meetings was intoxicating, but like taking a drug, it was only serving to distract her from the pain of her life.

She needed to confront her reality, not escape from it. She needed to mother her children and confront her husband. She had to have closure with her husband in one way or another before she could chase rainbows.

God must want that for her. Without drinking urine.

She grabbed her purse and within minutes, found herself at Vanessa's door.

Vanessa didn't look very well. Her hair was a mess, her skin was pasty and blotchy. A nauseating fishy odor hung in the air.

"I'm sorry to bother you," Cheryl said, nervously fiddling with her purse strap. "I was wondering . . . well . . . do you have any time?"

"Come on in."

Vanessa led her to the table.

"Has anything come to you?" Cheryl asked. "About my husband?"

Vanessa nodded. "Perhaps."

Cheryl's breath caught in her throat.

"I found another woman's husband. She is having the same thing going on as you. Her husband has been acting strange and then went missing. We found him, but he's not right. I wonder if your husband is with him."

"Not right? What do you mean?"

"I'm not sure what is going on. It could be very dangerous. Voodoo, maybe. At least, what little I know about it."

"The doll?"

"Yes, she had a doll too." Vanessa nodded to the altar, then stopped. She frowned.

"Oh, my." Vanessa went over to the altar. The dolls were gone.

"Where did they go?" She looked along the floor and started hunting along the bookcases.

"What?"

"The dolls. I had three dolls. One was yours. And now they seem to be missing."

"Great."

"I must have just misplaced them," Vanessa said hurriedly. She returned to the table and tried to focus on Cheryl.

"This is hard to believe or maybe not," said Vanessa. "But I guess I'll just say it."

"I can take anything. As long as I know what is going on. Not knowing is infinitely worse."

Vanessa took a deep breath. "There is a gentlemen's club called Decadance. A dance bar. I think that it is somehow connected to the disappearances."

"How?"

"I saw a ritual and there were many men there. Men that didn't seem quite right. Since I don't know what Tony looks like, I can't say for sure he was there. But I'd be willing to bet on it."

"A ritual?" Thoughts of urine-drinking flashed through Cheryl's head.

"It looked like voodoo. I'm not sure."

"Voodoo."

"I would suggest not going there on your own to see. I know you want to. But I'm going to try to find out what is going on and the best way to deal with it so that no one gets hurt."

"Tony wouldn't be into voodoo."

"Maybe not on his own free will. But there might be something more going on. That's what I don't know. And I want you to promise me you'll not go there till I understand what is going on."

"Should I call the police?"

"No. I would say for now that the police won't be any help."

"But he's a missing person."

"Yes. And we want him safe. If the police start nosing around, anything could happen. He might not be safe anymore. They could go underground and we'd never find them. We have to be smart."

"But the police . . . that's what they're for."

"The police don't have magic."

"Do we need magic?"

"I don't know. That is what I have to find out."

Cheryl was shaking. "Do you think really and truly that is where he is?"

"Yes. And I don't want you going there. We don't know who we are dealing with or what they want. Well, I can see she wants men for some reason."

"She?"

"The leader. The high priestess or whatever she would be called. The person leading the ceremony was a blond woman."

"The blond woman you told me about."

Vanessa nodded. "Probably the same. Please don't do anything until I tell you to. It might take a few days to sort it all out. I have to think. I have to proceed carefully. We don't need anyone to get hurt."

Cheryl bit her lip. "Is there hope? Is there hope he will come back to me? Ask the cards . . . please ask the cards."

Vanessa shook her head. "I won't ask the cards because I'm going to do my best to make everything okay. Go home. Be a good mom to your children. I will call you when I figure something out."

Cheryl's legs were wobbly when she stood up. Tears streamed down her face.

She left Vanessa's home in a daze.

*   *   *

Ashley sat in the little woods by the park where she had met that weird Molly lady. She often thought about Molly and half-hoped she would see her again. She wondered what Molly would make of the dolls. Ashley wondered if there really was power in these dolls, as Vanessa seemed to think. She wondered about the weird things she had heard Vanessa and David discussing.

It was as if she had fallen down a rabbit hole or maybe was whisked away by a tornado. The world was a topsy-turvey place and who knew what lay around each corner?

Did Vanessa's precious David know Alex was missing? How did she know that David had no clue about missing teenage girls. By the sound of the conversation she had overheard, David wasn't in on anything at all.

She wondered if maybe the missing men that Vanessa had talked about and Alex were connected. Were all the men dead like Alex?

Alex was near.

She could sense Alex just over her right shoulder. Kind of hovering, barely breathing onto her skin. However, when Ashley looked over, there was nothing there. Not even a shimmer of light. But she could feel Alex's presence as tangibly as if she were living and breathing right beside her.

She turned her focus back to the toys she had taken.

So what was with the dolls?

"Voodoo dolls," they had said. Voodoo seemed so . . . old-fashioned. It was a faraway thing that only really old and odd people did. She couldn't imagine its presence in a little coastal town.

Yet the proof was right here. Someone believed in voodoo, and because of their belief, a whole ripple was cascading through part of the town. If what she heard was right, strange women were bringing found dolls to Vanessa.

Goose bumps tickled her arms.

Did voodoo really work?

In the movies, there were so many horrible things that could happen in vodoo. There was the slaughter of animals, frantic dancing with trance drums, people getting decapitated like in *The Serpent and the Rainbow*. Then there was the worst of it. Just waking up one day dead or undead or a zombie.

Imagine that.

"Walking around with a broken brain.
There'd be no pain, no gain,
miss the train jump off the track,
there's no looking back.
Just walking around like someone who's insane.
Yet there's no one who knows how you feel no pain.
All around you life goes on.
But you stay focused on what you want.
Zombies are made to serve and obey.
So fuck them all, send them away . . . to . . ."

Ashley stopped. Her mind wasn't working well and her rap was suffering for it. No point in rapping if the words weren't piecing together right.

But all this zombie-voodoo-doll stuff. Was it really true?

Even Vanessa didn't seem to know.

Ashley emptied her pockets. They were full of the items of David's she had scored out of his jacket. When she was satisfied she had found all of his stuff, she surveyed her haul. She looked at the dolls.

The first thing she did was pick up each doll and turn it over in her hand. At last, she decided on the blond doll. She plucked David's hair from the comb and wrapped it tightly around the doll's neck. She had seen enough TV shows to know that she had to use his personal items to make voodoo work.

However it worked. If it would work at all.

She wrapped one of the tissues around the doll as well and stuffed the ends into the little pants it wore. She held the doll closer to her face and stared at its button eyes. What a weird-looking doll. The others were the same. They were creepy as hell, but if it meant she could somehow get back at that lying witch, then she would do whatever it took.

"Gonna get you back, you useless hag.
Gonna make your man be a real huge drag.
Gonna make him hate you, use you, abuse you.
Gonna make him leave you, betray you, lie to you,
break your heart, you worthless witch,
like you broke mine, you fucking bitch."

She danced the blond doll on her lap for a while, singing the song over and over again. Every now and again, she'd pick up the other dolls to dance with it.

As she sang and played with the dolls, she felt Alex's presence emanating with shuddery vibrations. There was a ripple in the air, and Alex shifted into view as a glowing glittering beam.

"Alex!" Ashley smiled as the luminescence surrounded her. "Make that bitch pay for what she did. Let's get her good." She laughed.

"Death would be too sweet for her. I hope she has a horrible bitter life."

The glitter glowed hot around Ashley. Her forehead beaded with sweat; the dolls in her hands were burning her fingers.

"Shit!" she cried out as she dropped the dolls. The glitter undulated around her, and then blinked off as if it had never been there at all.

Ashley sat in the darkness, blinking as she tried to adjust her eyes from the brightness of the light to the stars above her. Soon they shifted from a dull blur to pinpricks of knowledge.

Her heart was racing as she made a wish.

Chapter Fourteen

Vanessa paced around the house, a growing sense of unease consuming her. She moved her books from one shelf to another. She rearranged several knickknacks. Still she had that steadily increasing sensation of being watched. Her skin itched. Her mind conjured fantasies where she would go find David and run away where no one could find them. Where they could sit by the ocean day and night and make love and no one would ever know. She could do it. It was totally possible. She had done it before. Both she and Demian. They had just disappeared. And pretty much stayed disappeared as they drifted further away from each other's lives like roaming clouds.

If she ran away with David, would dissidence set in? Would her intrigue with him be consumed by malaise as she unpeeled his secrets and found that in the end, he was no more special than any other man? Or would she be so enthralled with each layer of him that she would spend the rest of his life discovering his deepest desires?

She fiddled with her tarot cards, shuffling and cutting them several times.

She and David.

Would it work?

Trembling, she pulled the first card. She set it facedown on the table. Her fingers tapped it thoughtfully.

No. She didn't want to know. What if there was something dire in the cards? She wouldn't be able to fix it until it was too late. Or maybe attempting to fix it would cause the dreaded chain reaction that she was trying to avoid.

Sometimes she really hated the vagaries of the universal laws.

So as much as she desired to know what her choices would bring, she put the cards down.

That brought her to her next dilemma.

There were women that were counting on her. On *her*. That was a switch. No one had ever depended on her for anything before without her expecting something in return. What these women wanted had nothing to do with her. She was only bridging a gap.

What would the reward be for getting involved with helping these women?

Maybe it would be a special spot in heaven for her. She laughed at the thought. Yeah, right. No matter how much penance she paid, she would never see heaven unless it was to clean the toilets.

No. There would be a reward. The pendulum always swings in the universe, and though logic would dictate that because she was helping others with no regard to herself, she would have something wonderful happen to her, in her experience it never turned out that great. Theoretically, if she could wish and manipulate, if she chose to wish and manipulate, she could suggest that in payment for her help she wanted a happy, peaceful relationship with David.

She was pretty sure that whether she helped them or not, the shit was going to hit the fan soon. And she was going to get spattered the most.

She didn't want to help them anymore. She felt sorry for their sad faces, for children asking about their fathers. But her energy was draining with every passing minute, like a battery running down. She had to boost her energy if she was going to go confronting some cult to free a bunch of men. Maybe the men liked being there. Maybe this was a path they had chosen, a way to get out of smothering marriages. She couldn't imagine it, though. Being a zombie in the basement of a strip club was no way to exist.

She was no hero.

She hated the thought of being a hero. She just wanted to get by, live her life quietly without any big adventure. She would be happy to continue living in her house, maybe even one day marrying David.

David.

What to do about him?

Whenever she thought of him, a warm feeling filled her. She was in love with him. She was sure of it. The more she thought about it, the more she was convinced that David was the soul mate she had conjured. How else could she explain her sudden passion? Her sudden realization of love that had happened so quickly, so suddenly? So completely? She didn't think he could do any wrong in her eyes. He was a simple man who appreciated her. He didn't have a bunch of fucked-up problems and issues. He didn't drink blood or turn into a werewolf or yearn for world domination. He was happy to go to work and come home, to relax in his spare time and hang out with her. And after they had finally made love, she knew he was the one she had been waiting a lifetime for.

How could she love him and lie to him at the same time?

That had been one of her wishes, hadn't it?

Telling the truth, always.

He'd told her the truth.

As much as she'd hated to hear it, she had heard about his unresolved feelings for Lizzie.

She was confident that the happier they grew together, the more distant his memory would be, until Lizzie was reduced to a sporadic whisper in his head.

Should she tell him that she had eternal life? He'd probably think she was nuts if he did. She had no idea what he really thought about her being a witch. Maybe he just thought it was some funky lifestyle thing and that there was no magic. No danger. No price to pay.

There was always a price. The universe thrived on balance. The cycle of nature. The circle of life.

What goes around comes around. His involvement with her would no doubt lead to trouble of some sort one day.

Could she spare him trouble? Even if she couldn't sidestep her own grief, maybe she could make things better for him.

If she bowed out of the missing-husband situation, she could ensure that for now, they could live peacefully. But then, she'd be letting all the women down. And she was getting more curious to find out what was going on.

She thought of Betty's husband dancing. Was Cheryl's there too? And Grace's? And Mrs. Bunting's? Were they all so enticed by exotic trappings that they didn't realize what was becoming of them?

Somehow she knew in her heart that everything was connected.

Everything was always connected.

Like a string of pearls, one thing leading to another until you were back at the clasp holding it all together.

That blond woman was connected to her somehow, but she couldn't remember ever meeting her before. She couldn't figure out where the connection lay, except that some of her clients had husbands missing. There was something bigger going on.

She was no hero.

What was the something bigger?

She could figure it out. She knew she could. But she still was hesitant. It was going to lead to ugliness.

She liked Cheryl and Betty. They were nice people and she had to help them.

She scratched at her arms. Damn, but she had to do something about her skin. She was going to have to get another virgin much sooner than she wanted.

Maybe she could do something to protect herself and David in the meantime.

She went over to the bookcase and pulled out a big old book. She carefully browsed through the thick yellowed pages until she found what she was looking for.

A spell of protection.

The procedure to brew the potion was complicated and tedious. It took her some time to gather the ingredients, tie various parchments and thread together. Cut and powder and set on fire one item after another.

As she cast the spell, the cauldron spit and bubbled. The smell filling the room was rancid. Mostly because of the dead animal parts she needed to add.

Katisha watched the boiling pot, tail twitching. A thick layer of foam bubbled to the top and began frothing over. Katisha hissed, spitting as she leaped around on all fours. Vanessa ran to stop the pot from boiling over as Katisha darted between her legs. Vanessa's foot came down on the cat. Katisha screamed as Vanessa hopped back, still reeling from the sensation of how hard her heel went through the cat's neck. Katisha howled and kicked her legs, her head hanging off kilter from her neck. Vanessa knelt down to examine her. Katisha twitched, blood running from her mouth. Her fur was matted and sticky, her eyes stared with bewilderment at her mistress. Vanessa touched her, feeling where Katisha's neck was snapped. She carefully scooped her up, petting her.

"Katisha! I'm so sorry."

She cried as Katisha mewed softly. She buried her face in the sticky fur. She thought about sending energy to the cat. She sent light and love. She knew she could send healing vibrations, and even could somehow weave bone back together within muscle.

Yet if she did that, it would drain her newly renewed resources, and she had no idea how long her new power would last.

As much as it pained her, Vanessa closed her eyes and stopped sending vibes to the cat. Katisha's breath was shallow, her tongue lolling out of her mouth.

"Poor Katisha." Vanessa stroked her fur.

The room grew cold. Vanessa shivered. She put the dead cat carefully onto the floor, near the altar. There was a low humming noise, and the windows were dark even though it was afternoon.

"Who are you?" she cried out. As she stood up, it was light outside once more. She touched her forehead, wondering if she was going to have a stroke.

The contents of the pot boiling over spit onto the fire, sending a thick haze of steam into the room.

The stench of it made her gag.

She took a heavy cloth from a hook on the side of the fireplace and lifted the cauldron out. The fire was pretty much out already.

She put the cauldron in the middle of the floor, and then poked at the embers until the last remaining remnants were out.

Every now and again she would look over at Katisha.

There was no breath, no mewing. No sound came from Katisha.

Vanessa's eyes welled with tears. She couldn't bring herself to touch the cat again. And even if she did, what was she going to do with her? She'd have to bury her, obviously, but the last thing she wanted to deal with was digging a grave.

Vanessa grabbed her purse and keys and ran outside. She looked quickly around the house, not knowing if she wanted to see anything there or not. There was nothing. No footprints. No sign that anyone had been there at all.

She still had blood on her hands from Katisha, and she wiped them on her legs as she hurried to the car.

She needed to get out.

Once in the car, she looked down at her blood-smeared clothes. She couldn't go out like this. People would think she was nuts or a murderer or some crazy chick who couldn't cope very well with her period.

Back inside she went again, walking carefully around the cat. As she set about the mundane task of changing her outfit, her heart stopped pounding so wildly. A moment of normalcy was all it took to keep her from trembling and bursting into tears.

Tears would get her nowhere.

Katisha was dead. She couldn't bring her back if she wanted to; she wasn't in a position to use up her beloved power.

The idea that someone was watching her didn't help at all either. She'd spent so much time lately peering over her shoulder and watching for demons or flashing lights or faces beneath faces. It was no wonder she was jittery. Odd happenings for an odder life. It had to stop somewhere.

At last she felt human. She walked around Katisha again and this time, didn't look at her companion's stiffening body.

She drove to the hardware store. As she entered the store, she felt that the energy was frantically disturbed. David looked terrible. His face was flushed with agitation as he tried to calm a surly customer. Vanessa watched the interaction for a while. The customer was yelling, slamming his hand on the counter. Vanessa narrowed her eyes, willing the customer to calm down. David continued to explain the store's policies in his gentle low voice, although he was shaking with rage.

The man flung up his hands and left the store. Vanessa turned to David.

"That looked tough," she said.

"It sucks."

David gathered up the defective merchandise the man had left behind and tried to piece it together.

"How's your day going otherwise?" she asked, leaning over the counter.

"Not well," he said, and dropped one of the parts onto the floor. It shattered.

"Goddamnit!" he shouted.

"Maybe I can . . ."

"Later, okay? I'm busy," he snapped as he knelt

to pick up the pieces. Vanessa stared at him in disbelief. His tone pricked her as surely as if she had been shot.

She turned on her heel and stomped out of the store.

The day had a chill in it. Winter was coming. She rubbed her arms, as if comforting and warming herself.

David's agitation crept under her skin. He hadn't been snapping at *her*. She knew that in her heart. But it stung, bursting the rosy bubble she had thought they shared.

He was only human. He was stressed out. That was all.

She was angry. Upset and angry.

Her cat was dead. Her boyfriend had other things on his mind. She felt alone.

Again.

Still.

She needed to find peace. To relax. To clear her mind and start again.

She went to her pond and tried to find solace there. She sat staring at the green algae, turning events over in her mind. She couldn't concentrate on anything for long. Ideas flitted from one place to another. A kaleidoscope of images wouldn't let her focus.

Her poor cat. Katisha had been a good cat. How could it happen that she tripped over her cat, as she had a hundred times, yet this time it killed her?

She threw a rock into the pond, watching the algae ripple. A crow burst from the bush and cawed loudly as it soared into the air.

Vanessa watched it until it was a tiny dot in the sky.

She sat thinking by the pond a very long time. Birds flew around her, frogs jumped and splashed. She tossed rocks into the pond, aiming for lily pads, and most of the time hitting them.

As day passed into night, she decided to go into town. Maybe she needed a drink and to be around people. Sometimes she forgot that humans were social creatures and once in awhile, needed to be surrounded by other humans.

Vanessa stood outside Velvet Darkness, watching the clubbers going inside. It had been a long time since she had been here, and she wasn't quite sure why she was even here.

She wanted to go in. She was drawn to the booming music and the young people wearing beautiful velvet outfits flowing in and out the door.

She remembered back to another time, when the Goth movement was new and fresh and seductive. When fetish gear was a hidden pleasure only revealed in secrecy to others that understood. Only punk rockers had tattoos, and no one outside of primitive cultures in far-away lands had much more than their ears pierced.

How dramatically things change.

She stood under the arched doorway and stared up at the leering plaster gargoyle. Artifice. Everything about culture now was artifice. The Goth culture was a medley of wanna-bes and earnest types.

The doorman waved her into the swelling pulsing darkness where lights flickered and dry ice wafted.

She wandered past the bar and through the first of three floors. By the time she made her way to the top, she knew why she had come.

She stared at the figure on the stage. A spotlight illuminated him and his burgundy guitar.

After all these years, there he was. Sitting on his stool, his fingers dancing along the guitar strings. Her heart pounded as it had the very first time she had ever laid eyes on him so many years ago. His music was still gentle and melodic, stirring her soul. His music still had the amazing power to set her legs trembling, her flesh yearning to touch him once more.

He looked up. He saw her watching him and he stopped playing. As if he forgot he was on stage, with an audience, he put down his guitar and stepped off the platform to walk toward her. She could feel the air between them thickening.

"Vanessa." He spoke her name the way he played his guitar. Gently, with so much unresolved emotion.

"Demian."

"I've missed you so much."

"Me too."

"Where have you been?"

"Traveling. Trying to forget you."

"Forget me?" Vanessa frowned.

"You know why." Demian looked down.

"I know. I wanted to forget you too."

"I see now that I can never be rid of you."

"You make that sound like a bad thing."

"You are evil, Vanessa. Everything you come in contact with ends up in destruction."

"I don't think so. Not everything. You didn't."

"Very nearly. You *know* how it was. And now, here we are. Still alive. Still beautiful," Demian said, touching Vanessa's hair. He twisted it in his fingers and pulled gently. Vanessa sighed as she stepped back. He released his grip.

She stared at Demian. He was handsome still. Now a man in his forties. His dark hair was only shoulder-length now, cut in the new modern style. She could even imagine him poofing it and spritzing it. He had always been clean and particular. Now as a man, a real grown man, she could see that he was neater than ever right down to his buffed nails. He wore a finely cut purple velvet shirt with three-quarter frilled sleeves and tight black leather pants. He was still slender, but not skinny as he had been twenty years ago. He filled out as a man fills out. His eyes were still vividly green, ringed with a touch of eyeliner that rendered him even more exotic-looking. His white teeth gleamed.

The crowd cheered and jeered for Demian to continue. He looked at them, at the anxious fans hungering for more. He took Vanessa's hand and kissed it.

"Will you stay until I am done?"

"Yes."

She watched the Goth children watching him. They stood, waiting, hypnotized by his brilliance.

He returned to the stage and resumed playing his guitar. The notes soothed with their hypnotic patterns, weaving a harmonic tapestry of sound. Vanessa had missed listening to him play. She could see he wove a spell on everyone within earshot.

277

Why had he not gone on to claim the fame and fortune that were so rightfully his?

She turned her attention to his admirers. She liked to watch the Goth children. They seemed so innocent sometimes, yet she knew from experience how not so innocent they truly were. One song led into another. She returned to the bar several times for refills, not wanting to stray too far from Demian.

At last, he had played his final song. He stood, facing his audience, and then took a little bow. He walked off the stage.

Vanessa moved over to the bar and sat on a stool.

Demian found her as the bar started to empty.

"Do you want to go for a coffee?"

"Yes."

They walked in silence to a nearby all-night coffee shop. A lot of the Goth children were there, sneaking glances at him as if to gaze directly at him would cause them to burst into flame. A celebrity in their midst.

"I've missed you," he said taking her hand.

"I've been thinking about you a lot," Vanessa told him.

"I wondered so often what became of you."

"Me too."

They stared into each other's eyes.

"Why don't you come back to my place? We can get to know each other again," Demian said.

"I can't. I have a boyfriend now."

"Oh, you do, do you?"

"He's very good to me."

"And I wasn't."

"I know you did so much for me. I'll never be able to repay you. But I've finally found someone that makes me happy." Vanessa looked down at her hands. She played with the hem of her sleeve.

"So tell me about this wonderful man," Demian said.

"I don't know what to tell," Vanessa said. "Why don't you come over for dinner and I'll introduce you. You can judge for yourself."

Demian winced. "Why would I want to meet your boyfriend?"

"Maybe we can all be friends. I bet he'd like your music."

"Friends . . . right."

"If you want to see me, you have to accept David. It's as simple as that."

"Fine. Then I'll come for dinner."

Betty stood in the bathroom of Decadance. She trembled with trepidation. Larry might be downstairs. No matter what might be going on, she had to see her husband. She had to get to the bottom of what was going on, once and for all. She lightly sponged her face with cool water, careful not to disturb her makeup. She stared at herself in the mirror. She had aged so much during these troubled times. Would her looks ever return to her? Would Larry ever return to her?

She braced herself as she opened the bathroom door. Instead of returning into the main club area, she turned down the hallway where the alternate staircase lay. She walked carefully down the stairs, checking behind her to be certain no one saw her. The basement was lit today. The doorway to the large room was open.

Fearfully, she peered through the doorway.

Then there was blackness.

Cheryl stood outside Decadance. She was sweating although it was chilly out. People were coming and going sporadically. She wondered what she would find inside.

As she made her way into the strip club, she searched every face for Tony.

She stood by the bar and ordered a drink, glancing at the dancers wrapping themselves around the two brass poles. Her gaze ran over the crowd of people watching the dancers. Some of the men looked so hungry. Desperation wafting from them in waves. Others seemed merely curious. Several joked with each other as they drank their beer, pointing to the girls and making comments.

So many men, and not one of them was Tony.

A beautiful blond woman walked by her. Cheryl felt a chill crawl up her back. Could this be the woman?

As if on cue, the woman looked directly at her. "Hello."

"Hello."

"What are you doing here all alone?" the woman said.

"I'm just seeing what it's all about," Cheryl said.

"Have you been downstairs?"

"No. What is there?"

"It's a more private area. Maybe whoever you are looking for has gone downstairs."

"What makes you think I'm looking for someone."

The blonde laughed.

"Of course you are. Why else are you here?"

"I'm just looking."

"For someone."

"All right, I'm looking for my husband. I heard that he was seen here a few times and I thought I'd check it out for myself."

"Catching hubby at playtime, huh?"

"Maybe."

"Then come along with me."

Cheryl followed the woman through the club and down the darkened stairway. There was no one around. They went down the hall a little ways and then suddenly, a hand wrapped around Cheryl's throat, while another shoved a cloth in her face. She fell limply to the floor.

Chapter Fifteen

When Vanessa returned to her home, there were several messages on the machine from David. Each one that she played sounded more upset, wondering where she was, sorry that he had snapped at her.

She wanted to phone him, but it was so late. Too late to disturb him. He would have to work in the morning.

She sat down, looking at Katisha, who still lay dead on the floor. A few flies buzzed around her.

It had been mind-blowing to see Demian again. She couldn't believe it. No wonder she had been thinking so much about him. He was right here.

She and Demian shared a lot of history. She could understand his disappointment at her finally finding someone else, especially so close to the time he came back into her life. But she couldn't help that. If she wanted things to work with David, she would have to be clear and straight with Demian.

A part of her heart would always be with Demian. But she had a new life now.

She scratched at her neck and then at her arms. She rubbed her nose. Everything was itching. As she dug her nails into her neck, a large flap of skin fell away.

"Goddamnit," she cried. She picked up the skin and flung it across the room. "When am I going to get the hang of this?"

She had to do something fast. Especially before she saw David again.

It wasn't that hard to find Ashley.

The girl was sitting alone in the park on a swing, humming to herself.

"Ashley." Vanessa stood before the girl.

Ashley's eyes grew wide. "What do you want?"

"I have some information for you. I think I know where your friend is."

"You said she went to California."

"So I was wrong. Everyone makes mistakes now and again," Vanessa said casually.

"What do you know?"

"I think I saw her. I want to take you there."

"Really?"

"You seem so surprised. Don't teenagers run away all the time?"

"But I thought . . . I thought . . ."

"What did you think? That you'd never see her again?"

Ashley swallowed. Her eyes filled with tears. "Yeah."

"Come with me. Hurry. Before we lose her."

Ashley followed Vanessa to her car.

"Did you tell the police that you saw her?" Ashley asked.

"Not yet. I wanted you to be the first."

Ashley hesitated before getting into Vanessa's car.

"How do I know that you are telling me the truth?" Ashley asked.

"Come or don't. It's all the same to me." Vanessa started the car.

"Okay."

Ashley sat in the passenger seat, staring straight ahead while fiddling with the Walkman in her pocket.

The trip was made in uneasy silence. As they drove up the driveway, Ashley peered out the window. She recognized Vanessa's house.

"Why would she be here?" Ashley asked.

"She wants to see you," Vanessa said, growing irritated. She scratched at her neck.

"You said . . ."

"Do you want to see her or not?"

• Ashley nodded. "Yes."

Vanessa led the trembling girl into her living room. As Ashley stood looking around the room, Vanessa slipped her anthame from her pocket. She walked up behind Ashley and held the girl by her head. Vanessa drew the anthame across Ashley's throat. Ashley screamed, trying to pry Vanessa's arms from her, as blood poured from her neck. Alex's spirit rose up in a mighty force, trying to beat Vanessa back from Ashley. Vanessa pointed her finger at the spirit. A blue bolt of light hit Alex. The spirit wavered, teetering and rolling in the air.

"Go back to where you belong!" Vanessa cried, hitting it again.

The spirit withered and dissolved.

"Alex," Ashley moaned as blood bubbled from her mouth.

Ashley's mind was filled with images of so many things. Of Alex and her watching the fish. Of her mother bandaging her knee. Of her glory at winning first place in the rap contest at the rec center. For a moment, there was a flash of a terrible creature with red eyes and a leering grin. A bright light blinked it away. TnT sang in her head as she collapsed to the ground.

Vanessa scooped up Ashley's body and dumped it into the Jacuzzi where Katisha's body already floated. She pushed the buttons for the jets, and poured various vials of liquid into the bubbling water. She stripped off her clothes and slid in. With great relish, she manipulated Ashley's body as she had Alex's until the Jacuzzi was a steaming mass of meat and blood.

Vanessa, Demian, and David sat around the table in Vanessa's home.

"Here's to an interesting evening." Demian lifted his glass. David followed suit, and Vanessa clinked both of them.

"It will be interesting," David said as he sipped his wine.

They ate in relative silence. David and Vanessa eating steak, Demian picking at a salad.

"Still not a meat-eater," Vanessa said. "After all this time."

"Just never got used to the taste," Demian said.

"I love meat." David cut into his steak and ate a large piece. "Delicious."

"I'm sure it is."

They continued to eat. Vanessa spoke softly.

"So, Demian. Tell us about your travels. You must have done a lot the past few years."

"Oh, just this and that. Clubs. Made a couple of CDs that went nowhere. The usual musician's story."

"Too bad," David said.

"Must get exhausting after a while," Vanessa said, anxious to keep the conversation going.

"Sure. But I like to keep moving. You know."

Demian winked at Vanessa.

"Trouble with the law?" David asked.

"No. Just itchy feet."

"I see."

They ate some more.

"Tell me, young David. What would you do if you could live forever?" Demian asked. Vanessa glared at him.

"Forever is a long time."

"It is, isn't it?"

"I don't know if I would want to live forever. My job is okay, but to do it . . . forever . . ." David sat and thought.

"You would probably find other ways to pass the time."

"I would hope so. I guess if I had my health, if I had my looks, it would be a helluva ride."

"Wouldn't it?" Demian laughed. "History is filled with people searching for that Fountain of Youth. For eternal life. Do you ever wonder if you've actually met anyone that had discovered the secret?"

David laughed. "I doubt I have ever met anyone. . . ." David took a sip of wine.

"What about you, Vanessa? What would you do if you had eternal life?" David turned to her.

"Me?" She laughed. "I don't know. Probably not much different than I'm doing now."

"Would you try to discover the secrets of the universe?" Demian asked.

"I'm always trying to figure out why things happen. I'm not sure having forever would make a difference. Everything is so elusive."

"Maybe, as time went on, you'd stumble across something that gave your life meaning," Demian said.

"My life has meaning," Vanessa said.

"What meaning? Have you gotten any further ahead than when last we met?"

Vanessa sighed. "I'm fine." She looked over at David. "I'm more than fine."

David grinned.

"What is it that you do to make Vanessa so enamored of you? Did you cast a spell on her?" Demian asked.

David laughed. "Me? Spells? I don't think so."

"Then I wonder what the attraction is." Demian stared at him.

"He doesn't need a spell to hold my heart," Vanessa said.

"Oh, he holds your heart." Demian nodded. "I once held your heart. Literally."

Vanessa coughed.

"Wonderful fall weather we're having," she said, desperate to lead the subject to safer ground.

"Yes. It is. I'm enjoying my stay in New England," Demian said, holding his glass up to the light. He studied the red liquid inside.

"What brought you here?" David asked.

Demian looked over at Vanessa. "Mostly work. And, of course, wanting to meet up with my dear old friend."

"How long are you in town for?" asked David.

"Only another week. Then it's back to New York."

"That's too bad," David said, leaning back in his chair.

"Yes. Too bad." Vanessa narrowed her eyes at Demian.

The main course eaten, Vanessa stood to clear the dishes.

"Here, let me." Demian stood and started to gather up the plates. David took the glasses, and soon the table was empty.

The rest of the night passed in casual chitchat. Vanessa held court, keeping the subjects safe and light.

At last, Demian stood up.

"It's time to call it a night," he said as he stretched. "Thank you so much for the wonderful food and hospitality." He shook David's hand.

He turned to hug Vanessa. "I missed you," he whispered.

Vanessa nodded.

When Demian was gone, Vanessa breathed a sigh of relief. "I hope that wasn't too horrible for you."

"Of course not. Have I told you how beautiful you look tonight?"

"Yes. But you can keep on telling me if you want!"

They laughed and went into the bedroom.

As David held her in his arms, nuzzling and kissing her, Vanessa had the sense of being watched. She peered over his shoulder to the window. A shadow passed.

David caressed her. Tantalized her with experienced hands. She closed her eyes and forgot about shadows and Demian and virgins.

She let David work his magic on her, and wished that they could stay in each other's arms forever.

Vanessa was back on the rocks. Sophie stood there, her arms crossed. There was no hazy glow surrounding her today. She watched Vanessa, her conjoined-twin piggy self merely a ripple in her face. Her face glowed with a rugged beauty, though her look was one of contempt.

"Did it again." Sophie shook her head.

Vanessa stepped toward her, raising her hands in a gesture of surrender. "What else could I do? There was nothing else I could do. David won't love me if I look old. And then there's all the scars. . . ."

"Poor Ashley." Sophie lowered her head in reverence. She prodded her fingers for a moment before looking up. "Who's next?"

"I wish there was no one else. I really do."

Sophie laughed. The sound rang hollow among the rocks till it was swallowed by the surf. "No. You love it. Blood sport. You are always bloodthirsty."

Vanessa flushed. "No, I'm not. Stop coming around to my dreams. I have enough problems without your comments on my life."

"You are playing a dangerous game."

"So you keep telling me. As if I don't know."

"What is going to happen now? You have Demian back as you always dreamed. You have David, who could be the love of your pathetic life. Who will you choose?"

"Choose?"

"You can't have them both."

"I don't want them both. I want David."

"No, you don't." Sophie sneered.

The rocks glowed with a reddish hue. Shadows of the virgins rippled as they tittered. Vanessa felt queasy.

"I want to wake up now." Vanessa walked away from Sophie and the laughter.

"You still love Demian," Sophie called after her.

Vanessa stopped walking and turned around to face her. "So what?"

"Demian knows your secret," Sophie whispered.

"That changes nothing."

"It changes everything."

Vanessa burst awake in a cold sweat. She looked toward the window. A shadow passed by, blocking the moon momentarily. A tree branch scratched at the side of the house. The wind whistled. Beside her, David snored lightly. She stared at him, marveling at his muscular back. Realizing that she would enjoy spending many years watching him sleep, she ran her hands lightly along his back.

"David . . ." she hummed almost imperceptibly. David stirred, flinging his arms around for a moment, then fell back asleep. Vanessa smiled.

A brilliant streak of light and the sudden sizzling sear of electric thunder shook her from her reverie. Rain pounded the window as the wind shrieked.

She listened to the wind growing steadily louder. The rain slamming harder. Her heart raced. Over on the shelf, the jars rattled. Little glowing globes swam inside.

One by one the jars smashed to the floor. David burst awake.

"What?" he called out. He rubbed his eyes and turned toward the sound. The last jar fell. Several swirling patches of light spiraled up from the broken glass, then dissipated into the darkness.

"What was that?" he asked Vanessa. She was trembling, but lovingly stroked David's arm.

"It was nothing, honey. Go back to sleep. Nothing but a bad dream."

David touched her face as he nestled back into the pillows.

"Some storm," he muttered, falling back to sleep.

Vanessa stared at the spot where the spirits had dispersed.

Where were they now?

Where would they go?

Vanessa opened the door to let in some of the morning air. The house was damp from the rainstorm and the musty smell was making her nauseous. She returned to the bedroom, where the shattered jars and all their various contents still lay on the floor. Blood, bone, lotions, herbs. She wondered what David thought they were as he left for work that morning. Had he noticed the bones and blood, or had he walked right on past it all in a sleepy haze?

He would have said something. Maybe.

She had been asleep when he left, exhausted from her nighttime vigil.

There would be no lotion from Ashley's remains. Or even Katisha's.

There would be no lotion or much of anything else save for what she had stashed in the bathroom. Three months at the most. Or maybe the more she used her power, the quicker she degenerated. She hadn't been able to figure out the equation over the years; it was always different. Except for the fact that it was happening more frequently.

As she cleaned up the mess, she wished that she could figure out another way to retain her looks. There had to be another spell that didn't involve murder. There had to be someplace she hadn't looked yet.

But what she had told Sophie was the truth.

She had spent years trying to find a better solution. To do anything but kill an innocent person. Virgins' souls. The poor souls hadn't even experienced one of the great mysteries of life.

Vanessa returned to the kitchen to throw out a bag of the mess. There was a figure standing in the front doorway.

It was Demian. Vanessa finished what she was doing and approached him.

Sèphera Girón

"What are you doing here?"

Demian smiled at her. He walked toward her and took her hand. His lips were cold as he pressed them to her hand. He released it and stepped back, admiring her.

"I wanted to see you."

"So you see me." Vanessa turned away from him. She walked into the kitchen and continued to package away the garbage.

"I wanted to tell you I love you."

Vanessa stopped rustling around and glared at him. "Too little, too late. Where have you been all this time? You couldn't expect me to wait forever."

Demian laughed. "But you have forever, remember?"

"Like that makes a difference."

"It would to David."

"Why?"

"What are you going to do when he is fat and bald at fifty and you still are young and beautiful? How will you explain that?"

"Plastic surgery, of course."

"It won't fly."

"Sure it would. Everyone has it done."

Vanessa returned to the bathroom and mopped up more of the wreckage. Demian followed her.

"Be with me, Vanessa. Give me eternal life and let's not be apart ever again."

"I told you before, eternal life is a curse and I won't let you do it. Besides, I don't have the book anymore."

Demian took her hand and put it on his heart. "Feel my heart. My pain. A day hasn't gone by that

294

I haven't thought of you. A moment hasn't passed that I don't crave to have you in my arms again."

"You despised me."

"I didn't like what you did. But I've had a lot of time to think. And we've both grown up so much."

"I love someone else now, Demian."

Demian's eyes flashed. How she loved his eyes when he was angry. "No. I won't have it."

"You can't make someone love you." Vanessa sneered.

"Sure you can. *You* can."

"I haven't and I won't. David loves me with his own free will."

"He loves another."

Vanessa stared at him. "What?"

"I know it. He loves another."

"How can you say that? Oh, yeah, that's right. You're Demian, the jealous."

"No. I can see it in his eyes. He has a hurt. A lost love. I bet I could bring her back for him, and then you can be with me and everyone would be happy."

"Just stop it already. You aren't going to change my mind."

"You'll love me and only me again, Vanessa," Demian said as he left the room. She heard the front door slam, the car start up, then race down the road. She sighed.

Demian.

He only wanted her because he couldn't have her. That was it. If she dared to give her heart to him again, he would just disappear on her, as he did before, as he did always.

She favored the reliability of David. He would never disappear for years on her. Would he?

Would he?

The hardware store was damp and musty like her house and everywhere else in the small coastal town. Vanessa hurried through the door, and saw David fussing around with something behind the counter. He was sweating and deep in concentration as he twirled a screwdriver into the little motor.

"Hi," Vanessa said.

David looked up. "Hey, hi!" His face broke into a smile. "What brings you here?"

"Just wanted to pop in and say hi," Vanessa said.

"Well, howdy, stranger."

They looked at each other and laughed.

"I had a good time last night," Vanessa said, amazed at how strange the words felt coming from her mouth.

"Me too."

"Maybe tomorrow night?"

"How about tonight?" David asked.

Vanessa paused. "I have a feeling I'm going to have to help those women tonight. The sooner I can get to the bottom of this, the sooner I'll be free to give you all my attention."

"Fair enough. But I'll miss you."

"Not as much as I'll miss you." Vanessa leaned over the counter to kiss him. He leaned over to kiss her. She savored the feeling of his lips pressed against hers. A brush of warm velvet. She left the store, amazed at how every time she saw him she felt like a young woman again. Maybe it was his age, or maybe it was that she was sickeningly giddy with love.

Maybe by tomorrow it would all be over. She could only hope.

Chapter Sixteen

Demian watched Vanessa leave the hardware store from his car. He watched her until she disappeared down the road. When he was certain she wasn't returning, he entered the store.

David was still sitting behind the counter, poking at the motor. He looked up at Demian.

"Hey." David nodded.

"Hey yourself," Demian said, looking at the contraption David held in his hands. "What're you doing?"

"Just have a jam in this thing. Trying to get the sprockets to grip properly."

"Oh." Demian watched him a moment longer. David put down the motor.

"Did you need a hand with something?" David asked.

Demian shook his head. "I wouldn't know what

to do with any of that stuff. I just came in to see if you want to go for a beer."

"I didn't figure you for a beer drinker."

"There's a lot you don't know about me."

"So what's the deal? Why do you want to go for a beer?"

"Drink a toast to you, buddy, for snagging the most beautiful woman in the world."

"Right." David looked warily at Demian.

Demian forced a large smile. "So what do you say? Come over and watch the game when you get off work."

"I . . ."

"I've got a big-screen TV," Demian said.

David grinned. He held out his hand.

"Sold."

Demian held a bottle of beer gingerly in his long slender fingers while beside him, David thirstily drank his in several gulps. Demian fidgeted with the label as David watched the baseball game unfold. They sat together on the long, red velvet sofa. It was old and battered, a remnant of many moves. The room was sparse and sterile. A lamp, a gleaming coffee table, two exquisitely carved wooden rocking chairs, and a small bookcase with a vase of fresh flowers on top. Nothing in the cases. The only area in disarray was where Demian's career lay.

In the far corner of the room were several guitar cases, a couple of amps, and lots of wire coiled around in bundles like snakes ready to strike. Papers with musical notation and scribbled jot notes littered the corner.

A music stand was set up, and there was a steel padded stool with a footrest.

Demian stood up and approached his music corner. He clicked his tongue at the mess and set to work rewrapping the cables. David was shouting at the TV set about some sort of play that had gone wrong.

Demian knelt by one of his guitar cases. He put down the cable and carefully snapped open the case. He lifted out his guitar from a blanket of crushed red velvet. Carefully, he touched the strings, just lightly enough that he could barely hear it as he held it up to his ear.

David sat back, his growling at the game over for a moment, and set to work eyeing the plays with a watchful eye, ready to pounce at the next mistake. Demian sat on his stool, watching David, thinking how raw and primal David looked in that moment.

But they were all beasts. The whole human race. All manner and pretense on the surface, but rippling deep in the belly was a gnawing hunger to rip and destroy anything weaker. His fingers lightly caressed the strings, adjusting the pegs to get the instrument tuned correctly.

Music is what lulled him from his primal state. In music, he could lose himself to vivid fantasies of his own choosing. He didn't need the power of someone else's mind to release his thoughts from the mundane task of living. He could tease them out on his own with no script, no actors, just him and his beloved music.

He watched David watching the game. He wondered what it was like to take such joy in watching other people conquer each other. Why waste time when you could be the one doing the conquering? Even sitcoms had merit in the inane ineptness of attempting to find humor in every man's faults. But to watch sports instead of playing them? It seemed ludicrous to him, unless a bunch of athletes were watching it for training purposes and exchanging observations on the strategy being used.

Still, he would rather play guitar. He softly strummed, keeping his haunting melody just below the sound barrier of the game.

At last there was a commercial. They were always long during these man-sport rituals. Demian returned to the couch. David sat in a daze, staring at a beer commercial with several buxom bikini-clad ladies battling in Jell-O.

Demian cleared his throat. He started to speak several times, each time stopping himself. David jerked his head, as if he had been sleeping, and looked over at Demian.

"Do you love Vanessa?" Demian asked. David laughed.

"Much as anyone, I guess," David said. Demian leaned close to him. David was aware that Demian was sweating. It seemed odd on the pale, fragile man. David wondered if he couldn't just snap Demian in half like a toothpick.

"Is she the love of your life?" Demian's eyes glowed as he peered at David's face. He tried to pull the thoughts from David's head, but he was no psychic. However, he was able to gauge thoughts from facial expressions.

David stared off into space as if lost in a dream.

"I knew it. You still pine for someone else, don't you?" Demian laughed triumphantly.

"Not really. I'm getting over someone that I thought cared about me. But she didn't. She ran off with someone else."

"That's not cool."

"No. But it's typical. Happens all the time."

"I know." Demian found his beer bottle and drank from it.

"Vanessa is great in bed, isn't she?" Demian said with a sneer.

"So you were her lover once. So what?"

"Maybe she still loves me. Maybe I can please her in ways you can't even conceive of."

"I'm no slouch in the bedroom from what I've been told. You know, she probably does love you on some level. Love doesn't just die, you know. I'm not stupid."

"Just like you still love that other one."

"Vanessa is a much better person."

"How do you know that she wouldn't leave you too? Run off with an old lover."

"I don't know that. But I'm willing to take a chance that she wouldn't."

Demian nodded. "It's all about chances, isn't it? Losing yourself to another, to music, to religion. Everyone has their muse. Their dance to dance," Demian said.

"I do love her."

"A leap of faith. I wonder if you love her enough. If you would truly withstand all that she could put you through."

"What would she put me through? She seems

genuine so far. I'm worried about something she's involved in, but she's chosen not to involve me, so I'll just wait until she's done."

"Don't like to jump into the thick of mysterious things?"

"Not really. I think she's dealing with a bunch of lunatics, for starters. People dependent on her for readings, and now, their marriages are under strain. They call on her all hours of the day and night."

"Like a doctor. A witch doctor."

"I guess. I hope these people are harmless. I want to help her, but I don't know if I can. I don't know anything about voodoo or witchcraft."

"You never felt the urge to follow her, to see where she really goes?"

"Not at all. We're not married. She's doing what she thinks she needs to do. I'm hoping she'll be through it all soon and we can get back to getting to know each other."

"What if she doesn't come through? What if something happens to her, sticking her nose in where it doesn't belong?"

David narrowed his eyes at Demian. "I don't know if it's life-or-death, what she's dealing with. They're just wacked. Probably a bunch of housewives turned heifers, too busy shoving their faces in the fridge, then tending to housework."

"Housework?"

"Women gotta keep their place, you know. I mean, sure there's equality and all, but let's face it. A man wants to look over at his wife and see someone young and beautiful, with a good ass and nice tits. Not some old saggy hag that bitches all the time."

"Well, I have to admit that I haven't settled down for pretty much that reason. We all grow old. And women, they can go from being so hot to so not," Demian said.

David lit a cigarette. "If I married, I would expect my wife to age, of course, but come on, there's no reason to look horrible. Diet, exercise, plastic surgery. We can be whoever we want to be in this society."

"Would you get plastic surgery?"

"Maybe. Depends how the looks go. If the hair falls out. All that. I won't stop my jogs or weight lifting, though."

"Ever see one of those shows where they take a person that isn't very good-looking and do a ton of plastic surgery on them? That's scary."

"It's too much at once. I mean, can you imagine how shocked their relatives . . . their kids would be? Coming home beautiful when you've known them their whole life as plain?"

"Imagine looking in the mirror. Wondering who that really is looking back. Would you recognize your own face?" Demian asked.

"It's freaky. I would go slow. One thing at a time, as it was needed."

"How's your beer?"

David held up his bottle. It was nearly empty.

"Want another one?"

"Yeah, sure."

Demian got up and went into the kitchen. He took a beer from the fridge and opened it. He took

a small vial from his pocket and poured some powder into it, as he had with the first beer.

When he returned, David was yawning.

"Man, rough day at work today. Seems like
everyone is so bitchy these days. Bitchy or just out
to lunch. Bunch of goddamn zombies running
around. Half-wonder sometimes if maybe the whole
town is doing some voodoo thing."

"You think?"

"Who knows?"

"Hey, let's drink a toast. To new friends."

They touched bottles and downed their beer. The
game was back on. David's attention turned back to
it. Demian watched the players preen and spit and
play with their bats.

"The pressure those guys are under with their
multimillion-dollar contracts must be incredible."
Demian said.

David grunted, his eyes half open. They watched
the game a while longer. David started to snore.

Demian smiled. "Hey, dude?" he said. David
didn't respond.

"David?"

David didn't answer as his breath grew shallow.

Demian watched him as he slept.

A slow smile crept along his face.

Vanessa dialed David's number again, and once
again she got his machine. She wondered where he
was. He was usually home at this time.

She called Betty and Cheryl and found there was
no answer, save a recorded voice.

It was so frustrating.

She went into the bathroom and combed her hair. She looked at herself in the mirror.

Who was she, really?

The woman staring back at her was so young and fresh-faced. She didn't look at all like the tired stressed woman peering out from inside. Did the young woman know the secrets that she sought? Did any of the young people she had devoured hold any knowledge that she was overlooking? Maybe there was something cellular that was bursting to reveal itself to her, but she'd been so busy that she couldn't hear it.

She sat down on the bed and closed her eyes. She tried to be aware of every part of her body, from her head to her feet. She opened her mind to listen to what messages there might be for her.

The resulting effect was noise bubbling in her head. A series of mutterings and whispers that clattered and chattered. Nothing was making sense. She saw images of color and shapes that swirled and morphed from one ring of turbulence to another. There were no answers for her here. Just a sense of dismay and despair. Those emotions would do nothing for her but put her in jeopardy.

She had to be strong.

She opened her eyes and the noise went away. She stared at the wall of her bedroom for a moment.

If she could get to the bottom of this, then she could hang out with David more. He was so different from what she was used to. Her bevy of boyfriends had mostly consisted of artistic types. Musicians and artists, with the odd wanderer thrown in. No matter what a person did for a living or what muse they followed, they had a story to tell. Sometimes the story was more challenging to draw out when patterns shifted from the usual path. Predictability turned to intrigue and a caution that no matter what, everything in the world is merely tangible and nothing more. There was no universal awareness to discover in another human being. That sort of secret had to be unlocked through other means. A fine-tuning to higher vibrations. Ones that were more accessible through music or skillful manipulation. She focused on the symphony of tremolos that sizzled through her flesh, into her bones. She moved cautiously higher, carefully raising the pitch until she felt a raw unhinged power surge through her.

There it was. The life-force of energy.

She grinned as she raised her hands and face to the heavens. Happily, she let the forces rain down on her as her flesh rippled with the screams of unrequited souls.

Vanessa turned up the radio. They were playing an old Our Lady Peace song, "Starseed," about astral projection. She remembered back to the nineties, when she had seen a Beavis and Butthead show where they were making fun of the same song because it started out on a mountaintop. She had laughed even though she had thought it was a pretty cool video for the times and the song. She sang along to the catchy song as she puzzled over what to do.

No one was answering her calls. No one had returned them. Even cell phones were ringing endlessly.

A chill ran through her. Things were not good at all.

She thought she'd better go check on Betty. The doll, the bird. Maybe her husband had finally returned home. Betty might be in bigger trouble than they had thought.

She flipped over a few tarot cards. Tower, Devil, seven of swords, eight of swords. None of it was good.

She turned one last card. High Priestess.

For a split second, she wished she were a mind reader. Oh, to know what was really going on. With the clients. With that blond woman. Then she banished that idea. Her half-assed wishes sometimes had a way of coming true, and she was still firmly convinced that she didn't want to know what rattled around in other people's heads, as curious as she could be sometimes.

She headed over to Betty's house.

Once more, she held hope that the woman would be home since her car was in the driveway. Once again, the doorbell ring was unheeded.

She walked around the house and saw that Betty wasn't there.

Damnit. She'd probably gone to Decadance. Vanessa couldn't blame her, she would have done the same. It had been too long to wait for answers. Every minute was an agony to a worried woman, and when pushed hard enough, even the meekest would take action. Betty was no weak woman, so it was no surprise if that was where she went. Or maybe she had gone to visit someone. Get away from all the sadness. Vanessa had been so busy with the men and Ashley that she hadn't been paying attention to time ticking on. What had been a side trip of necessity was a huge wall to someone else.

So if Betty had gone to Decadance, Vanessa would too. She was bubbling with power and ready to confront whatever darkness might lay before her.

When she got to Decadance, she opened her mouth in surprise. Before her, the boxy building looked like an old abandoned disaster. The windows and doors were boarded up. There was no sign that there had been anyone there in years, let alone a bustling hub of activity not that long ago.

"What the hell?"

She got out of the car and ran around the building. She found one of the side windows and pulled at a board. It was rotten and crumbled easily in her hands. Before long, she pulled several boards from the window. She heaved herself up and over into the dark hallway. She walked along until she came to the main room. The lights were off. She closed her eyes and willed the lights to turn up a bit. They flickered and glowed, loose wires buzzing. There were no chairs, no tables. No stage. No bars. Absolutely nothing. The place was empty.

It appeared like no one had set foot in here in a very long time. She saw an old battered dartboard on a far wall. It was the only object hanging anywhere at all. There weren't even glasses at the bar, or cash registers. It was as if Decadance had never existed at all.

Yet on the bar, there lay three darts.

Vanessa picked them up and fingered them.

The lights flickered.

She flung a dart at the dartboard.

It bounced off the board and landed on the floor. "Shit."

She took careful aim with the second dart, and succeeded in hitting one of the outer rings. She smiled.

With the third dart poised in her fingers, she willed the dart to hit the bull's eye. Almost in slow motion, the dart flew through the air, until it pierced the cork right in the center spot. Vanessa laughed and pulled the darts from the board. She laid them back on the bar.

With trepidation, she turned toward the hallway again. This time, she made her way down the stairs, willing the lights to glow as she walked past them. At last, she was in the big room.

There were no signs here that there had ever been anything more. No curtained rooms. No drums. No chairs. Just a big open space with naked lightbulbs fizzing yellow light.

It was all gone.

They had suspected a stranger in their midst and closed down operation. Anyone would do the same. Maybe Betty and Cheryl and who knows who else had come around too often for their liking?

She would go home to collect her thoughts and to see if she would hear from anyone at all.

When Vanessa returned home, the message light was flashing. Her heart raced. It was like taking a shower. The minute you step in, the phone rings. And that was what had happened. The minute she went out looking, they had all phoned her.

She pressed the callback, and was surprised to hear there was only one message.

It was from Demian. His gentle voice purred a message for her to call him.

Other then that, there was no David. No Betty. No Cheryl.

She dialed Demian's number.

"Hi. You called?" she asked.

"I want to invite you and David over for dinner."

"Today?"

"Yes. In an hour or two."

"I don't know. I was supposed to do something tonight." Vanessa said.

"Well, do you or don't you? Just for dinner. You don't have to stay all night . . . unless you want to . . ."

"It's late. Maybe I should come over for a bite. I don't know. I'll have to ask David."

"He's already accepted."

"Oh, he has, has he?" Vanessa nodded.

"I think he's already on his way. I guess he was bored."

"Then who am I to say no?"

She should try to get ahold of Betty one last time, but she dreaded hearing the click of the answering machine again.

If Demian was going to entertain both her and David, then she should take advantage of the opportunity. Demian's mood swings were notorious. There was nothing more she could do but see what happened next.

Vanessa went over to the window and stared out. Who was watching her?

Her fingers trembled. Her stomach rolled with anxiety. The darkening sky threatened rain again. Gray storm clouds tumbled into puffy white clouds, swirling together like a twist cone. Watching the clouds, Vanessa remembered a time that was much simpler. When the only decisions she ever had to make was what skirt to wear or what color eye shadow would enhance her outfit. If she went to work or danced to the band. Where late nights melted into mornings in a haze of booze and drugs and illicit sex.

Maybe once everything had calmed down, she could spend all night, all day making love with David. For a weekend. A week. A month. She needed loving. She needed to feel real and alive. Her taste of what he could do to her in bed piqued her curiosity. She was fascinated to discover what heights he could take her to.

When Vanessa pulled up to Demian's driveway, she didn't see David's car. She looked down the street, wondering if he would arrive shortly after her.

Demian opened the door before she even had a chance to knock.

"Where's David?" she asked, peering past him into the living room.

"I'm sure he'll show up shortly," Demian said. He checked out her ass as she pushed past him. "My, but aren't you pretty today."

"Thanks."

Vanessa walked into the house and breathed deeply.

"What are you making? That can't be meat I'm smelling."

"It is indeed. Only the best for milady."

They waited for an hour. David didn't arrive. Vanessa tried calling him several times, but the answering machine kept picking up.

"This is one of those cases when a cell phone would be a good idea," Vanessa sighed after hanging up the phone yet again.

"I guess it's just you and me then." Demian said as he carried a roast on a large platter into the room.

"That looks delicious," Vanessa said, eyeing the succulent meat surrounded by potatoes and carrots.

"Only the best for Vanessa."

He helped himself to the tossed salad, and watched Vanessa slice through the meat and raise it to her lips.

"So tender. It's like cutting butter," she said as she chewed.

"It's all in the marinating." Demian grinned.

"This is good. But I have to say, it doesn't taste like roast beef. What did you do to it?"

"All sorts of herbs and spices. Beer. A wonderful recipe."

"It is. I didn't know a vegetarian could cook so well. David is sure missing out."

"Ah, yes . . . David. Tell me. Now that you see me again. Are you really so in love with young David?"

"I told you before."

"You haven't known him long enough to get that attached. If he should suddenly . . . disappear . . . you would get over it."

"And go for you, no doubt."

"What if I told you he still loves that other woman."

"Lizzie?"

"Yes."

"We've been through this. You have to stop driving a wedge between us. Just get over it already."

Demian laughed. "You will be the one getting over it."

"What's that supposed to mean?"

"Nothing at all. Just eat up and enjoy."

"It is good." Vanessa ate more. Demian put on a CD of classical guitar. They let the music wash over them, their tongues dancing with culinary delight.

At last Vanessa was full. She wearily pushed away her plate.

"I'm done," she sighed. "That was amazing. But now, I'm afraid I have to get back to work."

Demian's eyes shone with a wicked gleam.

"I'm glad you enjoyed your meal."

Chapter Seventeen

Vanessa wondered what had become of David. She drove by his house on the way back from Demian's, but his car wasn't there. Maybe at the last minute he had decided he didn't want to sit at another awkward dinner party and had hit a bar. She couldn't blame him. Demian could be intimidating at the best of times.

Vanessa called Betty and Cheryl, and there was no answer at either woman's house.

She went into the bathroom and turned on the Jacuzzi. Maybe she needed to relax and open her mind. The answers were surely right there in front of her.

As the water poured into the Jacuzzi, she set to work organizing what little remained of her lotions and potions. She poured drops of soothing oils in that might open her up to higher vibrations.

The smell was sweet and alluring as the water

level rose. She peeled off her clothes. Her newest flesh was holding nicely. She ran her hands along her neck, her breasts, feeling the youthful smoothness of it. Her arms and legs were hairless and unscarred. Her face felt like a child's. A moment of remorse picked at her, but she figured that Ashley had been getting too close to her secret anyway.

Carefully, she stepped into the warm swirling water. It instantly soothed her as she sat down.

She leaned her head back against the ledge and closed her eyes.

As she grew to know David better, she looked forward to spending long winter nights sitting in the Jacuzzi, sipping red wine and planning their future.

Her stomach rumbled and she rubbed it.

She had eaten far too much at Demian's house. It had been so long since she had tasted his cooking. He had always had a grand flair for creating meals. Even back when things were a nightmare and she was barely functioning, he was able to coax and convince her to eat.

Whether it was something as simple as a fruit shake or as finicky as a roast, Demian had the knack for perfection. No matter how hard she tried, how closely she followed directions, she would never be able to create a slab of meat as amazing as the one she had had tonight. She would definitely have to pry the recipe from him.

Her stomach rolled again.

It wasn't like David, as far as she knew, to say he was going to be somewhere and then not show up. Part of her felt pissed off at him for not even leaving her a message about why he hadn't come.

The other part of her had too much on her mind to worry about it. He would come around. Wouldn't he?

Maybe he didn't like the fact that Demian was back in her life? Maybe he thought it was all too complicated and decided to take a step back.

She closed her eyes.

A sense of uneasiness washed across her. For a brief instant, she saw David's face, freeze-framed in terror, and then it melted away. Bile rose in her throat.

Maybe David had fallen victim to what had happened to the other men.

If that was the case, the urgency to discover what was really going on was now intensified.

Her man might now be affected.

Her hands trembled at the thought. If she wasn't in the tub, she would check her tarot cards to see if she should be concerned.

She was now worried, with or without tarot cards.

A wind rose outside the house, sending a wailing shriek through the windowpanes.

It was going to be a blustery fall evening.

She focused on what she needed to know. She needed a vision to come to her. Where should she start?

There was a pulling at the corners of her mind, and then a ripple. She was standing on the rocks looking out to the ocean. The sky was dark. The ocean was dark. The darkness was so bleak, so impenetrable, that she turned away from it.

Before her was a little house. It was about the size of her own cottage. Painted blue shutters slapped in the wind, the pale yellow door creaked open, and then slammed shut again. She walked toward the house, trying to make out the number on the wooden sign by the door.

There was no number, though. Just jagged letters. As she got closer, the letters shifted into a name.

Cozy's Cove.

Weird.

Cozy's Cove. She walked right up to the sign and with her fingers traced the letters that had been crudely burned into the wood. They were warm to touch, as if the sign were recently designed.

Cozy's Cove.

What did that mean?

Was the house cozy? Was the name of the cove Cozy? Was the owner of the house named Cozy?

Without thinking to knock, she put her hand on the doorknob and turned it.

When she opened the door, there was an earsplitting scream.

Vanessa opened her eyes and sat straight up in the tub. The bubbling had stopped. The lather was gone. The water was stone cold against her rock-hard nipples. Her arms were lined with goose bumps.

It took a moment to reacquaint herself with her bedroom. She looked over to the bed. The bed where David had lain sleeping on his stomach, muscular back naked to the room, arms hugging his pillow, breathing deeply and occasionally muttering. The bed where the sheets probably still smelled of their delicious lovemaking.

They would never make love again.

She shook her head at the intrusive thought. It

wasn't true. They were only beginning. She had a million fantasies in store for him.

Her stomach lurched, and she pulled herself out of the tub and toward the bathroom, just in time to empty out her dinner into the toilet.

She dared herself to look at the puke before she flushed it away.

Chunks of meat and bits of vegetables swirled around and were gone.

David.

She missed him already.

She'd go see him at work tomorrow and everything would be fine.

The sensation of a finger running slowly up her back made her turn toward the window. It was dark. That same dark that always made her feel like something was there.

Because something was.

This time, she ran to the window and flung it open.

The darkness shifted and the stars and moon were visible in the sky.

"Who are you?" she cried out to the night. "What do you want?"

There was nothing but the howl of wind, the scattering of blowing leaves, the last cries of crickets before the winter set in.

Clouds. Lots of clouds.

Fog and clouds. It was nearly impossible to tell one thing from another.

Never make love again.

No, she would never believe that. David was just

out and about. He just didn't want to deal with Demian and his pomposity. That was all.

She went over to the phone, picked it up, and
began to punch in the numbers. She hung it up
again. It was much too late to be phoning anyone.

She was too strong to be worrying like a teenager
over where her boyfriend was. Even if he had another lover, it wouldn't be for long. She had now let
her guard down a little more with him, and was
secure in the knowledge that it wouldn't be long
before they were exclusive. She had shown him that
Demian had no hold over her anymore. Why was
she letting stupid negative thoughts get in her way?

Then she smiled.

The blond woman knew she knew about her. It
was her sending the negative thoughts, trying to dis-
suade her from the mission.

Oh, yes.

Cozy's Cove was where she needed to go.

The image of the house was still there in her
mind.

There was probably a way to look up house
names somewhere, somehow, but it was late and
she wasn't into playing games. She went over to her
altar and said a little prayer of protection.

Might as well get going.

As she climbed into her car, a growing sense of
where she had to go ebbed through her. Her fingers
tingled, her feet itched. Her empty gut gnawed with
knowledge.

The car nearly drove itself through winding curv-
ing roads. The oldie-moldie rock station blared "Can

You See the Real Me?" from The Who's ancient but brilliant rock opera *Quadrophenia*.

As the song faded, she saw the house ahead in the darkness. She recognized the yellow door first, glowing in the night. The headlights shone onto the house. There were the blue shutters.

The sign COZY'S COVE lit up like it was on fire, then grew dark again.

She turned off the car.

Now what?

The owner surely had heard her car at this hour. Probably wondered who was sitting there.

The sign practically screamed at her that this was the place she saw in her vision.

She was being watched.

No question about it.

She got out of the car and walked up the pathway, dreading whatever it was she was going to find inside.

As Vanessa approached the house, the door slowly swung open. It was dark at the immediate entrance, but in the living room, a fire crackled in the fireplace. The smell was wretched. Dead things, fish things, herbs and food, and who knows what other rotten odors fouled the air.

As her eyes grew used to the dim light, she saw men hanging from huge meat hooks fastened in the ceiling. For a moment, she thought they were dead. Who wouldn't? A bunch of meat hanging down, like a human butcher shop. Yet the men didn't looked harmed.

She touched the closest man. A young handsome naked man, breathing lightly as he slept. She touched his smooth chest, feeling him breathe, studied the markings made with dirt and Lord knows what smeared across his body. He was beautiful from head to foot. Firm. Muscular. Even his sleeping penis evoked a sense of perfection. She stood on her tiptoes, lifting his head to view his face. He wasn't David, though he could have passed for his brother.

She walked from man to man. Touching. Examining body and face for David. But David was not here.

Larry was here. She recognized him. His gray hair askew, his dick hanging loosely between his legs. An urge to grab that flaccid dick and yank it right off rippled through her. It was that dick that had caused Betty so much grief in a lifetime. That stupid piece of meat.

She passed by Larry. She recognized a couple of the other missing men. Some she could only guess at since she'd never seen them.

She noticed, then, another pocket to the room. A smaller enclave where more bodies hung. Breasts and hips and curves marked the shadows.

Vanessa touched the first woman. Ran her hands along her body and felt beneath the clammy coldness of the flesh that the heart still beat, that breath still was being inhaled and expelled. She lifted the drooping head and recognized Cheryl.

"Of course . . ." Vanessa muttered.

She examined all the women, and found Betty, Grace, Mrs. Bunting, and several others.

Odd.

Very odd.

The hanging people slept, snoring lightly. Fingers and toes twitched as they dreamed.

Vanessa looked at the men again. Where was David? Her David?

She had been so certain she would find him here.

"So, you've come to see me at last." A woman's voice spoke from behind Vanessa. Vanessa turned around. The beautiful blond woman from Decadance stood there, grinning at her.

"Who are you?"

The woman tossed her mane and stretched out her arms playfully.

"Most call me Molly."

Vanessa looked at Molly, then returned to observing the slew of hanging people.

"Well, Molly, what is all this?" Vanessa finally said, putting her hand on the nearest man's chest.

"My toys. Temporary playthings. A way to amuse myself as the centuries spin past."

"Centuries?"

"All right, maybe not centuries. I've only been around eighty-seven years, but that's a damn long time sometimes."

Vanessa stared at the woman. "You don't look eighty-seven."

"No, I don't. Just like you don't look forty."

Vanessa gulped. "How do you know?"

"It took me a long time to figure it out. Who else was draining the energy coil? I watched and waited and finally I was able to track you down. However, now it is time to stop."

"Stop?"

Molly narrowed her eyes. "I had eternal life first.

And I don't need you messing around with my power."

"I don't know what you're talking about."

"There is only so much energy in the universe. And you are draining the pool. My pool."

Molly pointed a finger and a fireball flew out at Vanessa. Vanessa stepped aside quickly, her hair catching the brunt of it. The fireball crackled and smoked as it singed her hair.

"You can't hurt me," Vanessa said, pulling at her hair to make sure it wasn't on fire.

"Sure I can. Eternal life doesn't mean invincible. But you've been there before."

Vanessa wandered through the bodies, trying to stay out of a direct line of fire from Molly in case she tried another tactic.

"What are you doing with all these people?"

"I told you. They are my toys. My way of amusing the gods."

"Amusing the gods?"

"Of course. The gods grow bored, you know. They like to see us shake things up a bit. To have a bit of fun. Remember the ancient mythology stories."

"How is it fun putting all these people through this?"

"You're a fine one to talk. You go around murdering virgins. At least I don't do that."

Vanessa stared at her. "I'm not a murderer."

"Oh, you are. I was too, until I learned a better way."

Vanessa brightened. A cat meowed as it crept into

the room, watching the witches with bright yellow eyes.

"A better way?"

"Yes. Amuse the gods. I told you that. Give them some fun and they'll take care of us."

Molly reached down to the cat and picked it up. She held it in her arms, stroking it. It closed its eyes as it began to purr, its tail flicking contentedly. Molly wrapped her fingers around its neck. The cat yowled, frantically clawing at her as she tightened her grip. She slowly tore its head off. She held the head up for a moment, then tossed it aside.

"What the . . ." Vanessa gasped as Molly poured the blood from its body over herself. Molly flung the carcass aside, still smearing the blood over her chest.

"Amusing?" Molly asked.

Vanessa shuddered. "Not in the least."

"They're laughing. I can hear them."

"You're crazy."

"Oh, I am, am I?"

Molly flitted from body to body, anointing them with the cat's blood by rubbing her hands and her own body against each person.

"What are you doing?"

"I'm taking care of my loved ones," Molly said, her mouth twitching as she writhed against the most handsome man.

One by one, the prisoners woke. Larry grunted and his hands reached behind the back of his neck, fumbling for the hook. His legs kicked and flailed until his flesh gave way and ripped. Blood poured from his wound as he stood shakily facing his mistress. Vanessa watched as the men scrambled down from their hooks, some ripping themselves down, others still managing to unhook themselves without incident.

Betty and Cheryl shuffled toward her. Even in the dim light, Vanessa could see that their eyes were blank and unfocused. Their naked bodies were streaked with blood and ash and various markings.

"Come with us," Betty said. "See the sights that we see."

Her voice was without fluctuation. Her hand reached out and grabbed Vanessa's arm.

"What sights would those be, Betty?" Vanessa asked. Cheryl had her other arm.

"You can see God. All the gods. Right here. The pain takes you to a place of whiteness and knowledge. Come be one of us, Vanessa," Betty said.

"I thought I found the way, but now I see that this way is better," Cheryl said. Farah stepped forward and wrapped an arm around Cheryl.

"There are many ways to enlightenment," Farah said. She turned to kiss Cheryl. Their kiss was momentary passion, and when they released themselves from each other, their eyes and movement were dull once more.

"Renounce your powers and be one of us," Betty said.

The women pulled at Vanessa's arms. She struggled to escape their strong grips.

"You won't be able to fight all of us," Molly said. She was flanked by Tony and Larry. Tony's eyes were devoid of expression as his hands fondled Molly's breasts.

"Fight?" Vanessa asked.

"We have to fight, Vanessa. A battle to the death. There isn't enough room for two of us."

"There is no death. I've been down this road before."

"Oh, there are ways to die. You haven't been doing your research."

"I was ripped into a million pieces and didn't die. How else could I die?"

Betty and Cheryl ripped at Vanessa's clothes, clawing at her with long, predatory nails. Tony and Larry descended on her, as did the other shuffling zombies. They raked her flesh with clutching fingers. They pulled out clumps of her hair. Tore at her clothes. Her body.

She summoned all her energy, felt it coil and bubble inside of her, percolating as it wound tighter and tighter until she was ready to release it. She breathed out and a lurch of energy shocked the zombies from her for a moment. Several fell to the ground, where they lay twitching. Blue energy streaks circled and sparked along their bodies. The smell of burnt flesh filled the stagnant room. No sooner was she free of one set of hands than another snatched at her.

She pointed her finger at a handsome man gnawing at her ankle. He tore a chunk of flesh from her before the energy seared him. He fell back, clutching his mouth in agony as smoke steamed from his eyes.

Larry and Tony took her by each hand and proceeded to pull.

"Let go of me!" she cried out, flailing her arms to

no avail. Their grip was strong and the more she struggled, the firmer they held. Her arms were being yanked right out of their sockets. She shook them off with another electrical surge. They fell back, their hands blackened.

One by one, she battled the zombies, knocking each one to the floor in a daze. Rendering them unconscious by electroshocking their minds.

As the last zombie crumpled to the ground, she hunched over her knees, panting.

Molly laughed.

"Did you enjoy playing with my army?" Molly asked, dancing around Vanessa.

"What good does this do you?" Vanessa said.

"I don't answer to you," Molly said. She pointed her wand at Vanessa. Energy sparks shot toward her. Vanessa raised her hands and circled them, creating a blue ball. The energy engulfed the ball, ricocheting through it and back out at Molly.

Molly was sideswiped by the beam as it passed through her arm, burning a line through it. She howled with pain. She used her wand again. Repeatedly. Each time, Vanessa deflected the rays and they would bounce back to Molly or shatter against the wall.

Vanessa was weakening.

She had to remain aware as she drew upon more power.

Silently, she pleaded for the help of all whose blood flowed through her.

If they helped her, she promised to free their souls.

Help me please so we can all live.

At first, there was nothing. Then slowly, reluctantly, she felt their presence. Their young naive energy emanating from her and into the room like a beacon from the heavens.

Molly walked around the room, reviving her zombies with Vanessa felling them just as quickly. Molly's power was dissipating; the beams from her wand grew dull.

Vanessa's body bubbled with a life force more powerful than she'd ever felt before. The souls vied for her attention, tumbling within her, their energy angry and fearful. Trepidation and the suspension of belief that the witch would truly release them. Yet they had no choice but to try. Molly must be stopped no matter what the souls thought of Vanessa. They surged to her fingertips and back to her stomach, rolling within her like waves, awaiting their command. Mingled in among that youthful energy was an older male force. She closed her eyes, pinpointing the familiar sensation.

For a moment, she smelled David's cologne. His hair tickled her nostrils. It was like David washing through her, spinning his energy with the virgins. Vanessa glimpsed his face before her, urging her on.

Vanessa wanted to ask him how he got there. How did he know how to manipulate energy. But there was no time.

A pulse flooded through her. Ashley and Alex rapped a battle cry, while David filled her with masculine tenacity.

Vanessa repeatedly zapped Molly until she was able to grab the woman without being burned. Their energy mixed like dancing serpents in battle as Vanessa carried Molly to the nearest hook. She slammed Molly onto it, the hook piercing through her skull.

"You can't kill me!" Molly cried. "I'll never die."

"Your energy has run out," Vanessa said. "Your life force and your witchcraft"

Vanessa raised her hands and zapped the hook until it was glowing with heat. Molly screamed as her skull burned, the smell of cooking meat filled the room. Her eyes sizzled, bulging and bubbling until they popped like soft-boiled eggs. Her hair burst into flame, then turned to ash. Her skull split open. Her brains oozed out the cracks, dripping down her body in a spongy foam.

Molly's body hung limply as her insides leaked to her outsides.

On the floor, people moaned and twitched as if waking from a deep sleep. Cheryl raised her head.

"Where am I?" she asked. Vanessa knelt beside her, brushing her hair back from her face. Cheryl blinked and sighed in relief as she recognized Vanessa's face.

"It's all over. You're safe." Vanessa spied Betty and knelt by her.

"Betty. Are you all right?" Vanessa asked.

Betty moaned and rubbed her head. Vanessa helped her to sit up.

"It's all over." Vanessa hugged her. Betty looked at Vanessa as if she was a stranger. "There's Larry over there. You were both under a spell."

Betty looked over to where Larry still slept. Her lips trembled.

"My Larry?"

"Yes. And he's back to his old self now," Vanessa said, taking Betty's hand and leading her to her lost husband.

Betty knelt beside Larry and touched his chest lightly.

"Larry?" she asked. His breath grew deeper and he coughed. The coughing jag woke him up. He looked up at Betty. A smile crossed his face and he sat up.

"Betty!" he said, wrapping his arms around her. "I've missed you."

"I missed you too, Larry."

"What happened to me?" Larry asked, looking down at his naked filthy body. "Where am I?"

"I don't know the whole story myself, but we have the rest of our lives to remember."

Cheryl found Tony and was smothering him with kisses.

"Don't ever leave me again, Tony. Promise me."

"I love you, Cheryl. I love you and our children and from now on, everything is going to be different. It's going to be better." They hugged each other. Farah came over to Cheryl and Tony.

"This is my husband. He wasn't lost after all!" Cheryl laughed. Farah hugged Tony.

"I'm so glad she found you. She missed you terribly," Farah said.

"I hope we can all be friends. I have so much to tell you," Cheryl said.

All over the cottage, wives reclaimed their lost husbands. There was much crying and hugging as people struggled to remember who they were and where they were.

Vanessa stood staring at Molly.

Molly had eternal life.

If she didn't do something with Molly, the witch would be back for revenge.

Vanessa's body was still fueled with the energy of the souls. They throbbed and burned within her, awaiting their next instructions.

She raised her hands to the heavens and concentrated on erecting a cone of power. It was tedious hard work. Her energy was rapidly failing her, but the chorus of lost souls gave her just the spark she needed.

As the cone whirled around Molly, Vanessa pointed her hands at the body.

"Savor your victory.
As you blow through eternity,
as dust and debris and wind in the sky.
Go away far away, find a new way to die."

Molly dissolved into a pile of dust.

"Holy shit!" Tony said.

"I can't believe it." Larry shook his head.

"There's a lot of weird stuff in the world," Cheryl said to Tony. "A lot of weird stuff."

"I need everyone's help," Vanessa shouted. The room grew silent as everyone focused their attention on her.

"Molly was an evil witch. A terrible presence who truly can't ever be destroyed. But we can try. Each one of you take some dust and eat it. That way we can make it more difficult for her to rejuvenate."

Although several people winced at the concept,

each person approached the dust pile and put a pinch of Molly into their mouths.

After each person had a turn, Vanessa scooped up a big handful of the dust and threw it into the fire.

Sparks of brilliant colors lit up the room for a moment. The fire raged large and a billow of smoke emerged from the fireplace. Inside the smoke was a leering face with red eyes and a savage mouth. There were screams as people watched the monster roar and then disappear in a shower of smoke and vivid color. The fire burned out and there was nothing left but ash. Vanessa gathered up the rest of Molly into a bag.

Vanessa staggered out of the house. The sky glowed with early morning dawn. Behind her, people cried and chattered and puzzled over their lives. She held the bag limply in her hand and scattered handfuls of Molly along the grass, along the road, kicking her into the pebbles, throwing more of her into the sea at various places on her drive home.

Would it work?

She doubted it.

But it would buy her time to think of another plan.

When she entered the house, she headed directly for the phone. No messages, but of course, she had left so late, who would have called?

She dialed David's number and once more got the machine.

Inside of herself, there was rumbling and rippling. A great sense of unease. She smelled his cologne again, his fresh manly scent, and she yearned to feel his arms around her.

She sat in front of her altar and bowed her head.

"Thank you, blessed spirits and gods,
for guiding me to this path.
Thank you for victory.
Thank you for returning husbands to wives.
Please release these virgin souls.
Keep them in the light,
away from Solsucker,
away from harm,
Away from evil.
So mote it be."

A force propelled Vanessa backward as her flesh unknitted and flapped. Her blood boiled and bubbled up to the surface as the souls passed through her body and onward to somewhere else. It burned as they pushed and pulled through her. The pain was unbearable as she screamed.

"Go quickly," she begged, rolling on the floor.

At last, the pain stopped. There was a great sense of emptiness in her body. Vanessa lay sobbing on the ground. She looked at her hand. Her gaping hand riddled with open wounds and flakes of skin peeling off like a snake's skin. She gasped with pain, drawing in breath through torn lungs. She flopped over onto her back.

She was finally free. She had released all her prisoners. She could possibly find salvation after all.

No longer did she have to kill virgins for her body. It was as simple as amusing the gods.

However she chose to do it.

Chapter Eighteen

Vanessa wearily sat by the pond. Her body was scarred, pus flowed freely from gaping wounds. Her neck ached as though every time she turned her head, it would fall right off.

She stared at the water. She remembered the first time she had seen David. He had sat right over there. How long ago it seemed, though it hadn't been long at all.

How she wished he were here to hold her hand. To stare with her at the water. To talk about simple things that had nothing to do with the universe and the secrets that lay beyond.

Where was her David? He hadn't shown up at work. He wasn't at home. Could he possibly have gone back to Lizzie?

What was she going to do about her body now? David couldn't see her like this.

Molly had told her new secrets. Secrets that she

had learned, and now they were Vanessa's to carry.

Was Molly dead? Would her body somehow manage to knit itself back together one day? Did she have a lover who would find her parts and gather them?

They would never find all of her. Much of her was destroyed. Just as Vanessa had been so long ago.

Maybe Molly was relieved to be released from the burden of living. Or maybe she was still somewhere, waiting for her chance to return.

The universe as an energy coil.

That was what Molly had described.

Now it was Vanessa's turn to greedily suck at it as much as she wanted to, when she was better rested. Amuse the gods. And they would reward her.

"Did I amuse you enough? Will I get my body back to its youthful look?"

What would David say if he could see his lover now?

There was a glowing in the distance. It bobbed as it approached, green and purple flowing into each other like swirling balloons. The light diffused into two shapes.

Sophie walked toward Vanessa, holding David's hand. David shimmered with an iridescent glow. He looked confused and tired.

"David?" Vanessa was torn between running to him in relief and hiding her face. She pulled her sweater up over her neck and flipped her jacket hood up.

Sophie was fully human-looking, except for her

translucence. Her piggy features were gone.

"Yes, it's David," Sophie said. David stood silently, as if he couldn't quite understand what was transpiring. He looked at Vanessa with wide eyes.

"Why is he with you?"

Vanessa's heart started to race. Her palms were sweaty.

"He's not on the earth anymore, Vanessa. He's dead."

Tears welled in Vanessa eyes. Her body throbbed painfully.

"No. You're lying. It's a trick." She didn't believe the words even as she spoke them.

"Then where is he? Why haven't you heard from him?"

"I don't know."

"He is in you and around you and always will be."

"David?"

David nodded. He struggled to speak. His eyes glittered with tears.

"Good-bye, Vanessa," he said softly.

"But how? How did you die?"

"It's not important. You must go on now," David said.

"You can't leave me. I love you."

"I have to go somewhere else. I'll always love you, Vanessa."

David glowed brightly, then turned into a vivid kaleidoscope of color. In a blink, he was gone.

"No!" Vanessa scrambled to her feet and ran to where he had been. She wanted to touch him. To hug him. To smell him once more. To feel his strong arms wrapped around her.

But he was gone.

"Sophie. Tell me. What happened."

"It's better that I don't. Go home. Go to sleep, Vanessa. You will have to find a new way to amuse the gods."

Sophie glowed and then vanished as well.

Vanessa stared at the emptiness for awhile. She cried, aching for her loss.

David was dead. Somehow he was dead.

Slowly and painfully, she stumbled home.

Vanessa lay back on the couch, staring at the ceiling. David was gone. Her body was a mess.

But . . . there was still a life to live. She couldn't kill herself if she tried.

She closed her eyes and thought about David. Maybe Demian would have some insight. Maybe Demian could help her figure out what she needed to do next.

As she drifted off to sleep, she wondered if she would ever find peace.